SWEET SAVAGE SEDUCTION

Taking her hand, Sky Walker led her toward their tepee. After they were inside, he turned for her, and the hunger in his eyes told Brandy she must be wary.

"Don't," she said when he reached for her.

"Yes," he said, gently stroking her cheek with his hand. "I only wish to love you."

"Please let me go!" Brandy whispered.

"Go?" His eyes held hers, then his hands slid slowly down her back, and she shuddered again. "We are married now," he said. "You belong to me."

She watched him, fascinated. His ebony hair hung loose, his bronze skin glistened in the firelight. "But . . . it was a marriage in name only," she said. "The ceremony meant nothing . . ."

"Do not protest," he said. "I can feel the way you tremble in my arms. You want me to teach you the ways of husband and wife." His lips brushed softly against hers, and the shivers of desire that coursed through her were all the encouragement he needed.

"Let us remember this night forever," he said as he helped push her garments aside. . . .

FIERY ROMANCE

CALIFORNIA CARESS (2771, $3.75)
by Rebecca Sinclair

Hope Bennett was determined to save her brother's life. And if that meant paying notorious gunslinger Drake Frazier to take his place in a fight, she'd barter her last gold nugget. But Hope soon discovered she'd have to give the handsome rattlesnake more than riches if she wanted his help. His improper demands infuriated her; even as she luxuriated in the tantalizing heat of his embrace, she refused to yield to her desires.

ARIZONA CAPTIVE (2718, $3.75)
by Laree Bryant

Logan Powers had always taken his role as a lady-killer very seriously and no woman was going to change that. Not even the breathtakingly beautiful Callie Nolan with her luxuriant black hair and startling blue eyes. Logan might have considered a lusty romp with her but it was apparent she was a lady, through and through. Hard as he tried, Logan couldn't resist wanting to take her warm slender body in his arms and hold her close to his heart forever.

DECEPTION'S EMBRACE (2720, $3.75)
by Jeanne Hansen

Terrified heiress Katrina Montgomery fled Memphis with what little she could carry and headed west, hiding in a freight car. By the time she reached Kansas City, she was feeling almost safe . . . until the handsomest man she'd ever seen entered the car and swept her into his embrace. She didn't know who he was or why he refused to let her go, but when she gazed into his eyes, she somehow knew she could trust him with her life . . . and her heart.

COMANCHE EMBRACE

BETTY BROOKS

ZEBRA BOOKS
KENSINGTON PUBLISHING CORP.

Dedicated to: My husband, James,
The wind beneath my wings.

and to my four precious granddaughters:
Trisha Lynn Brooks
Tina Darlene Brooks
Skye Angelique Rayburn
and,
the newest addition to our family,
Brandy Danielle Harwell

ZEBRA BOOKS

are published by

Kensington Publishing Corp.
475 Park Avenue South
New York, NY 10016

First printing: March, 1991

Printed in the United States of America

Chapter One

May 1841
New Mexico Territory

Lady Brandy Tremayne crouched behind a boulder, curling her arms around her knees and hunching her shoulders. Hot lead whined like angry wasps around the cluster of rocks that sheltered her and her father. A bullet ricocheted, sending fragments of rock toward her.

"Ouch!" She grabbed her stinging cheek.

"Get down, Brandy!" Lord Tremayne snapped. He squeezed off another shot, then bent his dark head to reload. "We've already lost four men. I don't want you making the number five."

Four dead. Half their numbers depleted. Bile rose in the back of Brandy's throat and she swallowed around the nausea. Fear made itself known, tightening her stomach into a knot. She tried to pray, to concentrate on her father, tried to ignore the bodies on the ground a short distance away.

"Get down!" her father repeated.

Although there wasn't much farther to go, Brandy curled herself as tightly as she could. "Who are they, Poppa?" she asked anxiously.

The acrid smell of burnt powder hung heavy around them as Lord Tremayne squatted down beside her, slipped the ramrod from beneath the rifle's barrel, and reached for his powder horn. "Pedro thinks they're part of Emilliano Gallinos's renegade band," he said, dumping a good measure of powder in the barrel.

Becoming aware of a lull in the shooting, Brandy's anxious green eyes searched for Pedro and Jorge, the other two remaining members of their party. She saw Jorge's sombrero peek over the rock that hid him, then heard a shot ring out. With a muttered curse, Jorge withdrew.

"What could the renegades want with us, Poppa?" Brandy asked.

Lord Tremayne placed a patch and ball over the end of the barrel and tamped it down. "They're probably after our horses and supplies." A crack of rifle fire accompanied his words. "Dammit! Lorenzo swore New Mexico was safe now. Otherwise I would have left you home in England."

"You aren't really worried, are you, Poppa? Pedro and his men will drive them off, won't they?"

Bringing the rifle up, he sent a shot toward the stand of pine trees a hundred yards distant, and was rewarded by a loud yelp. He answered her question as he reloaded. "I hope we can drive them off, but they numbered twelve when they attacked us. We've hit a few, but we're still hopelessly outnumbered. We have to be prepared for the worst."

Her heart leapt wildly at his ominous-sounding words. "What do you mean?"

"These men are dangerous. Whatever happens, Brandy, you must not fall into their hands. Remember that. *You must not fall into their hands.*"

Although his words sent a tremor of fear through her, she managed to keep it hidden. Her father had enough to worry about already, without her falling apart.

During a lull in the firing, Pedro Delgado, their short, stocky Mexican guide, approached stealthily. His chin was covered with stubble and a curving mustache grew above his upper lip. When he smiled, which was frequently, he exposed large tobacco-stained teeth. Right now he wasn't smiling.

"We must speak together, Señor Tremayne," he said, nodding to a spot a short distance away from Brandy.

After a quick, uneasy glance at his daughter, Lord Tremayne followed Pedro.

Feeling almost stifled from the blistering heat of the afternoon sun, Brandy untied the bandanna from around her throat, wiped the dirt and grit from her face and pushed damp tendrils of golden hair back from her forehead. Her clothing was disheveled, her ecru blouse perspiration-stained. Her tan riding skirt was torn. So deeply was her training in the mores of society that she considered the damage for a bare instant; then she shrugged. She'd obviously left England — and civilization as she knew it — far behind.

The renegades began firing again and Jorge returned their fire. Brandy peered cautiously around the boulder toward the stand of pines. She saw a scurrying movement among the green and her gaze narrowed on the spot. A man, wearing a large sombrero and a colorful serape, dashed from the cover of the tree. A shot rang out and the man clutched his shoulder and fell.

Silence closed around them again.

Brandy and her father had left Sante Fe with a small caravan of eight mounted horses and two heavily laden mules yesterday morning, bound for Taos. They had reached the foothills of the mountains when the renegades had surprised them on a narrow trail. They'd barely reached the dubious safety of the rocks before two of their numbers had fallen. Since then they'd lost two more.

Why had they ever come to this savage land? she wondered. Why hadn't her father refused Lorenzo Vasquella's invitation to go on a buffalo hunt?

Beneath the gray sprinkled through her father's dark hair and thick brows, he wore a somber look.

She edged closer, straining to hear his words.

"Suppose we give them the horses," he was saying. "Do you think they would take them and leave us alone?"

"If it is the horses they want, señor," Pedro replied. He regarded the stand of trees.

"Spit it out, man!" Tremayne growled. "What are you holding back?"

"I think these renegades of Gallinos . . . I think they want the señorita."

Brandy felt the blood drain from her face, and a loud buzzing began in her ears. But her father's face reddened with rage and frustration . . . and another emotion she'd never before seen him wear . . . fear.

Oh, God! Could the renegades really be after her? If it were true, then she was responsible for the death of four men . . . and for her father's predicament.

8

"I think maybe they would not have stopped us if they had not seen her," Pedro continued. "But, then, maybe I am wrong."

Lord Tremayne clenched his hands into fists until his knuckles showed white. "This is all supposition," he said curtly. "I think we should talk to them. Perhaps we could make some kind of a deal with them."

"Renegades do not honor deals," Pedro said. "They will accept any deal you offer them, then when you are not looking, they will kill you and take whatever they want." His gaze slid over Brandy.

"What do you suggest then?" her father asked.

Pedro shrugged. "All we can do is wait, señor."

As though only now becoming aware of the lull in the gunfire, Pedro cast a frowning glance toward the stand of pines. "We must keep a closer watch, señor," he said. "The silence is not good. I think the renegades, they make plans."

"Perhaps they've had enough," suggested Tremayne.

"They will not give up so easily." Pedro said, his eyes dwelling again on Brandy. "We must take steps to remove your daughter from this place."

"You are right." Tremayne swiveled his head, considering the boulders in which they had taken shelter. The horses had been left confined in a narrow ravine a short distance away. "Unload the supplies from the horses," he said shortly. "We're going to make a run for it."

Pedro hurried away from them, bending low at the waist, darting from one patch of shelter to another.

Lord Tremayne took his daughter's hand and smoothed his fingers over it. "Brandy, it is time for us to consider the worst."

She didn't speak, knowing that her voice would re-

9

veal her fear. And here, under fire, she longed deeply for her father to be proud of her.

"Their numbers are too great and ours too few for us to win this battle," he said.

"You think we may die?" she whispered, fighting to keep her voice from trembling.

"We have to consider the possibility."

"I can help," she blurted. "Give me a rifle."

Her father's expression reflected doubt.

"I can learn to fire a rifle," she insisted. "There are extra. Just show me how one works while they aren't shooting at us."

Something about her words set him frowning. "Why aren't they firing at us?" he questioned. He rose to his feet and carefully searched the area in front of them. It remained quiet, ominously so.

Brandy's heart swelled with hope. "Do you think they've gone?" she whispered.

He remained silent, searching the trees, then the desert to their left and the sloping hills to the right.

"Dammit!" he shouted, his gaze on the gap in the hill above them. "There's a man in that notch above us. Pedro! Jorge! They're trying to get behind us!" He sent a shot toward the hill, sparing only a glance for the guide who was hurrying back to them, before bending to reload his rifle.

"Si, señor," Pedro yelled. "I see him." Dropping to his knees, he sent a shot toward the gap. The renegade dropped quickly out of sight, but only for a moment. His head reappeared as he returned Pedro's fire.

Brandy heard her father grunt with pain. Jerking her head around, she saw him crumple on the ground.

"Poppa!" Keeping her head low, she hurried toward

him, her eyes widening as she saw the shallow, bloody, two-inch gash the bullet had ploughed when it grazed his forehead. Blood seeped from the wound and dripped down his cheek. "Poppa!" she said again, taking his head in her hands.

Opening his eyes, he met hers. "Don't worry," he gritted. "It'll take more than one bullet to kill me." He struggled to his knees and picked up his rifle. "Tell Pedro to come over here."

But she didn't have to. Pedro had already covered the distance between them. The two men spoke together in low tones. When her father turned his attention back to her, she knew she wouldn't like what he had to say.

"Daughter," he said sternly. "Listen carefully to what I tell you. Pedro may be right. Women are scarce in this country and they may be after you."

"We can leave everything behind," she said. "The horses are strong. Thunder will outrun anything they've got."

"I'm counting on it, because he's all we've got left," Tremayne said gruffly.

She felt the color leave her face. "No!"

"Pedro's just come from there. One of the renegades was shooting the horses. Pedro killed him before he got to Thunder."

"All the horses . . . dead?"

"Yes. Which makes it obvious they weren't after them. I want you to take Thunder and leave."

"No!" she protested. "You can't mean that!"

"You must!" he ordered sharply. "I'll stand for no stubbornness from you. You must obey me without fail."

Brandy set her jaw.

"Don't fail me now, Brandon," Lord Tremayne said. "Not now. When I really need you. Our only chance is to make them follow you. You'll ride on to Taos and bring help back for us."

Brandon! His use of the name he'd given her at birth went a long way toward controlling her rising hysteria. "How far is it to Taos, Pedro?" she asked.

"If you ride hard you could reach it tonight."

"Tonight?" Her voice rose slightly. "I could never bring help in time!"

"You won't have to," her father said. "The renegades are sure to follow you. And the black stallion can easily outdistance them."

She swallowed convulsively. "Suppose they double back when they can't catch me?"

"By then we will be well hidden. Now don't waste any more time. Pedro will point the way. And when you leave here, don't look back!"

Realizing the sense of his words, she bent over and kissed him on the cheek. "I love you, Poppa," she said.

Was there a slight softening in his eyes. "You must be brave, daughter. Now go with Pedro."

"Come, señorita," Pedro urged from beside her. "You must hurry away from this place before they realize they have killed so many of us."

She stared at him numbly.

"Hurry," he urged, tugging at her arm.

Blindly, she allowed herself to be led away from her father, farther into the rocks behind them where they'd left their mounts. Pain stabbed at her as she picked her way through the rocks where the horses had been left. Why couldn't she be brave like her father? He had fought in the war against Napoleon. His courage in the

12

face of the enemy had won him many medals.

If she'd been a boy he wouldn't have sent her away; he would have allowed her to fight beside him.

She squared her shoulders. She'd never pleased him as a female child, but she could show him that she carried his strength and courage, even though her knees were weak, her legs trembling. She could prove her courage by leaving, and if the renegades were after her, then she could draw them away.

She spared little thought for the dead horses as she moved toward the black stallion.

"Keep your head low," Pedro said, holding the reins while she mounted. Brandy looked back toward the rocks where her father lay hidden, but there was no sign of him. "Ho, Thunder," she said softly, catching his reins and putting her foot into the stirrup. Without a thought for the amount of flesh she was exposing, she swung into the saddle.

She listened closely to the directions Pedro gave her even though she was already forming a plan in her own mind.

"Keep my father safe," she told him.

"I will do my best," he said. "Do not feel guilty for leaving. You are doing the only possible thing." His eyes softened as they met hers. "Believe me, señorita. There is no other way. To stay would mean certain death for all of us."

The rifle fire had started up again. How long before another bullet struck her father? Brandy wanted to scream, to cry, to rail at fate. Instead, she yanked her hat off, tore the pins from her golden blond hair and allowed it to fall in a wild tumble around her shoulders. "Since they seem to want me, let's make damn certain

13

they know just who's leaving."

Digging the heels of her boots into the flanks of her mount, she urged him forward, felt him bunch his muscles and gather speed. Then they were flying out of cover of the rocks, across the sandy plains, away from the place where her father lay wounded.

"Eeeeyaaah!" she screamed, intent on making certain the renegades knew who was riding the stallion.

Horse and rider seemed as one as they raced across the desert beneath the sun, keeping parallel with the mountains. She had no intention of going to Taos without her father. She would lead the renegades away, then she would lose them in the forest and double back for her father. Thunder was strong enough to carry both of them.

She leaned low over the stallion's neck, urging him to even greater speed. His hooves pounded in time with her heart, covering the sound of her pursuers.

A quick glance behind showed her a string of horsemen following. She was thankful for the endurance of the stallion who was leaving them far behind. It's working, she thought exultantly. The renegades are following me! Poppa will be safe.

The stallion's pace slowed ever so slightly.

God! Was he tiring?

She couldn't take the chance. It was time to seek refuge in the forest. Thunder responded quickly to her direction and soon they were in the pine-covered foothills. Brandy bent low across the stallion's neck to avoid a low-hanging limb, realizing she must slow his pace or risk injury.

Too late!

The horse stepped into a hole and sent her sailing

toward a dense growth of bushes.

Oh, God! She had time for no more thought before her head struck something solid and blackness closed in around her.

Chapter Two

The afternoon sun slid in golden patches through the canopy of pine needles as Sky Walker settled his gait into a holding lope.

He accepted the whim of the great spirit which had brought him miles west of his destination, but anger still surged through him as he imagined his hated enemies, the Apache, feasting on his horse. Only savages like they would eat the animal Comanche warriors considered extensions of themselves.

Sky Walker was, he knew, an extraordinary horseman, as were all his Comanche brothers. But, this morning, as he had ridden toward the mountains to elude a band of Apache, ten more waited in ambush for him. In the melee that followed, the horses meant as a gift for the Cheyenne were run off, and his own mount, a horse he had raised from a foal, had been killed . . . shot out from under him. Now he must travel afoot to the rendezvous for the Peace Council; he had to reach it before it ended.

Though he kept a steady pace, he remained ever wary. Already since he had eluded the Apache, he had almost been surprised by Mexican renegades. The mountains seemed to be crawling with the dark-skinned ones, who were obviously searching for something . . . or someone. This alone had kept them from noticing his passing.

Despite his hatred of the Mexicans, Sky Walker had had no thought of forcing an encounter with them. He had no time to spare for a matter so minor.

There was more at stake than his hatred for the Mexicans. The Comanche were at war with the Texans and had no time to worry about their neighbors to the south. It was for this reason the Comanche and their allies, the Kiowa, sought peace with the Cheyenne and Arapaho. The tribes must put aside their long-held enmity and band together. The Peace Council toward which he raced would provide that. When peace was declared among the Indian nations, then the Comanche would teach the treacherous Texans a lesson they would not soon forget.

Leaping lightly over a fallen log, Sky Walker wound his way through the pines and aspens that covered the mountain. Any other time he would have been alert for game, but not now. His every thought was focused on getting to the Peace Council as quickly as possible.

Sky Walker knew he was at a disadvantage on foot and must rely on his wits to elude his enemies. Directly in front of him lay a path, clearly blazed by game traveling through the forest and headed, more than likely, for the chuckling brook he could hear in the distance.

Realizing how soft the ground was and knowing his moccasins would leave prints that could easily be followed if he continued on the path, he narrowed his eyes on the dense growth of shrubbery on each side of the pathway.

The heavy thud of mounted horses in the distance brought him up short. He darted into a dense growth of ferns beside a plum bush.

Leaping lightly over the low-growing plum bush, Sky Walker's feet struck the ground with a soft thud. The earth shifted beneath him, and plunged down . . . down . . . into a waist-deep trench that had been hidden from his view by the spreading growth of the bush.

When Sky Walker landed, the impact knocked the breath from him. For a moment he lay stunned.

Hearing a soft moan, he jerked his head around, sucking in a sharp breath when he saw the girl lying limp beside him. Her golden hair tumbled wildly about her head and shoulders, concealing the upper part of her face. But he had little time to wonder where she had come from, because the moment he saw her, he heard a sharp crack, followed by the heavy thump of hoofbeats as the riders neared his hiding place.

"Oohhhh!" The sound came from the girl.

Sky Walker acted immediately, covering the girl's body with his and smothering her groans with his palm.

Her reaction was instant. Her lashes flew open. With a frightened gasp, she shoved at him. When he slipped an arm around her, fastening her arms to her side, her eyes widened in terror and she bucked and thrashed beneath him.

"Shhhh," he whispered, leaning his head closer and pushing the soft hair away from her face. "You must be silent or we will be found," he said in her English tongue.

Her head turned toward him and he found himself looking down into eyes that were the color of new spring grass.

For a moment, he forgot about his enemies, feeling almost mesmerized by her gaze. Never before had he seen such a woman. Sky Walker's blood began to boil from her nearness, but the fear reflected in her eyes sobered him slightly.

"Mmpphhh," she said beneath his hand.

Although he wanted to reassure her, a shout nearby stopped him. "Sshhh," he whispered again. "They must not hear."

She didn't heed his warning. Instead, she pounded her fists against his chest and shoulders, struggling against him. Realizing he must silence her immediately, he pulled back a fist, delivered a quick blow to her jaw, and felt her go limp beneath him.

Consciousness slowly returned to Brandy, and with it a feeling of being stifled. It took only a moment longer for her to realize it was human flesh that was almost suffocating her. Then, she snapped her eyes open and stared up at the Indian who lay on top of her.

God! She had been captured by a savage! Doubling a fist, she struck at him, but her blows were ineffectual against his greater strength. She squirmed beneath him, trying to free herself, wanting to cry out but remembering what had happened when she'd tried that before. He had struck her.

Feeling his body harden against hers, Brandy realized her movements were arousing the savage whose

19

body covered hers. Immediately she became motionless.

"Have no fear," he whispered against her ear. "I will not harm you, but there are others about who would."

The renegades!

For a moment she had forgotten about them! How could she have? She silently berated herself. Even as her heart fluttered with fear, hope stirred within her breast. If the renegades had followed her, did that mean Pedro's plan had worked and her father was safe? She could only hope that it was so.

Her thoughts were in turmoil as she lay quietly beneath the Indian, conscious of his hard body spread over the length of hers. And although he seemed to be listening with his whole body to the sounds of the forest, his dark, emotionless eyes continued to watch her steadily.

Finding his gaze completely unnerving, she tried to concentrate her thoughts on her surroundings. Her nostrils twitched at the moist, earthy smell that assailed them. Her mind shied away from the intimacy of her situation and she focused her thoughts instead on her father.

How long had she been gone? Had she succeeded in luring the renegades away from him?

The need to know the fate of her parent was almost overwhelming. How long would she have to stay hidden in this trench? Her wandering gaze returned to the Indian covering her body, and she felt a flush creeping over her face. Something flickered in his dark eyes as they touched on her reddened cheeks.

Brandy tried to control her blush. There was more to worry about than her embarrassment. The Indian seemed concerned about her. Perhaps he would be willing to help her. They had only been in this new land for a few weeks, but she had heard from several different sources that some of the Indian tribes were friendly. Perhaps the savage who'd found her must be one of the Pueblo Indians who lived near Taos.

An eternity seemed to pass until finally, when she felt she could stand the silence no longer, the warrior spoke softly. "I'm going to release you, but you must remain silent." His hand came away slowly.

She watched him warily, afraid to utter a word as he lifted his head and peered cautiously around.

Brandy lay silent, her heart fluttering wildly in her breast. It seemed anticlimactic when the warrior leaned down and pulled her to her feet.

He studied her searchingly. "Are you traveling alone?" he asked gruffly, speaking in perfectly good English.

"I was traveling with my father," she said. "Our caravan was ambushed by renegades and he sent me away." She plucked a leaf from her hair.

His eyes narrowed suspiciously. "He sent you away on foot?"

"I had a horse. Something happened. I think he must have stepped into a rabbit hole . . . or something. I was only going to lead the renegades away from my father, then go back for him. But I was thrown." She met his eyes. "I'm glad you came along. Now you can help me."

Leaping agilely from the hole, he reached down to help her out. "Come," he said. "The forest will be safe now. The dark-skinned ones have gone."

"Who are you?" Brandy asked. "And how do you come to speak my language? Are you one of the Pueblo

21

Indians from Taos?"

"I am Sky Walker," he replied. "My people are the Comanche. And many of us speak the language of the white-eyes. We learn from intermarriage and from white captives."

Brandy's stomach muscles tightened as fear reared its ugly head again. He'd said white captives. Was she safe with him?

"I intend you no harm," he said, seeming to sense her fear. "Where are you going?"

Her stomach muscles slowly uncoiled. "We were bound for Taos," she said. "My father was invited to attend a buffalo hunt with friends." She brushed at the dirt covering her skirt. "We were attacked by the renegade band, and four of our party were killed. Since our guide seemed to think they were after me, I took the only mount left and rode away, hoping the renegades would follow." She met his eyes. "I must go back. My father needs help."

"How many were there?"

"I'm not real sure," she admitted. "I think ten or eleven. Father can't be very far away. I didn't ride a great distance from him. We must go back. He needs medical help."

He glanced at the sky. "The sun hangs low over the mountain and I have a great distance to travel before darkness falls. You must find your own way back to your people."

"But"—Brandy stared incredulously at him—"you can't mean to leave without doing something. I told you my father needs help!"

"That is no concern of mine," he said. He lifted his right hand, pointed out a direction, and she noticed with surprise that he wore a ring with a large green stone on his little finger. The stone looked remarkably like an emerald. But how could an Indian acquire an emerald ring? "If you travel that way, you will eventually find Taos. And other white-eyes like yourself." Then, to her utter astonishment, he turned on his heel and hurried away from her.

"Wait!" she called, running after him and grabbing his arm. "Where are you going?"

He shook her loose. "I have already lost too much time," he said, frowning down at her. "I cannot be delayed any longer."

"You can't leave me here," she said with a spurt of anger. "I told you my father needs help. You must come with me."

But she needn't have bothered speaking, for he had already disappeared into the forest.

Chapter Three

For a moment Brandy remained motionless, staring in consternation at the place where the Indian had been. She could hardly believe he'd actually left her alone.

Finally, the reality of the situation galvanized her into action. "Wait!" She hurried forward. "You can't leave me here! You must help me!"

She might as well have been talking to the forest, because there was no one else to hear. Still, she pushed on through the dense growth of brush, unmindful of the limbs that clawed at her, intent on catching up to the Indian.

"Where are you?" she called. "Mr. uh . . . Sky Walker! Wait for me!"

When Brandy finally realized she was completely alone, that he had disappeared without leaving a trace of his passing, she felt like dissolving into tears. Instead, she took refuge in anger.

"Damn him!" she gritted, aiming a savage kick at a hapless daisy. "Why did I expect him to help me?" He was an Indian, not one of her own race. Even so, she had expected a little compassion from him.

Obviously it had been a mistake. The extent of her knowledge of the Indians of North America was what little she had learned during their stay in Santa Fe. And that wasn't much.

Realizing she was wasting time she could ill afford, she studied the area around her. She must return to her father and for the first time in her life there was nowhere she could turn for help. This time, she must rely on her own strength.

Her lips tightened grimly and she sucked in a calming breath. According to Sky Walker, Taos was on her left, but she had no intention of going there. After all, her father's plan had worked. The renegades had followed her and she had lost them. Now she could retrace her steps back to her father.

Remembering the blood flowing from his wound, she knew she must hurry. If only she had the stallion. What had happened to him? She hadn't seen him since she'd been thrown from the saddle. If the horse had broken a leg, then he would have been somewhere about. There had been no sign of him, so he must be safe. But she had little hope of finding him now.

Spinning on her heels, she faced the other way, realizing at the same moment that nothing looked familiar.

Had she become turned around while trying to find Sky Walker?

"Blast it!" she muttered. "Taos was northwest of us when we were attacked and the sun was on our right. All I have to do is keep the sun on my left and I should find the place where we were attacked."

With that bearing in mind, she hurried forward, winding through pine trees and aspens, keeping to game trails when it was possible and detouring around when it was not, always intent on reaching her father as soon as possible.

Sky Walker hurried on his way, taking care to tread softly in case the dark-skinned renegades were waiting in ambush ahead. Even as he ran through the forest, leaping over fallen logs and debris, his thoughts were on the golden-tressed woman he'd literally fallen over. If his mission had not been so important, he'd have taken her with him. He had found her incredibly beautiful, with her pale smooth skin and her eyes the color of new spring grass. It was obvious she had been blessed by the Great Spirit. Just the thought of her quickened his pulse and sent a yearning through him.

A rustling in the brush ahead gave him pause until he saw a rabbit dart from the cover of a bush. Realizing he must keep his mind on his mission, he forced the woman with the golden hair from his thoughts which he placed firmly where they belonged: on the rendezvous south of Bent's Fort, where he and other emissaries of the Comanche Nation were to meet with the Kiowa, the Cheyenne, and the Arapaho.

Brandy's blouse clung to her body like a wet rag. The pace she'd set for herself was draining and even though the sun was near setting, beneath the canopy of trees that covered the mountain the air felt hot and humid. There had been no sign of the Indian since he'd left her, and although she'd kept up a constant pace, she saw nothing familiar.

And night was falling.

God! what could she do?

Raking her fingers through her tumbled hair, she sank down on the leaf-covered ground. She, who usually had so much energy, felt drained and incredibly thirsty.

Closing her eyes, she leaned her head back against a tree. Poppa, she cried silently. Where are you? I'm so afraid.

Tears welled in her eyes and slid down her cheeks, but she swiped them away with the back of her hand. Tears would do no good and they were a weakness she could ill afford. She must concentrate her efforts on finding her father. But she felt so alone. God! She'd never felt so alone before, without another soul to depend on. But she must push on. Her father needed her.

Releasing a heavy sigh, Brandy pushed herself upright and continued on her way. She wasn't even certain she was going in the right direction, but her concern for her father would not let her rest.

When she heard the sound of running water, she hurried forward, pushing her way through saplings that grew thick and unchecked between the massive ponderosa pines and aspens. Breaking through the thicket into a clearing, she saw the chattering silvery creek. Along its banks grew willows and pines.

She shielded her face by bending her arms in front of her as she cut through the stand of willows. A rocky shelf bordered the creek and she lifted her eyes to the sky and gave heartfelt thanks.

Kneeling beside the stream, she scooped water in her cupped hands and tasted it. It was cool and sweet. After quenching her thirst, she splashed water on her face and then sank back against a tree, her mind filled with thoughts of her father.

How was he faring? Had his wound been bad? Suppose the renegades had gone back and found him? "Please God!" she whispered achingly. "Don't take Poppa from me." Covering her eyes with her palms, she swallowed hard. If only her father hadn't accepted the invitation to visit the New World and hunt buffalo. If her mother had been alive, she could have talked Lord Tremayne out of leaving England. Brandy was almost certain of that.

Why hadn't they stayed home? God! Why hadn't they?

Brandy's stomach growled and she realized she was hungry. If she were at Tremayne Hall, she would be in the drawing room partaking of tea and crumpets and buttered scones. Instead of a torn, sweaty riding habit, she would be wearing a gown of the latest fashion.

Sighing, she forced thoughts of England from her mind and stumbled to her feet. There was no way she could reach her father tonight. The shadows were deepening in the forest. She must find shelter before it became too dark to see.

Brandy had only gone a short distance when she stumbled over a fallen branch and went sprawling. As she picked herself up, she noted a stack of fallen logs a short distance away, obviously cut by beavers, lying in such a manner that a natural cave was formed beneath them.

Feeling tired beyond belief, she crawled beneath the tumbled logs, curled up into a ball, laid her head on her arms, and fell into a restless sleep.

Lady Brandy Tremayne dreamed that she was at Tremayne Hall, her home in England. Wearing a green

28

satin gown of the latest fashion, she picked up a buttered scone and bit off a small piece while her cousin, Miranda, sat across from her and sipped her tea.

"These Indian fingers are delicious, Brandy," Miranda said. "Why don't you try some?" Picking up a silver tray from a nearby table, she offered it to her cousin.

Brandy gave a gasp of horror at the tray her cousin held. It contained five human fingers, one of which wore an emerald ring. "Take them away!" she cried, averting her eyes from the platter.

"Don't you like them, dear?" Miranda appeared concerned as she studied the pale face of her cousin. "I thought buttered fingers were a favorite of yours."

With a gasp of horror, Brandy woke. Moonlight filtered through the gaps between the logs. For a moment she was disoriented . . . then memory returned.

She had become separated from her father. Now she was lost in the forest, taking refuge beneath a pile of logs. A cry sounded in the night and she shivered with fear, curling her arms around herself. "It's only an owl," she muttered. "Only an owl hunting for food." The sound of her own voice had a slight calming effect and she slowly relaxed her tense muscles. . . . Her eyelids became heavy and she slept again.

Sky Walker grasped the trunk of a sapling, leaned over the cliff and stared in dismay at the swollen stream far below him. There was no way he could continue ahead, nor could he cross the river. Yet he must go on if he was to reach the rendezvous for the Peace Council in time.

A heavy sigh escaped him. He would have to find another way across, and to do it he must retrace his steps.

Needles of sunlight pierced Brandy's closed eyelids and she stirred. She uttered a sigh that quickly turned into a groan, and cautiously opened one eye. The other one popped open and she stared at the logs overhead.

God! For a moment she'd forgotten her circumstances.

Peering from beneath her place of concealment, she decided it was safe enough and crawled out. After quenching her thirst at the nearby stream, she began to look for food to stave off hunger. When Lorenzo Vasquella had visited them at their home in England, he'd spoken at great length of the wild berries and fruit that were indigenous to the area. Moments later she was rewarded by the sight of a bush laden with berries. She hurried forward, picking one and popping it into her mouth.

Finding the fruit deliciously tart and sweet, she gathered a handful and stuffed them into her mouth, then another and another.

Then she realized this was the first berry bush she'd seen, which indicated the fruit wasn't as plentiful as Lorenzo Vasquella had indicated.

Tearing off a wide strip from the bottom of her riding skirt, she filled it with the ripe fruit. She'd nearly gathered it all, when the sound of thrashing in the bushes jerked her head up.

Brandy wasn't prepared for the sight that met her eyes. A black bear stumbled from the brush, moving in a straight line toward her, mowing down everything that stood in his path as he made his way toward the berry bush . . . and her.

Although fear streaked through her, Brandy had enough wits left to gather up the ends of the fabric containing her treasure before dashing toward the cover of the dense forest.

Her heart thudded frantically as she ran, expecting at any given moment to feel the hot breath of the bear as he reached out to make her his dinner. But luck seemed with her. Apparently the plums on the bush had been more appealing than her flesh.

Feeling relief beyond measure, she took her direction from the sun and made her way through the forest.

Hours later, having seen no sign of the bear, Brandy stopped for a short rest. It was only mid-morning and she was already exhausted. She'd been traveling as fast as she could and hadn't seen a creek since she'd left the plum thicket. Her store of plums had been eaten, used for water as well as food.

Hearing the sound of running water in the distance, she hurried through the thick forest, making her way toward the blissful sound. As she drew nearer, she could hear the murmur of voices. Her heart quickened, her spirits lifted.

Help was near.

She was certain of it.

She broke through the clearing, but before she could call out and announce her presence, her chest felt as though it were locked in a steel vise—then a rough palm closed over her mouth.

Chapter Four

Terror washed over Brandy like a tidal wave and her breath tore from her throat in high-pitched screams as she fought wildly against the hands holding her captive, striking out with her hands and feet. When she connected with her captor's shin, he muttered an oath and released the pressure against her mouth. Instantly, she sank sharp teeth into the leathery skin of his palm, feeling an immense satisfaction as he released a string of curses and tried to shake her loose.

Locking her jaws, Brandy hung on grimly, refusing to let go even when she tasted the warm copper flavor of blood in her mouth.

Cursing with pain, her captor released her. Swinging a heavy fist, he struck her a hard blow against her lower jaw that sent her senses reeling and the ground rushing up to smack her in the face.

A red haze formed around her, turning to smudges of charcoal and black. God! She was going to faint! Brandy shook her head, trying to clear her befuddled brain, intent on keeping awake, knowing if she gave in to the shrouding darkness, she was surely lost. Her heart thudded wildly as she lay there stunned.

Above her she could hear cursing, and focused her eyes on the voice. The man was big: at least six feet tall, with shoulders and chest built like a wrestler's. No wonder his blow had packed such a wallop. She was lucky he hadn't killed her. Her gaze lifted to his unshaven face, and his eyes, which fastened on her like hard, black marbles in ice.

"Bitch!" he growled. "You'll be sorry for that!"

Brandy was certain she would, if she stayed around. But she didn't. As he reached for her, she drew a long breath into her burning lungs, then rolled quickly to one side and scrambled to her feet. Before he could comprehend her actions, she was off and running, leaping over fallen logs and debris that lay in her path.

Realizing she had gained only a little time by her actions, Brandy ran mindlessly through the forest, deflecting the backlashing branches with her upraised elbows, the throbbing of her own heart covering the sound of pursuit.

Boots pounding on the forest floor, crashing over fallen branches. The sound of thundering heartbeats, throbbing temples, breath coming in short, painful bursts as her lungs strained for air—these things filled her world as she raced through the forest on her headlong flight for safety.

But she should have known it couldn't last.

She should have known she would be caught.

Somehow, Brandy knew he was there, felt his presence before she felt his hand in her hair and the painful yank that brought her up short. She fell to her knees, tears of pain and despair squeezing through her tightly closed eyelids.

She heard a cruel laugh, coming from somewhere above her, then felt a hand around her neck . . . fingers squeezing tightly, choking the life breath from her body. Her head began to spin, spots appeared on the back of her eyelids . . . her muscles loosened as she lost her grip on consciousness and sank into a gray mist.

A harsh male voice woke Brandy.

"You shouldn'ta choked her so hard, Toby. She's still out!"

"Damn bitch bit me!" snarled a voice several feet away, obviously belonging to the one called Toby.

"What'd'ja expect her to do?" grated still another voice.

Brandy stirred and a groan of pain escaped her lips.

"Think she's coming to."

"It's about time," Toby said.

Brandy forced herself to remain still. Even with her eyes closed, she knew she was being watched . . . the hair at the base of her neck prickled. If only she could make them believe she was still unconscious.

Heavy boots crunched over gravel and stopped beside Brandy, and she felt a sharp jab just below the left side of her ribcage. She willed herself to lie still. "Thought you said she was waking up." The voice belonged to Toby. "She's still out cold."

"Like I said, you choked her too hard," the man next to Brandy said.

"I reckon you'd'a just thanked her politely for taking a chunk out of your hand," Toby snarled.

"Toby, you and Clem both shut your faces," a harsh male voice said. "I'm tired of hearing the two of you bitching. If you got that much energy left, then maybe we ought to just keep riding instead of making camp here."

"Now wait a minute, Franko," whined Toby. "We been in the saddle and still got plenty of time. They ain't no sense in us pushing ourselves."

"All right," Franko agreed. "But I don't want to hear no more arguing out of the two of you. Understand."

"Sure, boss," Toby said. "No sense in arguin' with fools noway."

"Yeah, boss," agreed Clem. "They surely ain't."

Brandy could sense the tension in the silence that followed, a silence that was broken by Franko. "Ben. See to the horses. Clem, fill our canteens with water and check our backtrail. Toby—you get the supplies off the packhorse and fix something to eat."

"Dammit, Franko," Toby said. "I cooked last night. What about Clem doing it tonight?"

"Snap to it, Toby," Franko said.

Brandy's pulse sounded loud in her ears as she listened to the footsteps moving away. How could they keep from hearing the beating of her heart? But evidently she had fooled them and they had left her alone. But had they? She had heard four voices. Three men had left the camp. Did that mean Franko was still nearby? She dared not open her eyes to see. She would have to wait, but not too long. She was determined to escape. And this time no one would catch her.

The silence lengthened and Brandy continued to hold her breath. She was on the verge of taking a peek when she heard the footsteps and felt the eyes on her, inspecting her face for any sign of consciousness. If she could just hold still enough, she could fool—

"I know you're awake," Franko said coldly. "No one can keep that still. Or hold their breath for that long."

Fear shuddered through her as she released her breath in a sigh, opened her eyes, and looked up at him. She met his eyes, cold and gray, studying her as though she were an insect, and found not a trace of pity for her plight. Was he waiting for her to beg for mercy? Her lips tightened, her eyes darkened. He'd wait until hell froze over before she'd give him the satisfaction.

"Who are you?" he asked shortly.

She lifted her chin slightly, tried to sit up, then realized her wrists were bound together. "Lady Brandy Tremayne," she said haughtily. "Who are you?"

"The man who is holding you captive," he said. He squatted down beside her. "So you're a lady are you? Royalty from England. What're you doing out here?"

"None of your business," she snapped.

He slapped her across the face. "All right," he said. "We'll try it again. What are you doing here?"

She stared up at him. "I came with my father on a buffalo hunt. Is that all right with you?"

"With your father?" He looked toward the forest as though expecting to see someone break into the clearing. "Where is he?"

She considered lying to him, telling him her father would be back momentarily, but her hesitation proved to be her undoing. Drawing a knife from a scabbard at his waist, he held it in front of her face. Then, slowly, as though savoring the moment, he placed the blade of the sharp knife against her neck.

Brandy's eyes widened with fear as Franko grabbed her chin with his other hand to hold her face still. He needn't have, for there was no way she could have

36

brought herself to move. Not with the cold steel pressed against her flesh in such a manner. She hardly dared breathe for fear the slightest movement would cause the blade to slip and slice through her flesh.

A long silence stretched out between them as she waited for him to grow tired of his game, waited for the pain of the knife, the gush of her blood.

Suddenly, he laughed and sat back on his heels. "You've got guts," he said. "I'll give you that."

His gray eyes were hard, filled with malice, and something in them, in the hungry way he looked at her, filled her with terror. She made herself hold his gaze, swallowed hard against the terror that filled her, while she fought hard to stop the racing of her heart, to get a firm grip on herself.

A thrashing in the bushes told her the others were returning.

"Well, well." She turned her head, recognizing Clem's voice. His unsavory, unkempt appearance did nothing to reassure her. "Look at the little yellow bird," he said. "She's done gone and woke up."

" 'Bout time," said Toby, tossing to the ground the pack of supplies he carried. "Now they ain't no reason to be skeered of us, Yellow Bird. We ain't gonna hurt you." As he bent over her, his heavy breath washed over her, making her want to gag.

"They ain't no time for that," growled Franko. "Be enough time later."

"Later," Toby said, making it a threat. "Little Yellow Bird, we gonna have us some fun." He squeezed her breast and she gasped in pain, then lashed out with her foot, aiming at the soft spot between his legs. If the blow had landed, it would have put him out of commis-

37

sion, but all it served to do was anger him.

"Bitch!" He hooked his fingers in her blouse and ripped it down the front.

"Toby! That's enough!" Franko said. "We got work to do, things to work out and plans to make."

"Aw hell," Toby said. "We could take a little bit of time off to enjoy this little lady. After all, it ain't ever day we find someone like her out in the bushes. Hell! It ain't ever day we even see the likes of her."

Franko ambled over to them, but even though he seemed in no hurry to reach them, Brandy felt the power of his presence, the danger confined within his body. "You decided to take over as boss of this outfit?" he asked softly, his gaze never leaving Toby.

Brandy winced as Toby's fingers tightened, digging into her flesh, before relaxing slightly. "Reckon not, Franko," he said. "but I don't see no harm in enjoyin' ourselves for a bit. It ain't like we gonna find that Injun. We ain't seen hide nor hair of him since yesterday. He's long gone by now."

Injun? Were they referring to the Comanche warrior, Sky Walker?

"I ain't worried none about the Injun," Franko said. "He was wearing the trappings of the Comanche, and this ain't Comanche territory. He musta been passin' through for some reason or another. Sure ain't likely he would stick around and face up to the four of us. He was traveling by foot and the odds was too uneven."

"Then why can't we . . . ?"

"Dammit, Toby!" Franko said. "We ain't got no time for lollygagging around. We gotta decide what we're gonna do about that shipment of rifles."

"Hell, Franko! We already told Gallinos we'd sell 'em

to him. Ain't we on our way to meet him now?"

His words startled Brandy. It seemed this was not a part of Gallinos's band. Instead, they were gunrunners. The knowledge didn't help to make her feel better.

"Just because we're meetin' up with Gallinos don't necessarily mean we're gonna sell to him," Franko said. "Fact is, I already got an offer from the Apaches for them rifles."

Toby's voice warred between anger and fear. "You never said nothin' about dealin' with Apaches."

"Maybe I don't tell you everthing," Franko said. "Way I see it, Gallinos offer's gotta be a whole lot better'n he's made so far, 'cause this is Apache country. They ain't no way the Apaches would like us sellin' guns to Mexicans. If we risk our hides doin' it under their noses, then it's gonna have to be worth our while." His hard gray eyes moved to Brandy. "Now leave that bitch alone."

"Looks like you'll have to wait awhile," Toby told Brandy. "But soon as we finish our business, I'm gonna have the rest of the night for you." Brandy was unable to control the shudder that swept over her. "I can see you're lookin' forward to it as much as I am," Toby said, a wide grin spreading across his face. "Too bad we have to wait." Turning his head, he said, "Ben, bring me some of that rope."

"I'm usin' this," Ben said. "If you want some rope, then get it your ownself."

Brandy had little time for thought before a man appeared with a coiled rope across his arm.

"Dammit. Clem!" Toby swore. "I ain't plannin' on trussin' her up like a Christmas turkey. All I need is enough rope to tie her to the tree so she can't get away."

"I ain't cuttin' my rope up!" Clem said shortly. "Use it that way or not at all." He tossed the rope on the ground and stalked away.

Muttering curses, Toby reached for the rope and Brandy acted. Her foot lashed out and caught him between the legs.

Yelping in pain, he fell to his knees, and Brandy sprang away. But she had only taken a few steps when she was flung to the ground. Toby's hard eyes pinned her like a butterfly to a board as she struggled to escape him.

"That wasn't very smart," he snarled, his eyes blazing with fury, his fingers biting cruelly into the flesh of her arms. "Bring me that rope, Clem. I'm gonna teach this bitch a lesson she'll never forget."

"What'n hell is goin' on," Franko growled.

"She tried to run away, boss," Toby said.

"Well, what'd you expect her to do? Spread her legs when you asked? Now get up from there and leave her for Ben to take care of."

"Why Ben?"

"Because he's the least likely to take his time with her."

"Shit!" Toby said. "He's been feedin' you that line about bein' a woman hater."

"I don't hate women," Ben said. "Just ain't got no use for 'em. They get in the way of a man's good sense. Take right now for instance. That woman's all you can think about. You done forgot about the money we stand to make on this deal when the rifles are delivered. Now get up and leave her to me."

Brandy wondered if she could make another run for it when Toby stood up. But there was no time. Ben's hands were on her feet, holding them together while he tied them securely. Pulling her by her bound hands, he dragged her over to the nearest tree and tied a short length of rope to it. Then, without uttering a word, he left her and joined the others.

A cold dread settled over Brandy, and despite the warmth of the day, she felt incredibly chilled. Her body trembled despite her efforts to get a grip on herself. While the renegades hunkered over a fire and made alternate plans to sell the shipment of rifles to the Apache if Gallinos didn't come up with enough money to suit them, Brandy's mind whirled frantically, concocting and discarding plans to escape. Testing her bonds, she discovered the old man had been more than efficient in his efforts to keep her under control. Her ankles were bound so tightly that her feet had begun to tingle. She was afraid the circulation had been cut off. And if that wasn't enough, she was lying on something hard and sharp.

Hard? Sharp?

Her heart leapt with hope. Perhaps it was a rock. If she could wriggle around, perhaps she could get it with her hands and saw through her bonds. Her first attempt told her there was no way she could do it. Ben had left very little room between the tree and her wrists. There was no way she could reach the rock, or move it to her wrists.

But she must get loose. She must.

Becoming aware again of the men around the campfire, she searched each of their faces for any sign of compassion, any sign of sympathy for her plight — and found none. Her gaze rested on Franko, the leader of the gang. He was older than Toby and Clem, probably around her father's age. As though becoming aware of her gaze, he looked up and the malice that filled his eyes served only to increase her fears.

Brandy turned her head quickly, searching the forest nearby, hoping for some sign of help. Nothing. Tears of hopelessness filled her eyes. Why had she and her father come to this savage land?

She'd never dreamed when she'd begged her father to allow her to accompany him that she'd wind up the captive of renegades. If only she'd tried to talk her father out of coming instead of being excited at the thought of visiting the New World. Her cousin, Miranda, had been horrified when she'd heard of the planned trip.

"How can you even think of going there?" she had asked. "The place is full of wild savages. Painted Indians shooting bows and arrows and taking scalps."

Brandy remembered how she'd laughed at her cousin. "That doesn't happen anymore," she'd replied. "The Indians are civilized now and most of them are confined to reservations."

What a fool she'd been. Too trusting. Too complacent. She'd found there were Indians on reservations, but not as many as there were running loose. Still, it wasn't the Indians that were causing her harm. It was the so-called civilized people. But Brandy, always a tomboy, always searching for adventure, had not let her cousin's concern sway her. She had felt the greatest adventure of her life lay in the New World.

Now she was here.

But where she'd sought adventure, she'd found danger, perhaps even death.

Suddenly she was brought back to reality. She caught her breath. Something was tugging at her bonds. Jerking her head around, she caught a glimpse of a moccasin, barely hidden behind the tree. Her eyes flew back to the men gathered around the fire and she counted them.

One, two, three, four.

They were all there.

All accounted for.

So who was behind her?

Chapter Five

Turning her head cautiously, Brandy met the dark gaze of a warrior.

Sky Walker! He had returned for her.

Brandy stilled her breath, afraid the renegades would hear the pounding of her heart that even now fluttered wildly in her breast.

Raising a finger, Sky Walker placed it across his lips in a gesture of silence, then began sawing at her bonds again. A few moments later her hands were free. Then he started working on her ankles. She kept an apprehensive gaze on the men hunkered beside the fire as she scuttled like a crab into the concealing shrubbery.

Although she felt the need to hurry, to put as much distance as possible between the renegades and herself, her legs refused to cooperate. They seemed made of jelly, threatening to buckle beneath her weight.

Becoming impatient with her weakness, Sky Walker wrapped an arm around her shoulders and forced her along with him. Brandy was alarmed at her weakness, and the pace the Indian set didn't help her recover her strength.

When they neared the horses she felt a measure of relief. If she had a horse to ride, then she'd have no trouble escaping from the gunrunners.

The warrior released her and coiled his fingers through the mane of a brown mare. Brandy's legs felt like rubber, her knees buckled beneath her, and she stumbled against the horse. The mare shied away and bumped into the pinto nearby. Immediately chaos reigned as the horses whinnied and kicked out their annoyance.

Brandy heard a shout.

What's wrong with the ho—Dammit! She's gone!

The alarm was given.

Panic washed over Brandy. They didn't have enough of a lead, were sure to be caught if they didn't run the horses off. Her panic caused her to fumble in haste. As though sensing her terror, the horses reacted to it, rearing and shoving and kicking out at each other. Suddenly, they were running, and taking with them her only hope of escape.

But even as the thought came, Sky Walker's hand snaked out, his fingers wrapped around her wrist, and she found herself thrown over his shoulder and carried toward a bluff with bushes growing at the base. She was looking at an upside-down world and didn't see the crack in the rocks until they were inside. Sky Walker carried her a good thirty feet into the shadows before stopping and lowering her to the ground. She waited, her eyes filled with fear as she heard the sound of boots crashing through the underbrush. Surely they were going to be discovered.

But to her astonishment, the noise slowly dimmed and she knew their hiding place had not been found.

"We must not linger," Sky Walker said. "When they do not find us, they will return. The opening to this place will not remain hidden for long. Can you walk?"

She nodded, hoping she could. "I think so," she said. "The ropes had cut my circulation off. But the feeling is coming back in my feet."

He nodded and moved toward the slit of light about thirty feet away, seeming to take it for granted she would follow. They were in a crevice that seemed to be formed by two large boulders that had somehow been pushed together, leaving only a space of about two feet between them. She had only time for a quick glance before she hurried after him. The sounds of pursuit had completely died but Brandy feared he might be right. The gunrunners were sure to return and find their hiding place, but it was still hard for her to step out into the open. She could do nothing but place her trust in the Indian.

They traveled through the forest for what seemed to be hours before they came to a bluff. She looked over the edge. Surely he didn't mean to make her climb down the cliff? She felt a measure of relief when he pulled a bush aside and exposed a cave that slanted downward.

At her questioning gaze, he said, "I saw a rabbit take shelter from an eagle here." He went down first, and she followed, picking her way carefully past fallen rock and debris.

Sinking gratefully on the ground, she leaned back against the wall of the cave, closed her eyes, and fought to control her breathing. "I must thank you," she murmured. "That's the second time you've saved my life."

"It was not your life they wanted," he said.

She blushed, realizing the truth of his words. "I know," she admitted. "And I'm grateful for your intervention. How did you know I was in trouble?"

"I did not know."

"Yet you returned for me."

"Not for you."

"The why did you return?"

"These mountains are unfamiliar to me," he said. "When I found I could not cross the river upstream, I came back to find another way across. I had just found a crossing when I heard you scream. Now I find myself delayed again."

Anger surged through her. He was callous and she had been feeling grateful to him.

"I apologize for causing you an inconvenience," she said stiffly. "But had you taken me with you in the first place, then I wouldn't have found myself in trouble."

His lips curled in a wry smile. "It seems you are not unlike the women of my tribe."

Was he laughing at her? She lifted her chin a degree higher and stared at him with stormy green eyes. "How so?" she asked, her voice dripping ice. She tried her best to look down her nose at him. Of course, it was impossible since he towered above her, but she gave her best impression of their butler, James, confronted with a tradesman who had dared summon him to the front door.

Sky Walker's grin became more pronounced. "Like all women, you must have the last word. What are you called?"

"I am Lady Brandy Tremayne," she intoned imperiously. "How long must we remain here?"

"The palefaces will not leave very soon." Reaching

47

out, he picked up a lock of golden hair and let it slide through his fingers. Her heart skipped a beat, then picked up speed. "Your hair is the color of the white man's gold," he said. "They will not let you go easily and that will make my task harder."

"What do you mean?"

"I cannot leave while they are about." Releasing her hair and leaning back against the cavern wall, he opened a hide pouch at his waist. "You must be hungry," he said, "Eat this."

She looked at the round patty he'd handed her. "What is it?" she asked.

"Pemmican. Dried berries and meat. Very good."

Very good? She bit into it and, despite her hunger, chewed slowly. He'd said it was very good. Well, she had to admit it wasn't bad, though she wondered if her hunger didn't have something to do with her enjoyment of the pemmican. Then, she put aside all thought of analyzing the reason and set to eating.

When she had finished and satisfied her thirst from his water skin, she leaned back against the rock wall and closed her eyes.

How was it possible that she, Lady Brandy Tremayne, had come to this state? She had never realized before how pampered and protected she'd been all of her eighteen years. Her thoughts turned to her father. Had he managed to survive the attack? She prayed it was so.

"Stay here," Sky Walker said, recalling her to the present.

"Where are you going?" she asked, springing to her feet.

But he didn't answer, he had already disappeared

48

through the opening. Her heart began to race and she hurried toward the entrance. Stepping outside, she listened to the silence. He had left her alone again. God! What was she going to do? Casting a glance at the sun, she judged the time to be three or four in the afternoon. Only a few hours before dark. Another night alone in the forest!

She didn't hear him approach. One moment she was alone, the next moment the bushes parted and Sky Walker stepped forward.

"They are gone," he said. "It is safe to continue." He handed her a pouch. "You will need that," he said. "And you may take the water skin with you."

When he stalked away, she hurried after him. "Wait," she said. "You're going too fast!"

Frowning, he turned back. "Taos is that way," he said, pointing a direction. "I am not going there. You must go on alone."

"No!" Fear of the unknown surged through her. "You can't leave me behind again!"

"You must listen to me," he said patiently. "I have no time to take you to Taos." There was pity in his eyes. "I understand that you are afraid, but I cannot help you. I have done all I can by giving you the water skin and some food. You must do the rest yourself."

Her lip quivered and she set her jaw, pressing her mouth into a thin line. His pity, combined with his unyielding stand, firmed her resolve. How dare he pity her? Anger surged forth, swamping her fear. "I demand that you take me with you!" She absolutely refused to stay behind. She didn't know where he was going, but there must be people there. Someone who had more compassion than he did, someone who would help her.

Someone with more sympathy for her situation than this savage.

Sky Walker stared grimly at the girl who stood just outside the cave. Although she tried to look angry, she only succeeded in looking lost and forlorn.

His hands clenched into fists. The woman was not his responsibility. He had already lost time by stopping to help her. His duty was to his people and he had no reason to protect the paleface woman. Her green eyes glittered.

Despite the angered outrage she presented, he felt she was close to tears, saw it in the barely concealed quiver of her chin. Despite himself, he felt touched by her plight.

It went against everything he believed in to leave her alone again, to desert her in her time of need. If he didn't take her with him, she'd probably die in the forest.

Could he live with that? He didn't think so.

"You may come with me," he said grimly. "But I cannot take you to your people until I have completed my mission." Relief showed in her face. "If you cannot keep up, I will leave you behind," he warned.

Without waiting for an answer, he strode away, fully conscious of the girl hurrying after him, matching his long strides as best she could.

They stopped that night in one of the numerous caves that covered the mountain. Brandy knew the elevation was high because the air was chill, colder than it

50

had felt the night before. She shivered, wrapped her arms around herself and watched him reach for the hide pouch that held the pemmican.

"A-are you going to build a fire?" she asked.

"No. The cave is shallow. A fire could be seen by our enemies." He handed her a piece of pemmican, then settled back on his haunches and began to eat."

With a tired sigh, Brandy bit into the cold pemmican. It seemed her dreams of a hot meal would remain only that . . . dreams. If only it wasn't so cold. The thought had only formed when her teeth began to chatter. She hurriedly stuffed the rest of the pemmican into her mouth, hoping the nourishment would serve to warm her body somewhat. But the hope was in vain. When she'd finished her meager meal and drank from the water skin, she was still shaking with a cold that seemed to reach into her very bones.

Brandy moved farther back into the cave, hoping to find a warm spot. But it didn't seem to help. Her teeth kept chattering.

She was vaguely aware of Sky Walker leaving the cavern. When he returned he carried an armload of pine boughs. "W-what are you—"

"Making a sleeping mat," he said, arranging the branches near the back wall. "They will help keep the cold at bay." When he had finished, he waited until she curled up on the improvised bed, then settled down beside her.

"W-what are y-you d-doing?" she chattered.

"We must share our body heat."

Realizing he was right, she swallowed her apprehension and lay still. As the heat generated by his body slowly warmed her, her teeth stopped chattering and she began to relax. Her eyelids became heavy . . . then closed.

He shifted his body closer to her and her eyes jerked open. She stared up at him, her green eyes glittering with fear. "Go to sleep," he murmured huskily. "I will not harm you."

Brandy didn't know why, but she trusted him. Her eyes closed and she tried to relax her body. But her neck felt stiff and soon began to ache and, she shifted her shoulders and upper body around until she found a comfortable nest for her head. Then she slept.

It was barely dawn when Brandy woke. She stirred and sighed. Her pillow felt hard, uncomfortable. Doubling up a fist, she punched at it, trying to force the lumps into a softer shape. But it remained firm, rock hard. Opening one eye, she blinked in confusion at the copper-colored flesh beneath her head.

Flesh?

Both eyes snapped open and her body went rigid with shock. Her mind tried to deal with the broad expanse of chest that she had been lying on.

Oh my God!

Chapter Six

Somehow in the night she had crawled into the Indian's arms. The realization sent a surge of heat through her body.

God! How could she have allowed herself to do such a thing? She wouldn't dwell on what he must be thinking of her. But then, perhaps he wasn't aware of where she'd slept. Perhaps he was still asleep. If he was, maybe she could wiggle away from him before he woke up.

Suiting action to thought, she tensed her body, preparing to move away . . . and became aware that his arms were around her. Although she was held loosely, any attempt to escape his hold would surely wake him.

Had he planned it that way?

Don't be crazy, a silent voice whispered. You didn't know you'd crawled into his arms. More than likely he didn't realize he held you.

But what was she to do?

Carefully, she lifted the hand that was spread across her hips, placed it against the pine boughs, and waited a moment to test his reaction.

He lay still, his breathing regular. Good. She hadn't woke him.

She tried to reach the hand pressed against her back and in doing so, found her breasts pressed firmly against his naked chest.

Was it her imagination, or had his breathing changed?

God! she silently prayed. Please don't let him wake up.

Holding her breath for fear the slightest sound would wake him, she lifted her eyes to his shoulder, then higher, until his copper-colored chin came into view. Funny. She hadn't noticed how square it was: ruthless, determined. And his mouth, soft, yet perfectly formed. His nose was just the right size for the rest of his face, and his eyes . . .

His eyes, so dark and fierce, were open. Staring into hers with something like amusement.

Was he laughing at her?

She swallowed hard, her cheeks flushing pink with shame and confusion.

Gathering her wits about her, she pushed out of his arms, struggled to a sitting position, and pushed her tangled hair back from her face.

"Sorry," she muttered.

"Sorry?" His dark brow lifted slightly and his eyes glinted.

"Yes. I didn't realize I was . . . was . . . crowding you," she added lamely.

"Crowding me? I do not know this word . . . crowding. Explain it please."

Explain it? She looked at him in consternation. How did she explain the usage of such a word? What other word would have the same meaning?

"I am waiting," he said imperiously.

"It means to . . . uh, shove." She stopped, shook her head. "It means to . . . to take up your space."

"But the space is not mine," he said reasonably. "It belongs to everyone."

"The . . . . the space close to you should be yours," she said disagreeably. She didn't like this conversation and wanted to end it.

"You are welcome to it," he said magnanimously. "You may use it anytime you wish."

Unless she was mistaken he *was* laughing at her. Deciding this conversation had gone far enough, she blew a silky strand of hair out of her eyes and climbed to her feet. "Shouldn't we be leaving soon?" she asked.

Her words seemed to remind him of his errand, the mission that was so important that he couldn't take her first to Taos, and he leapt lightly to his feet and started for the cave entrance. After commanding her to wait inside, he disappeared through the opening.

Left alone, Brandy combed her fingers through her hair, hoping to obtain some kind of order in an otherwise tangled mess. When he returned they ate a meager meal of pemmican and water, then left the cave.

They traveled in a northwesterly direction, following ridge trails and creeks. Sky Walker allowed her little rest, growing impatient each time she started to fall behind.

Brandy was determined to keep up with him, even though she suspected her muscles would soon be protesting against the pace he'd set for them. Her thoughts returned often to her father and the way he'd looked the last time she'd seen him. She carried the hope in her heart that all the renegades had followed her when she'd left, allowing her father to escape. She held on to thoughts that she would find him waiting for her when she arrived in Taos.

They had been climbing steadily for the last hour, treading through sloping meadows covered with wild flowers of every imaginable color. But Brandy had little time to admire the beauty surrounding her. Her breath came in harsh gasps and her knees felt weak, scarcely able to hold her upright.

Lifting her gaze to the pines and cottonwoods rearing high above, she stumbled over a fallen log, grabbed a sapling to steady herself, and paused to catch her breath.

God! It was hot! How could it be so hot during the day and so cold at night? she wondered, pushing at the damp tendrils of golden hair curling around her face. Could the heat be responsible for her weak-kneed condition?

How would she find enough energy to go on?

"We will rest for a time," Sky Walker said from beside her.

Brandy released a grateful sigh and slumped down on the carpet of green, breathing in the heady scent of wild grasses.

"You are not used to the high altitude," he said. "It drains you of energy."

"Is that the reason I feel so tired?" she asked. "I thought perhaps it was the heat. It doesn't seem to affect you, but then, you must be used to it."

"No," he denied. "We do not have such high mountains as these. But I have been used to traveling."

She was barely listening to his words as she studied

the area around them. "How far is it to Taos?"

"I do not know," he said. "These mountains are un-known to me."

"Yes. You did say that, didn't you. I had forgotten. Is it far to your home?"

"Yes. Very far."

He offered her the water skin and she drank thirstily before handing it back to him. "You said you were on a mission for your people. What kind of mission?"

"I am going to a Peace Council," he said.

"You are? Then there will be white people there. They could—"

"No!" he said, cutting her short. "There will be no white-eyes there."

"But you said a Peace Council."

"Yes. But it is a gathering of Indian tribes. The Co-manche and Kiowa are meeting with the Cheyenne and Arapaho."

"Oh." She looked at him curiously. "I'm afraid I don't know much about your people. I guess I assumed all the Indians were friendly to each other."

"If only that were true," he said. "If all the tribes were at peace with each other, than we could unite and drive the white-eyes from our land."

"Why don't you just make peace with the white eyes . . . uh, my people?"

His gaze was scornful. "We have tried to live in peace with them. But the white-eyes are treacherous and can-not be trusted." His expression became hard, uncom-promising, and when he spoke, his words were sharp, cutting. "Only two moons have passed since the Texans invited our people to a peace conference in San Anto-nio. But instead of peace, the great chiefs who went

57

there found death." His fists clenched, his body was strung taut, and his eyes flashed fire. "There can be no peace for us. But we will not let the Texans get away with killing our people."

"What . . . what are you going to do?"

"They must be taught a lesson," he said. "They must be taught they cannot offer words of peace and then make war on our people."

She shuddered. What was he planning? Whatever it was, she certainly didn't want to be on the receiving end of his wrath.

Leaning back against the trunk of a pine tree, Brandy tried to relax her tense body, but the feel of the rough bark through the rips in her blouse served to remind her of the danger surrounding them. Civilization had never seemed so far away before as it did now. The breeze blew a lock of golden blond hair across her face and she flipped it back, tucking the unruly strand behind her right ear.

Closing her eyes for a long moment, she breathed in the fresh scent of pine, the fragrant scent of blossoms. Feeling Sky Walker's gaze, she looked up to see him studying her with a peculiar intentness. "W-what's wrong?" she asked, her voice betraying her nervousness."

Instead of answering her question, he asked one of his own. "Why do you speak differently than others of your race?"

"I don't live in this country," she said. "My home is in England."

He frowned. "England. I have heard of this place. But I am told it lies across the big water. The one the white men call ocean."

"Yes," she said. "The journey can only be made by ship."

"I have traveled on such a vessel," he said. "Many seasons ago I went to a place called New Orleans with Hawkeye in search of his wife who had been stolen from him."

"Hawkeye." She tested the name on her tongue. "Who is he?"

"Like me, Hawkeye is a Comanche warrior," Sky Walker replied. Abruptly, he changed the subject. "Are you hungry?"

At his mention of food she suddenly felt ravenous. "Yes."

Reaching for a leather pouch hanging at his waist, he opened it and extracted two strips of dried meat and handed her one of them. "We cannot build a fire," he said. "Perhaps tonight we will find a safe place where the smoke cannot reveal our location. It would be good to have fresh meat."

As much as Brandy wanted the warmth of a fire and some cooked meat, she also wanted safety, protection from Franko and his bunch. "You don't think the gunrunners are following us, do you? I think they were supposed to meet with someone."

"I believe the men who captured you are not important. The Apaches are the ones we must worry about."

She studied him closely. "I don't know much about your culture," she said. "But I gather you don't like the Apaches."

"No." His voice was hard. "The Apaches are enemies of my people. And they are the reason I travel by foot."

"They stole your horse?"

His expression darkened. "They killed him and made

59

it impossible for him to reach the happy hunting ground."

"But I understood that your happy hunting ground was—" she broke off, searching for the words. "Isn't . . . isn't that where you go when you die?" He nodded. "Then how did they make it impossible for your horse to go there?"

"They ate him." The words were flat, harsh, and cold.

Brandy shuddered. Obviously Sky Walker had been fond of the animal. "I understand how you must feel about the Apaches eating your horse," she said. "Back home in England we have several horses that are more like pets than livestock. But I don't understand how that could keep your horse from going to his reward. In this case, your happy hunting ground."

"A warrior and his horse must be whole to make the journey. Otherwise he will dwell in the place of the spirit void forever."

She studied his bent head, recognized the sadness he was feeling. "It's obvious you cared very much for your horse," she said gently. "But you need not worry about him. I am sure your Great Spirit is much like our God, the creator of all things. If so, he is just. He would never allow any of his creatures to be damned forever just because they were not whole. I'm certain if your horse is not in your happy hunting ground, then he is in heaven, the place where my people strive to go after leaving this life."

"Do you really believe this?" he asked.

"Yes."

"Then I will consider the possibility."

When he fell silent, she began to wonder about him.

"Tell me something about yourself," she said.

"What do you wish to know?"

"I know nothing about your way of life. It must be very different from my own."

He smiled. "Yes. I am sure it is."

"Then tell me how you live. Tell me about your family. Do you have brothers and sisters?"

"Hawkeye is my blood brother."

"He's your blood brother? What does that mean?"

"Our blood has been mingled together so we are the same as brothers."

"Have you any other brothers? Ones you were born with?"

"No. Hawkeye is the only brother I have."

"How about sisters?"

"I have one sister," he said. "She had hoped she would be Hawkeye's wife. But when his eye fell upon another maiden, my sister accepted what she could not change and went to another's tepee."

"If she really loved him, why didn't she fight him?"

"The women in your land fight each other for men?" He seemed to be astounded.

"Not with weapons," she said with a grin. "But yes. We do fight."

"How strange. Would you fight for a man that you wanted?"

She hadn't ever considered it before. She studied him from beneath lowered lashes, feeling totally aware of the masculinity he exuded. "Yes," she finally said. "If I loved a man, then I think I would fight for him." Sky Walker said he'd been to New Orleans. She wondered what he'd thought of it, wondered as well, what he would think of her world. "Are you married?" The

61

words came huskily.

"You mean do I have a wife?" His lips curled in a smile. "No. I have no woman to warm my bed at night. Would you like to come to my tepee and do that?" His dark eyes twinkled at her.

She blushed. "Certainly not!"

"Why?"

"Why—why—I'd have to be in love with the man I marri—" She broke off, her cheeks flushing bright red, realizing he hadn't mentioned marriage. "We . . . people don't do that in my world."

"They don't?"

"No!" she snapped, her eyes flashing emerald green. "I think you're teasing me. I am sure there are plenty of women waiting for your return."

"Perhaps," he said. "But none such as yourself. None of them have golden hair and grass green eyes."

She shifted uncomfortably, feeling a shiver run down her spine as he continued to stare at her. Leaning over, she picked up a twig and twirled it idly between her fingers.

"Do you have brothers or sisters?" he asked.

"No. But I have a cousin who is like a sister to me. In fact, she is a double cousin."

"I have never heard of this word. A double cousin."

"Her mother was a sister to mine."

"Oh. Yes. That happens very often in my tribe. But we call the offspring of our father and mother's sister a brother or sister. We do not call them double cousins."

She laughed. "It would be the same in my world if our mothers married the same man. But they didn't. Our fathers are brothers."

He picked up a curl and let it slip through his fingers,

seeming to be more interested in the color and texture of her hair than her words. Their eyes met and locked for a long moment. She seemed to be drowning in his and it took a great effort to pull her gaze away.

He seemed to shake himself. "We must be going," he said gruffly. "Even now it grows late."

The trail led them up the side of the mountain. Blue spruce and aspen stretched out on both sides of the path. Billowing clouds lay like puffs of cotton in the clear blue sky and she could hear the sound of rushing water coming from just below the trail. The high altitude, combined with the exertion of climbing the steep trail, was making her heart beat fast and her breath come in short gasps.

When the trail widened and they came upon a quiet glade dappled with sunlight, she reached out and hooked her fingers around a limb. "Wait," she gasped. "Could we stop and rest?"

He frowned at her. "Only for a moment," he said.

Brandy sank gratefully down on a carpet of green and waited for her breathing to return to normal. But Sky Walker didn't join her. Instead, he headed for a large boulder that nestled against the mountain. Something about the way he held his body made her uneasy. Was he concerned about something?

Brandy watched him climb the boulder and stare out over the valley below them, but she could tell nothing from his expressionless face.

Deciding he was only being cautious, she turned her attention to her surroundings. The clearing abounded with blue columbines and other wildflowers that she didn't recognize. A movement in the corner of her vision turned her head and she saw a chipmunk peeping warily around a dead stump. For a moment they stared at each other, then the chipmunk darted away in the brush.

"Come," Sky Walker growled from beside her. "We must go."

Reluctantly, she rose and followed him up the trail. For some reason, he seemed to hurry faster than he had before. And the going was harder, steeper, and the trail seemed to be moving away from the creek. Although the air was getting colder, the steady climb kept Brandy's blood circulating and her body created its own warmth.

They hadn't gone far when the first patches of snow appeared. Brandy's foot slipped on a wet patch of ground and she flung out her arms to regain her balance. It wasn't long before they encountered a stretch of snow that covered the pathway completely for about ten feet. Gingerly, she made her way across the slippery surface until she had reached the other side. Only then did she breathe a sigh of relief.

They were nearing the summit of the mountain when the sound of water became a muted roar. As she rounded a curve in the path, she stopped short to stare in amazement. Torrents of water cascaded down the side of the mountain, plunging over a ledge into a pool twenty feet below. Sky Walker wouldn't let her stop and rest. He seemed in a hurry to be gone.

Perhaps it was because the ground was completely covered by a blanket of snow and he realized they must find a better place to shelter for the night. Whatever the reason, they continued to climb up the path.

Soon the trees to the right of the path fell away and she could see the creek rolling in a swollen current far below. On her left was a chalky cliff streaked with red and white rubble. She had left the forest behind.

The ground beneath her feet was rocky and the heat of the sun had melted most of the snow away. She took one look over the side to her right and felt a sudden dizziness as she realized how far it was to the bottom. Yet the roar of the swollen creek was so loud in her ears that it seemed to drown out all other sounds. She backed quickly away, hugging the cliff to her left.

The trail had become a rocky ledge, not more than five feet wide, and for some reason, Sky Walker had chosen to bring up the rear. She had no thought of danger from another source, no hint that anything was wrong, until she heard Sky Walker shout, "Flee!"

Instead of obeying, she whirled back to face him. Only then did she realize what had concerned him. It was the renegades she'd escaped from. They seemed to have appeared out of nowhere, more than likely the roaring of the water had covered the sound of the horses hooves.

"Run!" the warrior shouted.

Even though she turned to flee, one foot caught in the tear in her long skirt and she stumbled and fell. Now she could hear the clatter of hooves on the loose shale. Struggling to her feet, she tried to still the panic that turned her feet to lead. She watched with sick fascination as a horse and rider drew abreast of Sky Walker. She saw the rider urging the horse nearer the drop, saw Sky Walker stumble, his arms flailing out as he tried to regain his balance.

"No!" she screamed.

But it was too late. The ground shifted beneath Sky Walker's feet and he plunged over the side of the cliff.

Brandy stood stunned. One moment he was there, the next he was gone! She realized she should run, but her limbs seemed frozen, unable to move. For a second or two she looked at the place where the warrior had disappeared. A strange dizziness crept over her, settling in a huge dark mass behind her eyes . . . and Lady Brandy Tremayne fainted.

Chapter Seven

Slowly, Brandy regained consciousness. Her lashes fluttered. Awareness crept over her at the same moment she felt the stab of pain in her temples. Her head throbbed, beating with the steady rhythm of hooves clattering against rocky ground.

Horses!

Brandy opened her eyes, glimpsed an upsidedown world, and blinked in confusion. But the confusion lasted only a moment, a beat of the heart, because the ground-rocking motion, combined with the jostling she was receiving lying on her stomach, brought full clarity to her mind.

She had been captured! Now she lay face down across a horse.

That accounted for the sore, queasy feeling in her stomach, for the bile that was rising in the back of her throat. Was she going to be sick?

Her head whirled, darkness closed in around her, and she feared she was going to pass out. Then she wished she would. At least for a time she would be rid of the sick feeling, of the aching in her body, the throbbing of her temples.

When she tried to move, she found her wrists were bound together with a leather thong that ran beneath the horse's belly. Since she couldn't move her feet either, she suspected that her ankles were tied together with the other end of the strip of leather.

Brandy groaned and turned her head . . . and met the cold gray eyes of her captor.

Franko!

Controlling a shudder, she held his gaze for a long moment, clamping her lips together, refusing to allow herself to beg for mercy.

The horse stepped in a depression and stumbled, jostling the already bruised muscles in Brandy's stomach.

"Ohhh." Despite her efforts at control, the cry escaped her lips.

"Uncomfortable?" Franko's grin bordered on sadistic. "Leastways you're alive. That's more than the Injun can say."

Sky Walker!

He had fallen over the cliff, undoubtedly to his death. And the fault was hers. The realization brought a stab of pain. Although she'd only known him for a short while, he had done his best to help her. His sympathy for her plight had brought about his death.

Suddenly Brandy felt cruel fingers twist through her hair. Tears of pain stung her eyelids and she blinked rapidly, unwilling for the outlaw to see her tears.

"I'd be willing to let you ride astride if you give your word you won't try to escape," Franko said.

"Go to hell!" she gritted.

"Have it your way." His voice was absolutely emotion-

68

less and it chilled her. "We'll be stopping soon. And after me and the boys tend to some business, we'll have time for some fun."

Brandy turned her head away, trying to keep a grip on her fragile control.

"You say something, Franko?" asked a voice just out of the range of her vision.

"Just talking to our prisoner."

"She finally awake?"

Brandy swiveled her head slightly and recognized Toby. The look he gave her was hungry, possessive, almost savage, and she shivered with fear.

Franko's voice came from above her. "Toby, you ride on to the hideout. If Gallinos and his bunch are there, tell 'em we're on our way. If they ain't then check all around. Make sure we ain't riding into a trap."

"Thet don't make sense," Toby grumbled. "They want the rifles we got to sell. Why'd they want to ambush us and ruin their chances of getting the guns?"

"They don't know we ain't bringing the rifles with us," Franko said. "I didn't tell 'em. Figgered it'd be better if we got half the money before we bring 'em. You can't trust those renegades."

His words struck a chord of humor in Brandy. Franko was not unlike a pot that was calling the kettle black. She tried to concentrate on the conversation between the two men, realizing the more she knew about them the better her chance for escape.

"Stop arguing' with me," Franko snarled. "What I say goes. I told Juanita we'd be there before Gallinos. And he's expectin' to meet us before dark. No way we can make it with me ridin' double. But if you hop to it, you can make it there in no time. Wanta be sure we ain't ridin' into a trap."

"So if they are setting a trap, then I'm gonna be the one to fall in it? Is thet what you're after?" Toby's face was grim and set as he eyed Franko. "You trying to get rid of me?"

"Don't be stupid!" Franko growled. "There's gonna be enough gold for all of us. Why should I want to cut you out? It's gonna take ever gun we got to put Gallinos down. He ain't nobody to double-cross."

Double-cross? The word echoed through Brandy's head. So the gunrunners were double-crossing the renegades. Perhaps there was some way she could use the information to her advantage.

"If Gallinos is so bad, why're we risking a double cross?" Toby asked.

Franko grinned. "Them rifles is goin' to bring us more money than Gallinos would pay," he said. "After we get the gold from Gallinos, we're gonna sell the rifles to the Apache."

"I don't know about thet, boss," said another voice that Brandy recognized as Clem's. "The Apaches got no cause to like us. And they ain't nobody to fool around with. I ain't so sure it's a good idea to supply them with rifles."

"They don't have to like us," Franko said. "All they gotta do is pay us. An' they'll pay a damn sight more than Gallinos will."

"I don't know thet's such a good idea, boss," Ben said. Up to this point he'd kept silent. "We gotta get the rifles past the Texas Rangers if we sell to the Apache."

"You let me worry about that," Franko said. "I got me

70

a man in the Rangers that will take care of everything." His gaze went to Brandy and he frowned. "You been gettin' an earful ain'tcha, little bird. That ain't so good. Maybe we'll have to do something so you can't give away our plans."

"You ain't goin' to cut her tongue out like you done to that Apache woman?" Toby whined. "She wasn't much good after that. Made those godawful noises all the time. It was enough to turn a man's stomach."

Brandy's eyes widened with fear. "You cut out her tongue?" she whispered, her voice betraying her horror.

"Kept her from talking," Franko said.

"I won't say anything," Brandy said with a shudder.

"Dammit, boss," Clem said. "I can watch her and see that she don't talk. I'll gag her. That way it'll stop her tongue." He seemed almost as horrified as Brandy over Franko's words.

"Toby!" Franko said sharply. "What're you hanging around for? I told you to get on to the hideout. I don't want Gallinos gettin' there before we do."

Brandy watched Toby ride off, muttering curses beneath his breath. That left Clem and Franko and Ben with her.

"I ain't so sure about thet Ranger, boss," Ben said. "He seemed a mite too eager to help us to suit me."

"We don't have to worry about Clay. Texas don't pay its Rangers much. It ain't nothing besides what we're paying him. And all he's got to do for it is turn a blind eye when we come through with the shipment."

Ben spat a long stream of tobacco juice at the ground. "I still don't like it," he growled. "And I think we all oughta have a say in what goes on. It's for

71

damned sure thet ranger ain't the only one thet'll hang if we get caught. All our necks'll be stretching ropes."

"You saying you want out?" growled Franko.

"All I'm sayin' is we oughta have a say in whether or not we deal with Gallinos or the Ranger. Gunrunnin' ain't the safest business to get into."

So they *were* professional gunrunners! By their conversation, Brandy had suspected as much. She had heard about men such as these. It seemed she had indeed fallen into a bad way.

"Don't know about that," Franko said. "But if we get found out by anybody, at least we'll have weapons for fighting them." He looked at Brandy again and his big hand came out to caress her buttocks.

Shooting him a look of hatred, she tried to wriggle away from him. The only thing she accomplished was an ache in her stomach and a nasty laugh from Franko. "One thing for sure, I'm gonna take some time out to enjoy this piece."

"Thet's what I like to hear," Clem said. "But maybe we should stop off and get a piece now. Gallinos and his boys might want a piece of the action."

"They can have her when I'm done."

The two lapsed into silence and Brandy thought about what they'd said. Apparently they were meeting the renegade, Gallinos, at a cave. Could he be the same Gallinos whose men had attacked her father's caravan?

Pedro had suspected their attackers were part of Emilliano Gallinos's renegade band and surely there could not be two men with the same name. Perhaps when they stopped at the cave she would get a chance to escape. It was a certainty that she could not do anything about it now.

Revulsion filled her as the outlaw caressed her buttocks again, and she squeezed her eyes shut tight. She must hold her silence, make them think she was too frightened to try anything. And the moment they grew careless she would make an attempt to escape.

She held on to the thought that she could escape from them. It was the only way she could retain her sanity. It was dusk when they entered a high valley dominated by an insurmountable cliff. Dark patches dotted the face of the cliff. Brandy saw a dark-haired girl, probably in her early twenties, step out into the sunlight. Only then did Brandy realize the dark patches were caves, obviously serving as temporary headquarters for the gunrunners.

Brandy's spirits lifted as she saw the girl, then just as quickly plummeted when the girl cried, "Franko!" And laughed and ran toward him. Her long black hair fell against her thin blouse and her floral cotton skirt swirled around her ankles as she ran. She laughed as she threw her arms around Franko, obviously pleased to see him.

Toby stepped out of the cave to stand beside the girl. "No sign of Gallinos," he said. "Looks like they're late too."

"Good," Franko said, urging his horse into the cave. After he'd dismounted, Clem helped Toby free Brandy from her bonds, and then pulled her from the horse. But her knees were weak, unable to hold her weight, and her legs buckled beneath her. She fell to the ground.

"What is she doing here?" the girl hissed. Her eyes were malicious, glinting with rage. She seemed to take

Brandy's presence as a personal threat.

"She is here because I wish it," Franko said, his authoritative voice cold, almost threatening.

"I only wondered," she muttered, casting a baleful look at Brandy.

"Toby! Tie her up again," Franko said gruffly. "Then take the horses to the creek and water them."

"Hell, boss," Toby said. "Since Gallinos and his bunch ain't here yet, seems like we could enjoy ourselves a little." His leering gaze told Brandy what he had in mind.

"There will be plenty of time for that later," Franko said, turning to leave the cavern. "Nobody touches her until I've had my fill."

"Thet ain't right, Franko," Toby growled. "I'm the one thet found her."

Franko's hands rested on his gunbelt and his eyes were cold. "You didn't keep her, did you? Anyway, I'm the boss of this outfit. I get first choice on everything. Especially any women brought along. There'll be plenty left for the rest of you whenever I'm finished with her."

Toby's face was suffused with anger as he knelt beside Brandy and bound her wrists together. After he'd finished securing them, he did the same for her ankles. Then, rising reluctantly, he left her alone in the shadowy cavern.

Brandy's gaze swept the dimly lit interior, searching for some means of escape. She'd be damned if she was just going to lie there quietly, waiting for whatever fate the outlaws had planned for her.

Some way, somehow, she would find a way to escape

74

from them.

But how?

She had little hope of rescue, because the casual observer would have thought the caves uninhabited, but it was obvious the renegades had used them time and again by the way the central cavern was set up. The walls of the cavern were creamy limestone. Off to one side she could see smoke drifting upward from a fire. A table, built from rough-hewn logs, was set about five feet from the fireplace. It provided a workplace for the girl, who obviously cooked for the men . . . and served other purposes as well. When Brandy saw the break in the back wall of the cavern, her heartbeat quickened and her gaze narrowed, tracing the outline of the crack.

Was she imagining things? Could that be a narrow tunnel? If so, where did it lead?

Her pulse accelerated and she maneuvered her body to the left until she could see a dim light slanted on the dirt floor. The light could only be sunlight, coming from another exit.

If only she weren't bound hand and foot. If only . . .

Suddenly, she felt a painful stab. Her wriggling movements had brought her in contact with something hard . . . and sharp. She twisted her body to the right until she was free of the hard protrusion, which proved to be a rock with sharp angles.

Brandy sucked in a sharp breath, realizing the rock could be her means of getting free of her bonds. Keeping a cautious eye out for her captors, she inched her way carefully until she could reach the rock. Then she began to saw at her bonds.

The thudding of hoofbeats and the creaking of saddle

leather told her she had run out of time. But she wouldn't stop her efforts to saw through the ropes. She couldn't!

When Sky Walker regained consciousness, his eyes snapped open and he stared up at the sky overhead. His last memory was of falling into space and with that in mind, he moved his head cautiously, realizing that something must have broken his fall.

Fifteen feet above him was the edge of the cliff. Slowly, he let his gaze roam downward, over the face of the cliff until his eyes reached the height of his shoulder. It was then he realized he was lying on a ledge, an incredibly narrow ledge upon which clung a stunted tree, with skeletal branches reaching for the sky as though hoping for a drop of moisture.

The wind gusted and the branches of the tree rattled like the bones of his ancestors high atop the burial structure.

Carefully, he pushed himself to a sitting position and took stock of his situation. The sides of the cliff were sheer rock, with no indentations he could use for hands or feet. There was no way he could climb it.

A quick glance down sent his senses reeling. It was several hundred feet down to the canyon floor. For an instant he felt as though he were a tiny replica of a man, suspended in a vast universe, and then the illusion passed and he was a mere man, peering down into a rock canyon far below.

How could he possibly make such a descent? Then again, how could he not? Brandy had been taken by men intent on doing her harm and there was no way he could leave her to her fate. Only now did he realize how much she had managed to get under his skin. He had never felt in such a way before about any woman. He'd always kept his emotions under control, eager to take what the women of his village offered him. So why should he feel committed now? He didn't want to, and yet there was nothing he could do about it.

Sky Walker looked down again, this time examining the rock wall closely, swallowing the bile and dizziness that accompanied the act. If there was a way off this ledge, then he had to find it. He was not yet ready to sing his death song.

Brandy's gaze moved past Juanita, bent over the fire tending supper, to the men who sat around the campfire, deep in conversation.

Gallinos and his men—she'd counted four—had arrived a short while back. Although Gallinos had spared only a glance for her, she'd felt the eyes of the others, cold, hungry, glancing often at the shadowy corner where she was confined, while pretending to listen to their leaders who were bargaining for the rifles.

Despite the unease the glances generated, she remained quiet, trying to be as inconspicuous as possible, hoping they would forget about her.

But she should have known they wouldn't. Toby, unable to stand the distance that separated them, stood and crossed the cavern to her.

She shrank back against the cavern wall as he knelt beside her. He ran a rough hand across her cheek, his

77

fingers lingering on her lips for a long moment before continuing down her neck to her breasts.

A cold knot of fear closed her throat but she made herself hold still, her gaze fixed unwaveringly on his, as she vowed silently to kill him if she got half a chance.

Brandy was astonished at her feelings. She'd never before had the desire to take the life of another human being. But then, she'd never been in such a situation before either.

"Get away from her, Toby!"

Toby jerked his head around and stared at the man who had spoken. "She belongs to me!" he snarled.

"I said get away from her," Franko repeated, getting to his feet. His hand hovered inches above his holstered gun.

"Wait a minute, Franko," Toby said in a whining voice. "They ain't no call fightin' over her. I'm willing to share with you and you can have her first."

Gallinos had been quietly watching the proceedings. Although he remained where he was, there was a quiet authority in his voice when he spoke. "The girl is mine," he said.

His statement was no surprise to Brandy. After all, hadn't Pedro said they were after her? And ever since Gallinos and his men had stepped into the cavern and saw her, she had felt Pedro had been right.

"How do you figure she belongs to you?" Franko asked coldly. "We found her."

"I lost six men over her," Gallinos said. "And I figure she's already bought and paid for."

"I don't agree," Franko said. "Our deal is for guns. Not women."

78

"Perhaps I would pay more gold for the woman."

"How much?"

Gallinos shrugged. "Who's to say. Perhaps I must try her out first to see what she's worth."

"The girl's a virgin," Franko said. "After you try her out, she won't be."

"You are right, amigo," Gallinos chuckled. "And after she has Gallinos, she will be spoiled for any other man." He shrugged. "It is always the way of women. One night with me and they beg for more."

Franko looked at him coldly. "She ain't for sale. Now let's deal on the guns."

"Perhaps the rifles no longer interest me," Gallinos said softly. "After all, we can get guns from others. But such a woman is not easy to find." His gaze was possessive as he studied Brandy, and her blood ran cold.

"Listen to him, Franko," Juanita said. "She's no good to us anyway. She's just—"

"Shut up!" Franko snarled.

Feeling the need to hurry, Brandy began raking the fibers harder across the rock. She must escape before they could do what they intended to her. But there were so many of them. How could she hope to fight seven men? And yet, how could she give up and allow herself to be used in such a manner?

She couldn't.

She would fight until there was no breath left in her body, even though she knew it would be useless in the end. She would never willingly submit to the degradation they had in store for her.

"Suppose I agree to sell you the girl?" Franko was saying.

79

"You would be wise," Gallinos said.

"How much would you be willing to pay?"

The two men started discussing figures and Brandy continued sawing away at her bonds.

"Toby," Franko suddenly said. "Sounds like something's disturbing the horses. Go outside and check on them."

At a nod from Gallinos, three of his men rose and followed Toby from the cavern.

Brandy saw the look that passed between Franko and Ben. Were they distrustful of Gallinos's reasons for sending his men with Toby? Apparently so, because at Franko's nod, Ben rose to his feet, looked at Clem and jerked his head toward the cave entrance. Clem rose to his feet silently, picked up one of the two rifles leaning against the wall, and muttered, "Goin' outside."

Juanita's dark eyes followed the men, then settled on Franko and Gallinos, who remained seated on the floor of the cavern.

Realizing a confrontation was imminent, Brandy twisted her hands, pulling hard at the frayed rope that bound them.

Dammit! She must get free.

Suddenly she felt the rope give . . . the fibers parted and she was free. Clumsily, with her ankles still tied, she sprang for the rifle, snatched it up, and pointed it toward Juanita and the two men.

"Don't move or I'll kill you," she said.

Gallinos grinned. "So the señorita has fire," he said softly. "That is good. But you must not test my patience. Put the gun down before I grow angry."

"Whether or not you get mad doesn't concern me,"

she said coldly. "I want some answers from you before I kill you."

"What kind of answers?"

"Where is my father?"

"Dead."

A wave of grief swept over Brandy. Her father was dead! How could she bear the pain the knowledge brought with it? Tears blurred her vision of the man before her. The man responsible for her father's death. Hatred surged through her, drying her tears. Her eyes blazed emerald green and her mouth stretched tight with pain.

Without a thought for the consequences, her finger tightened on the trigger and the gun exploded.

Chapter Eight

A gust of wind trailed its cold fingers through Sky Walker's dark hair, as he clung to the face of the cliff. His muscles strained with his efforts to find a cavity in the rock below with the toes of his right moccasin while the toes of his left moccasin were jammed with all the force he could apply into a narrow crevice.

Don't look down! he silently told himself. Forget about the distance you must go. Concentrate your thoughts on finding the next toehold, the next groove for your fingers and toes.

When he encountered a rough protuberance with his toes, he balanced himself on three points; both hands clinging from above and left foot clinging below. He tested the strength of the protruding rock, and when it held, he tried to move his right hand lower . . . and found he couldn't let go!

Grim lines of pain and exhaustion settled deeper into his bronzed skin. Let go, he silently commanded his limbs. Move! Or you will fall to your death. But try as he would, his muscles refused to obey his command.

Sky Walker was disgusted with himself. He had gone

through training as a child, endured pain until he could will his conscious mind to ignore it. And now he was stuck here on this cliff, unable to move an inch.

Realizing he was too exhausted to continue, he closed his eyes and allowed his head to fall forward. Taking a deep breath, he exhaled slowly.

Inhale . . . exhale . . . He concentrated his mind on his breathing, gathering strength and will from deep reserves.

Think of the girl, he told himself. She needs your help. You must find her!

He clenched his fingers, then forced them to open. Sweat beaded his forehead with his efforts at control. Suddenly, as if his muscles were released from a stranglehold, he lifted his right hand, moved it lower in search of another crevice, another groove, one small indentation upon which to fasten his fingers. His fingers nearly passed it by in his desperate search for it. Just a small crack in the rock, but when he probed with it, his forefinger found an opening.

But would it hold his weight?

Suddenly he remembered his knife!

With it, he could deepen the opening

Digging his toes harder into the narrow crevice below, he pulled the knife from his belt and started chiseling away at the opening until it was larger. Then, using the knife, he began to chip away at the rock. Fragments flew up, striking his face, but he paid them little heed, his every thought concentrated with his efforts to make another groove for his fingers.

When droplets of sweat dripped into his eyes, he brushed his face against his arm and continued chipping away at the rock, then testing it for strength before inching his way slowly down the cliff. First his right hand, then his left. Then his right foot, followed by his left one.

The minutes seemed to last an eternity, the hours stretched into aeons. And all the time he kept the memory of the girl's face before him, forcing himself to concentrate on her need. He couldn't let exhaustion overcome him. He must get off the cliff, must get to her before she was harmed.

Turn loose with the right hand, search below and grip. Loose with the left hand, search and grip. Reach out with the right foot, dig in. Out with the left foot, search and grip.

And so it went. Over and over again. Breathe in, breathe out. Concentrate. Ignore the strain, the exhausted limbs. Even when the wind howls around your body, threatening to tear you from the face of the cliff. Hold on. Concentrate on getting to the bottom of the canyon.

He was impatient with the progress he was making. At the rate he was going, night would find him clinging like a fly to the face of this cliff.

He found another spot for a toe and inched a little farther down the cliff.

When his other foot found the crevice, he sighed with relief and, after testing it, allowed it to take his weight. So far, it was the largest, and strongest, resistance he'd encountered.

Something in his mind clicked. When he'd looked down hadn't he seen a narrow ledge? He was almost certain of it. But it had been so narrow, perhaps only four inches wide, that he'd completely discounted it. Perhaps if he followed it he would find a rougher surface, better suited for his needs.

Indecision weighed heavily on him, but he realized he was failing to go forward. Could he be any worse off if he did move over a few feet? He didn't think so.

Realizing he had nothing to lose, he began searching for a hold on his right. His fingers found a nook, and latched on to it. Slowly, he pulled his body to the right until he could put his other foot on the ledge.

For a moment he clung there, breathing hard. He'd actually made it! And his position was more secure, if only slightly. When his breathing became normal, he inched his way slowly across the face of the cliff until his right hand suddenly encountered emptiness. At first he thought the cliff had come to an end. Then he frowned. The cliff couldn't end here. He was certain it ran the length of the mountain.

Swiveling his head, he found himself staring at the black maw of a cave. Set close against the cliff and masked by tumbled boulders, he had failed to see it from up above.

With great relief, he entered the cavern. Then he stopped—staring at the panther flattened against a rocky ledge. The cat's sensitive ears were held tight against her golden head, her fangs bared as she hissed her outrage that her lair had been invaded. Flexing her muscles beneath her tawny coat, she let out a great roar and launched herself at him.

It was several moments before Brandy realized her shot had missed. She lay on the ground, stunned from the powerful recoil of the rifle, while Gallinos slowly rose and crossed the cave to her. His eyes were like coals of fire, his face set in grim lines. Leaning over, he struck her a hard blow across the face that sent her senses reeling.

"You need to be taught a lesson," he said, bending over her and securing her wrists with rope once again. "And it looks like I'm the one to do it."

"Turn her loose," Franko growled.

"Stay out of this," said Gallinos. "This is between me and the girl and none of your business."

"She belongs to me. And anything to do with her is my business."

Feeling totally defeated, Brandy listened to the two men argue over her. She had tried to escape . . . and she had failed. Now her fate was sealed.

Listen to you, an inner voice chided. Are you just going to give up and take whatever they have planned for you? You're supposed to be a fighter. It was the only reason father allowed you to come.

Father!

The thought of him had her straightening her shoulders. He'd be ashamed of her if he knew how cowardly she was acting, how easily she had given up.

She was a fighter. And she would be damned if she'd give in without giving a good accounting of herself. Before she was through with them, they'd at least know she'd put up a good fight.

The two men seemed to become aware of the sudden change in her demeanor and turned their attention back to her.

The mountain lion's roar sent chills up and down Sky Walker's spine. He brought his knife up, held it before him. Just in time! The animal was upon him in a moment. The weight of the beast flung him to the ground with a heavy thud. But he quickly rolled over and brought his knife into play, stabbing it down into the animal, over and over again until the lion lay still.

Rolling out from under the weight of the beast, Sky Walker stood up and began a systematic search of the cave. The lion had found a way to get in the cave, and wherever the entrance was, Sky Walker intended to find it.

Brandy opened her eyes a slit. She could see the men sitting around the fire. Since she'd tried to kill Gallinos, no one had come close to her. Although she intercepted glances from Juanita and the two men, they kept their distance, probably instructed to do so by their leaders.

Gallinos and Franko had gone out of the cave together and when they came back inside, she knew they had come to an agreement of some kind.

She was soon to learn what it was.

Gallinos crossed the floor of the cavern and stood grinning down at her. "I paid much gold for you," he said. "Let's see if you're worth it." Reaching down he pulled her to her feet by her bound wrists and led her toward the entrance of the cave.

"Where you going with her?" Franko growled.

"Outside. I have no wish to have others watching me while I perform."

Brandy allowed herself to be pulled along behind Gallinos into the night, realizing one man would be easier to defeat than many. And if she were successful, than the darkness would provide a cover for her escape.

Gallinos led her through the forest until they reached a shallow stream that flowed briskly over a rock bed.

Then, with a calmness that was in itself dangerous, he hooked his fingers in the neck of her blouse and ripped it in half. She uttered a gasp and struck out at him. But to no avail. He stripped the torn blouse from her body, shoved her to the ground, and followed her down, covering her body with his own.

Sky Walker worked his way closer to the cave. He could hear several men deep in conversation a short distance away.

"I don't like what's happening," said one man. "I didn't bargain for a girl in the deal."

"Ain't none of my business," said another voice. "I just do what I'm told and collect my pay."

"Man could get himself killed by not asking questions," said the first voice.

"In this outfit you could get yourself killed if you do ask questions. I'll be back in a minute. You watch them horses."

"What do you think's going to happen to them?"

"You can't never tell when you're dealin' with a bunch like the one thet runs with Gallinos."

"You think you're any better than them?"

"Shut up and watch the horses." The man headed into the forest toward the warrior who lay hidden.

Sky Walker decided to take care of him first.

The man unbuttoned his breeches and while his hands were busy, Sky Walker struck. His knife came up and down in one smooth stroke and the man lay dead at his feet.

He moved toward the other men.

"Franko is beginning to get on my nerves," a man was saying. "I ain't so sure about this plan of his. It don't sound so hot to me. Texas Rangers ain't to be trusted. Going against the Rangers ain't a very good way to stay alive."

"Hell, Ben! Franko says we ain't going against the Rangers. According to him, that Ranger is with us."

"The whole thing stinks to me," Ben growled. "If I didn't need the money so bad, I'd tell him to go to hell." He raised his voice. "Hey, Toby. Hurry up and get back here." He turned back to his companion and said, "Toby wants the girl bad and I'm afraid it's going to lead to trouble for all of us."

Sky Walker's blood boiled as he listened to the men talk. Although he had no idea how much she'd been made to suffer, at least Brandy was still alive.

"Dammit! I guess I gotta go after Toby," Ben said. "Boss is gonna have a fit if he ain't here when he's needed." He strode toward the bushes that hid Sky Walker.

The warrior's knife was held ready as he waited silently for Ben to reach him.

Suddenly, there was a rustling in the brush beside him and the fine hairs on his neck prickled. He had the feeling he was being watched. His fingers gripped the hand of his knife tighter, his muscles bunched.

Slowly, he swiveled his head, his gaze falling on a rabbit just as it made a mad dash out of the underbrush, straight across the boots of the man he'd been intent on killing.

"What in hell?" Ben growled. Then he laughed harshly. "Nothing but a rabbit. Must be getting jumpy."

His boots thudded against the hard ground as he went on his way.

Sky Walker watched him, realizing he must let him pass, for the other man had become curious at the noise and was even now approaching.

"Toby!" a man called. "Get in here! I wanta talk to you."

"Toby's takin' a leak, boss," said the remaining man.

Franko frowned. "Ben with you?"

"He went after Toby."

Franko muttered something under his breath and came closer. "What's wrong?" he asked sharply.

"Nothing, I reckon. Just Ben's imagination working overtime."

"Find them," Franko snapped. "Get them both in here." He turned to leave as Clem disappeared in the forest. Sky Walker caught Franko before he reached the cave.

But something must have warned the other man. He dodged the blow that would have killed him. The fight between the two men was hard and silent. Franko was on top, but Sky Walker rolled him off and plunged the knife downward. He missed and the man cursed as they struggled silently for the possession of the knife. It was a silent battle that raged between the two men and all the time Sky Walker felt the need to hurry. He must find Brandy before harm came to her. When his blade finally found its mark, he drew it out and prepared to strike again. That's when he heard the scream.

Leaping to his feet, he ran toward the sound. When he entered the clearing he saw Brandy struggling with Gallinos. Sky Walker's knife swung up and he struck downward, over and over again, his rage almost consuming him.

When Gallinos lay dead at his feet, Sky Walker pulled Brandy into his arms. "I thought you were dead," she sobbed. She lay against him, trying to still the tremors that shook her body.

"They killed my father," she sobbed against his chest.

"Hush," he soothed. "We must leave this place before others come." Taking her hand, he led her through the night, toward the clearing where the horses were stabled. But before they reached the horses, they knew they'd been discovered.

"It's an Injun and that girl!" a man shouted, lifting his revolver and sending a shot toward them.

"Did'ja get him?" another man yelled.

Brandy didn't hear the reply, because the sound of voices raised in the distance told her their flight had been discovered.

"Come," Sky Walker said, gripping her arm with fingers of steel, tugging her toward the cover of the dense forest. "They cannot follow us with their mounts."

After traveling several hours, Sky Walker decided they were safe enough to rest for a time. He found a narrow gorge with a rock overhang where they would be hidden from prying eyes while they rested. Then, silently, he held his arms out to her and she found shelter there. Brandy felt his sympathy pouring over her and it almost proved her undoing. He caressed her until her sobbing finally ceased.

Grateful for his comfort, she lifted her face and softly kissed his cheek. "Thank you," she said softly. "You've been so kind."

Suddenly she became aware of the ragged tempo of his breathing, of the tender way he held her. She was by no means blind to his attraction, but such an attraction would be perilous. Her eyes widened as his head lowered and his lips found hers. She felt a tingling jolt in the pit of her stomach, felt an electrifying need to be crushed in his embrace. His obvious male virility was arousing erotic feelings deep inside her; feelings that were better left dormant. The purely male scent of him filled her nostrils and she breathed deeply.

The smoldering flame in his eyes kindled a fire deep within. Mindlessly, she wrapped her arms around his waist. The action brought her body firmly against him and with a low growl, his lips found hers again.

Brandy was powerless to resist her feelings. Her feet seemed to be drifting along on clouds as she wrapped her arms around his neck, twining her fingers through his dark hair. When he burrowed his face against the tender skin of her neck, she shivered delicately and goose bumps broke out on her arms. He chuckled at her reaction, nipping playfully at her earlobe. A tightening started deep within her body and her breasts rose and fell with her quickened breathing. Her stomach seemed to have butterflies in it and her heart beat faster. But so did his. When she placed her head against his chest, she could hear his heart beating in rhythm with her own. His hand clasped the firmness of her breast, his fingers on her nipple. She caught her breath, feeling astonished at the tingling, electric sensation he'd caused. His mouth lowered, his tongue traced the curve of her neck. Pushing aside her blouse, he kissed the swell of her bosom, then his head moved lower and his lips found one taut peak and closed over it.

Brandy dredged up her last ounce of common sense.

"Don't," she gasped. "You must not do this."

He lifted his head and his black eyes narrowed to points of steel. "You don't mean that," he said in a hard voice.

"Yes. I do!" she cried. "It's wrong."

At first she thought he was going to ignore her; then he rolled over on his back and lay breathing heavily. When she started to move away, his hand reached out and stopped her. "Stay!" he said harshly.

She subsided and lay quietly beside him until his breathing slowed and became normal. "Sky Walker," she said hesitantly, "I'm sorry. But what you wanted was what a man and wife should have."

"You wanted it, too."

"That doesn't make it right," she said, unable to deny his words. Her voice came in harsh gasps. She felt ashamed for having allowed their feelings to become so aroused before calling a halt. She supposed it was because she felt indebted to him for saving her. But what he'd offered had been purely physical, and for a while, she had been grateful for it. Now she would not think of it more. She was surprised that she'd been able to stop him. His culture was so different than her own, she hadn't known what to expect. But he was obviously a caring man. Even though he was honor bound to carry out his mission, he'd taken time to help her. Somehow that thought consoled her. She didn't know what awaited her at their destination. But whatever it was, she would find the courage to face it.

Chapter Nine

The sun hung low in the western sky, painting the horizon with hues of red and gold, but Brandy had little thought for the beauty of the sky. The discomfort she was feeling, the weariness of mind and body, served to sap her strength until she walked with head bowed, trying to forget the overpowering thirst that was consuming her.

"It is not far now," Sky Walker said. "Soon we will have water, for we are close to the river."

Brandy swallowed hard. Her mouth seemed to be filled with cotton and what she could see of her skin looked gray with a coating of dust mixed with sweat. She had not realized they were climbing steadily until she topped the rise and saw the river only a short distance away. It was spread out before them, sparkling like a silver ribbon beneath the sun.

Her pulse accelerated. Water! A weight seemed to leave her shoulders. They had actually made it.

Forgetting her weariness, she hurried forward, stopping at the edge of the water only long enough to strip off her boots. Then she stepped into the water, feeling the wet coolness against her feet and ankles, swirling around her legs and thighs as she made her way deeper into the river.

And then she sank into the water, opened her mouth, and allowed the cooling liquid to flow inside. Joy bubbled in her laugh, shining in her eyes as she filled her lungs with air and submerged.

Brandy splashed and frolicked in the river for a while; then, exhaling a long sigh of contentment, she waded toward the shore. She was unaware of Sky Walker's gaze, taking in the way the wet fabric molded itself against her rounded thighs.

"Come on in," she called.

He smiled at her and shook his head. "I will wait until later," he said, turning to stare downstream. His gaze narrowed on a thin thread of smoke beyond the bend on the other side of the river. "Come. We do not have far to go now. Then we can rest."

"We are that close?" she asked, looking beyond the bend at the smoke drifting upward, faint against the dark backdrop of clouds.

He nodded his dark head. "Yes."

For some reason, the hair lifted at the base of her neck and fear trickled down her spine. Although she told herself there was no reason to fear, her mind refused to accept it. Her footsteps were slow as she followed Sky Walker down the riverbank.

When they rounded the bend, she stopped abruptly. Indian tepees were spread out as far as the eye could see.

Her green eyes darkened and her heart pounded wildly as she stared at them. There must be several hundred of the tepees. Brandy swallowed a bilious swell of panic. She had never dreamed there would be so many of them. What did it mean? And would it be safe for her to go among so many Indians? What would happen to her?

Suddenly she remembered stories she'd heard. Stories about Indian massacres and what happened to women taken as captives. Her father said they were stories designed to frighten, but those things didn't happen anymore. Not in these enlightened times. But how could he know for certain? He was only repeating what he'd heard.

Had she been stupid to come with Sky Walker? Her thoughts were frightened, jumbled as she turned eyes glimmering with fear on the warrior.

"Why . . . why have you brought me here?" she asked, her heart beating like a wild bird trying to escape from a cage.

His brows drew together in a heavy frown. "You insisted," he reminded her.

"I—I thought you were going to a town."

"I never said so."

"No, but—how far are we from Taos?"

He shrugged. "It makes no difference." He took her arm, pulled her toward the river. "Come."

Brandy dug hard into the sandy earth with her heels. She didn't want to cross the river, was suddenly fearful of being among so many of the Indians.

"What is wrong?" he asked impatiently. "You have nothing to fear as long as you are with me."

His words, rather than calming her fears, had set off an alarm in her already turbulent mind. "You have nothing to fear as long as you are with me," he'd said. But suppose she'd stumbled alone across this? If she had been alone what would have happened?

Shuddering, she pushed the thought from her mind.

Despite her efforts at control, her chin trembled and her eyes glittered with fear. Gulping in several deep breaths of air, she looked back at the Indian encampment. In this day and age, even friendly Indians commanded fear and respect. And how could she know that all the Indians would be friendly?

But friendly or not, she had no choice except to go ahead. Even now several warriors had spotted them and were moving toward the canoes that had been drawn up on the bank of the river.

Two braves left the others and with one man on each side, they pushed a canoe into the river and leapt lightly into the craft. While Brandy stood frozen, the canoe moved toward them, gliding silently through the water, trailing a little wake of ripples behind it.

Brandy wanted to run, cry, scream, anything except stand there and watch the Indians come closer. She stared at the boat and its occupants, her eyes locked in frightened anticipation.

"Do not worry, Sky Walker said. "You will come to no harm. And when I am finished here, then I will take you to your people."

"Is this the Peace Council you spoke of?"

"Yes."

Peace Council. That doesn't sound so ominous. She found a slight reassurance from his words. "I hadn't expected to see so many of your people," she said. "How long must we stay here?"

"We will speak of it later," he said impatiently. "Now my brothers, the Kiowas, are here to greet us."

Brandy heard the canoe bottom scrape against the gravel shoal. The two braves jumped out of it and approached them. Sky Walker hailed them, speaking in a guttural language that she could not understand. Her mind was a whirling vortex of confusion as she watched the warriors cautiously.

Like Sky Walker, they wore buckskins. Although both men talked with Sky Walker, one of them had his gaze fixed on her. The hairs at the base of her neck crawled with fear as she forced herself to meet the eyes that resembled black marbles set in ice . . . and quickly looked away.

One glance was all she needed and his image was embedded firmly in her mind. He had black hair parted at the center and worn loose around the shoulders. When he'd turned his head she could see one narrow braid running from the top of his head down to his back. Long strands of green beads ending with tassels of fur were fastened in his hair, while around his neck he wore a green scarf.

He turned to Sky Walker and spoke in the guttural language the others were using and somehow she was almost certain he was asking about her. Sky Walker answered shortly, then turned to her. "Buffalo Grass is a Cheyenne warrior. He wishes to be made known to you." Pointing at the other warrior, he said, "His companion is Long Knife. His people are the Kiowas." Before she could respond, he motioned her toward the canoe. "It is time to join my people."

Frowning, she stepped into the canoe, feeling it dip beneath her weight, then right itself. She seated herself in the bottom of the craft and Buffalo Grass stepped in beside her. To her consternation, he stayed there, picking up his paddle and waiting for the others. After a frowning glance at them, Sky Walker stepped into the canoe and seated himself at the other end. Then they began the journey across the river.

By the time they had landed, word had spread of the presence of a white girl among them, and the Indians stopped their work to stare at her.

A lean dog, with a wolfish look, came forward barking. He circled around her, little ridges of bristling hair along his spine, tail wagging suspiciously. Brandy felt she could hardly breathe; the musky smell of the Indians was close and she'd never heard so many voices speaking at once, not even in London. The babbling of voices rolled over her in waves and the Indian women came closer, their gazes fixed on her hair, shimmering gold beneath the sun's last rays. One of the women, bolder than the rest, reached out and touched her hair with curious fingers.

Brandy shrank closer to Sky Walker as she was poked at and stared at like she was some specimen in a zoo.

The dust was thick and she licked her dry lips. She grabbed Sky Walker's arm and clung tightly. At least he was someone familiar. But he seemed impatient with her fears. Shrugging her away, he joined the other men who had gathered near a large tepee that stood in the center of the compound. Brandy was left alone with the Indians staring at her, women, children, and men alike, their eyes never leaving her as they stared and stared.

Someone laughed, an ugly sound that broke the silence that had fallen over them. Sun-bronzed hands reached out and pulled at her clothing while others reached for her golden locks of hair.

Feeling a painful tug, Brandy whirled toward her tormenter. "Don't," she cried, tears filling her eyes. "That

99

hurt!" Sharp nails raked down her arm and she stared in horror at the blood welling up from the long scratch. "Leave me alone!" she cried, holding her arms up to shield her face.

But the Indians paid no attention to her words. The painful pinching and hair pulling went on. From the innermost regions of her mind she recalled her father's words: It is said the Indians admire courage and despise cowardice. Never lose your dignity before them. And above all else, you must never allow them to see your fear.

Suddenly, pain stabbed at her cheek. She swiped at it with her fingers, then stared at the blood. Anger surged over her, swamping her fear. But it wasn't so much anger at the woman who had struck her with the rock. Rather, the anger was directed at Sky Walker, who had said she'd be safe with him. The woman who'd thrown the rock had another one in her hand. She raised her arm, ready to let it fly.

"Don't you dare throw that!" Brandy snapped. Her green eyes were blazing, startling in their purity. The woman fell back a step, taken by surprise. But it lasted only a moment and Brandy found herself pushed toward the center of the compound, forced there by a wall of human flesh.

"Sky Walker!" Brandy shouted. "Where the hell are you?" Her father would have been shocked to hear her words, but she was so angry the words seemed appropriate. She tried to ignore the faces of the savages around her. Above all, she must not let her courage fail.

When she thought she couldn't take any more of their abuse, Sky Walker returned. She gripped his arm as though she were a drowning woman who'd been thrown a lifeline. "Where've you been?" she demanded.

He motioned toward a tepee. "Come with me," he said. "You will need to rest."

Rest? she stifled a hysterical giggle. Rest? She didn't need to rest. What she needed above all else was to get out of here, to leave this place of madness. But she kept silent and followed Sky Walker to the tepee. She felt a little easier when they were inside the buffalo hide lodge with the faces of the Indians shut away from sight.

"They were like savages," she said. "Look at my arms." She pulled the sleeve of her blouse up, showing him the reddened skin that was fast turning into bruises. "See what they did to me? And my face! Look at it! One woman hit me with a rock. Dammit, Sky Walker! You said I would be safe with you."

He seemed unimpressed with her wounds. "You are not badly injured," he said.

"Not hurt! Not hurt?" Her voice rose hysterically. "Look at the blood. What do you call hurt?"

"Calm yourself," he said. "They were only testing your strength."

"They were testing me? Do you mean they do this to all their visitors?"

He gave a long sigh. "You are making too much of this. I have no time to discuss it now. We will talk later."

When he turned to go, her fingers clutched at him. "Where are you going?"

He frowned at her. "A woman does not question her man."

"You're not my man!" she snapped. "And I'd damn well like to know what I'm supposed to do while you're off gallivanting about."

He lifted a dark brow. "You will prepare a meal, of

101

course."

"Of course," she muttered, slumping down on the sleeping mat. "How?"

"How?" His expression was incredulous. "Do you not know?"

"No."

"How can this be?" He studied her curiously. "Have you not been taught to cook?"

"No," she repeated, suddenly feeling inadequate. "There was no need. There was always someone else to do it for me." She looked around the sparse dwelling. Various leather bags and pouches hung from the ceiling while several clay bowls and pots rested beside a fire. "I don't think skills learned in my father's kitchen would help me here. There is no cookstove."

"Such things are for the white man," he said. "My people do not need such trappings."

"Well, I'm not an Indian!"

"No. You are a useless white woman. But you will have to manage."

"How?"

"I do not know, but I cannot ask for help from the other women. If I did, then everyone in the village would know how useless you are."

"Stop calling me useless!" she snapped. "And if you don't ask someone to show me what to do, then we won't eat."

"We will eat," he said grimly. "Even I can make a meal. I will build up the fire and show you how to prepare it. Then I must leave."

Brandy could see he was impatient with her inexperience. But, dammit! It wasn't her fault nobody had ever taught her to cook. And she hadn't asked to be brought here, had she?

Yes, an inner voice chided. You did.

"Go get some wood," Sky Walker said. "And I will build a fire."

"Where will I get it?"

He snorted impatiently. "I saw some outside the dwelling. It should be enough for tonight's meal. Tomorrow you must go out and gather buffalo chips to cook with."

Buffalo chips? Did he really expect her to cook with them? God! She hoped he was only joking. But somehow she felt he was not. Well, she'd just worry about that tomorrow.

Stepping outside the tepee, she found the wood. After gathering an armload, she hurried back inside, where Sky Walker was already searching through leather pouches for food. He handed her a handful of some kind of dried vegetables and told her to prepare them for the pot and fetch water to boil them in.

A scratching at the door caught his attention and he spoke in a guttural language, obviously bidding whoever was out there to enter. The hide covering was thrown back and an Indian girl stepped inside. Barely above five feet tall, she was slender, with lustrous black hair, her eyes dark and luminous.

Sky Walker's expression lightened when he spoke to the girl and he actually smiled. "Yellow Moon," he said, his dark gaze traveling over her womanly curves, barely hidden by the shapeless buckskin dress she wore. The two spoke together for a moment in the language Brandy couldn't understand, then he turned back to Brandy.

"This is Yellow Moon," he said. "She speaks your language and is willing to show you how to prepare the meal." His brows drew together and he said darkly, "And she will be silent about it." With that he turned and left the dwelling.

Yellow Moon watched him leave, then turned back to Brandy. "He is much man," she murmured. Although she had strong-boned features, there was a softness about her that lent beauty to her face. "He could have his pick of all the maidens. And yet he has chosen you."

"Oh, no," Brandy hurried to explain. "He didn't . . . we aren't going to be married. He's just helping me."

The girl raised dark eyebrows. "How is he helping you?"

"I was lost. He's taking me to Taos."

"Did he say so?"

"Yes, he—" She stopped. Did he say so? She couldn't remember. But he was, wasn't he? Suddenly she wasn't so certain. Did he have an ulterior motive for bringing her here? The thought continued to worry her mind, still didn't leave even after the meal was made and Yellow Moon had left. Brandy paced the tepee waiting for Sky Walker to return, afraid to go outside where the others were. Why didn't he come? Damn him! Why didn't he?

It was late when she ate a small portion of the food Yellow Moon had helped her prepare. Then, leaving the rest of the stew in the pot, she settled down on the sleeping mat. But her troubled thoughts kept sleep at bay. She was frightened and alone. And even Sky Walker had deserted her.

Chapter Ten

Sky Walker's mind was absorbed with thoughts of Brandy even as he hurried across the compound, intent on joining the other warriors in the council lodge. Although he'd appeared callous to her injuries, he wasn't. The sight of her scraped and bruised skin had pained him, but it would do no good for him to sympathize with her. She must continue to be strong, to face her future with the same courage she had shown on their journey.

He was so intent on his thoughts that he failed to see Long Knife until he collided with him.

"It is plain who occupies your thoughts," Long Knife teased, clapping Sky Walker on the shoulder with one hand. They had known each other since boyhood and each knew he could always trust the other. "But I do not blame you. The woman is good to look upon. You are very lucky to have her."

"She is not mine," Sky Walker said. "I found the girl lost in the forest. I could not leave her there or she would have died."

Long Knife suddenly looked grim. "The paleface means nothing to you?" When Sky Walker remained silent, Long Knife continued, "It would be unwise to let it be known you place no claim on her."

"Why?"

"I overheard Buffalo Grass speaking to his chief, High Backed Wolf. It seems the girl has found favor in the eyes of Buffalo Grass and his desire to possess her is strong."

A heavy weight settled on Sky Walker's shoulders. He recognized his predicament. High Backed Wolf was an important Cheyenne chief. Sky Walker's mission was to help bring about a friendly alliance with the Cheyenne and Arapaho. Perhaps he had made a grave mistake in bringing Brandy with him. But what else could he have done? Left her with the gunrunners?

"We have brought many presents for the Cheyenne and Arapaho," Long Knife continued. "Many horses and other gifts. But what better gift could be found to show our friendship than a woman with golden hair and grass green eyes."

No! Everything within Sky Walker cried out against it. "Buffalo Grass cannot have the woman," he said grimly. "If she must belong to someone, then she will belong to me." He squeezed his friend's shoulder. "Thank you for warning me," he said. "I should have realized this would happen. My thoughts were only on reaching the conference on time and eluding the enemies who would have stopped me."

"What will you do?" Long Knife asked.

"Tell them the woman is mine," Sky Walker said. "Then I will not be expected to make a gift of her to the Cheyennes."

Suddenly they were hailed by Little Wolf, a Comanche warrior they both knew well. "You must hurry," he told them. "All the chiefs are gathered now. They are only waiting for Hawkeye's representative."

Bidding them good-bye, Sky Walker hurried to the council lodge, where the others had already gathered. He sat down beside the Kiowa chief, Three Feathers.

The four tribes involved in the Peace Council spoke five distinct languages, but communication was not difficult. Many of the tribesmen were multilingual, while nearly every leader spoke more than one language. They had developed an abundance of interpreters from captives and intermarriage and, in addition, all the Plains tribes were proficient in sign language.

The peace pipe was lit and the chiefs smoked together, made speeches, and praised each other's worthiness and bravery. The climax of the chiefs' meeting came when the Kiowa Little Mountain rose and issued a long-awaited invitation.

"Now my friends, when the sun rises on a new day, I want you all, even the women and children of your tribes, to come to my lodge." Sky Walker knew his lodge was set apart from the rest. "Let all come by foot," he continued. "They will leave on horseback."

A mutter of approval followed his words, then everyone rose to leave. When Sky Walker would have followed them, Three Feathers reached out to stop him. "Stay a moment," he said.

When everyone had left, he spoke. "My brother Hawkeye did not come with you?"

"He could not," Sky Walker said. "The white man's disease swept through our tribe during the cold season. Hawkeye's wife has still not fully recovered." He knew he didn't have to explain what the woman was recovering from, for her fame as a healer had spread far and wide. "Many lives were taken by the sickness. But those brought

107

to She-Who-Heals recovered. Now she must regain her strength in order to bear Hawkeye's child safely."

Three Feathers looked grim at the mention of the white man's disease. Smallpox. Both the Kiowa and the Comanche had been decimated by an epidemic of smallpox during the previous winter. "When you return, give them both my good wishes. She is not only a good woman, obedient and thoughtful, but she is much needed by our tribes."

Sky Walker nodded and waited silently, knowing Three Feathers still had not revealed his reason for keeping him there.

"I noticed you brought no gifts to the Council," he said. "Did Hawkeye not send any?"

"Yes, he sent them," Sky Walker said. "He sent fifty horses and many rifles. But I was attacked by the Apaches who stole them from me. Please assure High Backed Wolf that other gifts will be sent to replace them."

"There is another way," Three Feathers said.

Sky Walker knew his words before they ever left his mouth.

"I am told you bring a paleface woman with you."

"Yes."

"The Cheyennes want her. She would make a pleasing gift to replace the ones you lost."

"I could not do that," Sky Walker said. "One does not make a gift of the woman he is to wed."

Three Feathers sighed. "You would not consider choosing another? There are many maidens who would consider it an honor to share your lodge."

"It would be unthinkable," Sky Walker said.

"Very well," Three Feathers said. "I will lend you fifty horses to give the Cheyenne. You may repay them whenever it is convenient."

After expressing his gratitude for such a generous offer, Sky Walker fell silent, waiting for Three Feathers to continue, for he had not indicated the conversation was over.

"Perhaps it would be a good thing to have the marriage ceremony here," Three Feathers said. "Yes. That would be good. A wedding feast is a festive time. Everyone enjoys such a celebration."

Everyone except perhaps the reluctant bride and groom, Sky Walker silently told himself.

"Although you were unable to bring gifts for the Cheyenne and Arapaho, you brought an occasion to celebrate. That is good. We will arrange to have the ceremony when the sun sets on the new day." Pleased with himself for his idea, he terminated the meeting and went on his way, leaving Sky Walker to deal with the situation.

Brandy was alone in the tepee when she woke. She must have slept late because she could hear children laughing and playing outside and dogs barking. She rose and dressed quickly, and had barely finished when someone scratched at the tent flap. It was Yellow Moon.

"Come," the girl said. "There is much to do before the feast tonight."

Brandy didn't want to go outside. Not without Sky Walker. But she hadn't seen hide nor hair of him since he'd brought her to the tepee. "Have you seen Sky Walker this morning?" she asked.

"He went hunting with the other men before sunrise," Yellow Moon said. "Four of the hunters have already returned carrying two deer. Some of the women have already set to work preparing it." She picked up the empty water container. "I will show you the spring," she said. "After you have replenished your water and fire chips, then we must help prepare the meat for tonight."

Although Brandy had dreaded moving about among the Indians, they paid her little attention. The hatred they had shown the day before was as though it had never been. Although she wondered why their attitude toward her had changed, she made no reference to it, perhaps fearing subconsciously the slightest mention of it would call forth the same hostility.

Brandy was dipping her water jug into the spring when she saw two warriors step from the grove of pines nearby. They were obviously returning from the hunt, for they were carrying a deer that had been strung to a long pole between them.

Apprehension settled over Brandy when she recognized Buffalo Grass as one of the warriors. Trying to still her fast-beating heart, Brandy ignored them, focusing her attention on the sparkling water that filled her container. She felt eyes on her, demanding to be recognized.

Don't be a coward! a silent voice chided. You can't stay here all day.

Her water jug was full. She lifted it out . . . and met the eyes of the Cheyenne warrior. The impact was like a sharp jolt. Fear shivered over her. She had seen that same look of wanting in Toby's eyes, and in the eyes of Franko and Gallinos. But the way they had looked at her was a pale comparison to the way Buffalo Grass looked.

An angry voice jerked her head around. Yellow Moon spoke harshly in the guttural language they used. Buffalo Grass spoke in kind. Yellow Moon's normally placid expression was angry, hard.

"Come, she told Brandy. "We must hurry back to the village."

Buffalo Grass spoke again. He seemed to be asking a question. Angry words were exchanged between the two. Then Yellow Moon hurried Brandy along the trail leading back to the village.

"You must not let him catch you alone," Yellow Moon said.

Brandy didn't have to be warned about Buffalo Grass. She had no intention of letting any of the Indians find her alone. "What did he say?" she asked.

"Never mind," Yellow Moon said. "He is only making noises."

Brandy's curiosity was aroused. "What kind of noises?"

Yellow Moon sighed. "He wanted me to tell you that you will be welcome in his lodge when you grow tired of Sky Walker." Her lips tightened grimly. "Do not tell Sky Walker about it. There would be trouble and we must have peace with the Cheyenne."

"Why would his words make Sky Walker angry?"

"His words were meant as an insult to Sky Walker, meant to suggest Sky Walker could not keep a woman happy."

Brandy laughed. "I don't think Sky Walker would take offense. He doesn't care if I'm happy or not."

Yellow Moon flashed her a secret smile. After the water had been left at the lodge and fire chips — which proved to be Buffalo droppings — gathered, Brandy and Yellow Moon set to work helping the other women. Brandy sliced deer meat from the carcass and handed the strips of meat to Yellow Moon, who placed it over wooden racks constructed above the glowing embers that had been raked from the fire. Several women were performing the same tasks while another group was absorbed with filling a huge communal pot with meat and vegetables.

"They prepare the meal for the feast," Yellow Moon explained.

"Who is the woman who keeps staring at me," Brandy whispered.

"She is White Owl, the sister of Buffalo Grass."

"I don't think she likes me very much," Brandy said.

Yellow Moon shrugged. "Perhaps not."

Brandy wondered what she'd done to cause White Owl's enmity. After all, the other women seemed to have accepted her presence among them. Why should the other woman's reaction be so different?

They worked in companionable silence all morning and Brandy noticed how easy the Indians were with the children, who had the free run of the camp. They climbed all over the women and men alike and ran through the camp playing their games. She reflected on how stiff her upbringing in England had been and how the Indian way of life was freer, more relaxed. They stopped at midday to eat a portion of the roasted meat before resuming their work. By nightfall she was weary but felt good knowing she had done something useful.

"Now you must be made ready for the celebration," Yellow Moon said. "Wait in your lodge until I come for you."

The other woman was gone before Brandy could protest that she'd rather not attend the celebration. She was tired, wanted nothing more than to rest.

Pushing back her golden hair, she allowed the air to cool her neck. After entering the tepee, she frowned down at her torn clothing. It was soiled and her blouse was held together by a knot tied at her midriff. If she must attend the celebration, then she would have to do something about the tear. Untying the knot, she slipped the blouse from her shoulders and bent her head to examine it.

Suddenly the entrance flap was lifted and Sky Walker stepped inside.

"What are you doing here?" she gasped.

Sky Walker's lips twitched as Brandy clutched her blouse against her heaving bosom. "Would you please leave?" she asked haughtily, her cheeks flushing bright red.

"Would you ask your husband to leave his own dwelling?" he asked.

"You're not my husband!"

"We will soon remedy that."

"We will do what?" Her emerald eyes glittered brightly. "Exactly what does that mean?"

"We are to be married." The words were said coldly. Sky Walker was still angry at being put in such a position. He had not the slightest wish to be married. A woman would only clutter up his life. If he had need for a woman, there were plenty of them eager to warm his bed . . . without any emotional tangles.

"Married?" Her voice raised to a hysterical pitch. "You've got to be crazy! I have no wish to marry anyone. Especially not you."

"Nevertheless, you shall do so."

"Please turn your back while I dress," she said haughtily. "Then we can sit down and discuss this like rational human beings."

"There is nothing to discuss. Although I have no wish

113

to take a wife, your foolishness has made it imperative that we marry."

"My foolishness? What do you mean?"

"You insisted I bring you with me. Now Buffalo Grass wants you."

"Suppose he does?" She stared at him with wide eyes. "What difference does that make?"

"You wish to be given to him?"

"Of course not!"

"I have told you how important this gathering of the tribes is. We cannot risk alienating the Cheyenne. I have told them you are mine. Three Feathers, chief of the Kiowas, decided a festive occasion, such as a wedding celebration, would help relations between the tribes."

"I won't do it," she said.

"You have no choice. If you do not become my wife, then you will become his."

"I don't see any difference," she snapped.

"Very well," he said. "He may have you."

"No!" Her eyes had become wide and fearful. For some reason she hadn't expected him to say that. "You can't mean that. You wouldn't really have me marry him."

His lips tightened. "It makes no difference to me."

"You said you would take me to Taos."

"If I am to help you, you must obey me."

"But to become your wife . . ."

"You have no need to fear me." His dark eyes were like stone. "I have no wish to be saddled with a paleface for the rest of my days."

"I'm sorry," she muttered, feeling curiously hurt. "I do appreciate what you've done for me. After we reach Taos, you need never see me again."

"It is agreed then. We will marry now and when the

peace council is over, I will take you to the white-eyes and leave you."

The drums sounded loudly in the night. Thrum . . . thrum . . . thrum.

She was dressed in white doeskin, an ornate beaded dress that had been given to her by the Cheyenne. Now Yellow Moon finished combing her hair and gave a final pat to it.

"This is a special night," the woman said. "You are envied by many. Especially, the girl, White Owl. It is said she wished to have Sky Walker for her own." She began to rub sage on Brandy's arms. "You will not find the marriage without pleasures," Yellow Moon continued. "Sky Walker is much man. He looks as though he would know how to make a woman feel pleasure in the bed."

"Oh, but—" Brandy stopped, realizing she had been about to say there would be no consummation of the marriage. She must learn to curb her tongue. It had a way of running away with itself and getting her into trouble.

Suddenly the flap was thrown back and a young girl entered. After giving Brandy a shy smile, she spoke to Yellow Moon.

"It is time," Yellow Moon said.

Curbing her fears, Brandy rose to her feet, reminding herself there was no need to be concerned. The wedding would not be binding in her world.

What about Sky Walker? an inner voice cried.

We will see the last of each other in Taos, she silently answered. He will be free to take another wife.

Somehow, the thought of another woman in his bed left a bad taste in her mouth, which was a peculiar thing, for

115

she certainly didn't want him herself.

Then she remembered how his lips had tasted when they covered hers, how his hands had felt on her body. Brandy flushed at the memory; her heart quickened, her green eyes glittered. She must not think of such things. Not with him waiting to wed her. It would be a wedding ceremony that was necessary, but not binding. Suddenly she wondered if he understood that.

Chapter Eleven

Brandy's courage nearly failed when she stepped outside the tepee and saw all the people waiting for her. With Yellow Moon beside her, she moved toward the huge bonfire in the middle of the compound.

A woman blocked her way. It was White Owl, the Cheyenne girl. "You will never hold Sky Walker," she said. "He will never be happy with a paleface. But you can never return to your people."

"Pay her no attention," Yellow Moon said, keeping a firm grip on Brandy's arm as she tried to edge past the other woman.

"I am surprised you have not tried to dissuade her," White Owl said to Yellow Moon. "It is said you favor the Comanche warrior yourself."

"Get out of the way, White Owl," Yellow Moon ordered. "You are interfering in things that do not concern you."

The girl's eyes flashed with anger. "You will be sorry for this night," she hissed. Then, reluctantly, she moved aside and let them pass.

Yellow Moon steered Brandy toward the bonfire.

Poppa! Brandy cried inwardly. Where are you?

If only she'd had more time. But one look at Buffalo Grass's expression told her there was no way out for her.

Suddenly she saw Sky Walker striding toward her. The firelight cast flickering shadows across the hard planes of his face. Uncertainty settled over her like a dark mantle. Was she foolish to go through with this? But what else could she do? And the marriage would not be valid in the white world. It was a Comanche ceremony, a way of saving her from the Cheyenne warrior who had thought to possess her.

The drums beat loudly in the night, shutting out every other sound. Sky Walker's eyes had never left her face since she'd stepped from the tepee. Now she felt the pull of them, almost mesmerizing in their intensity.

He stopped before her and reached for her hand. "Come," he commanded. "It is time."

She swallowed hard. "I . . . Sky Walker," she said, resisting the tug of his hand. "I . . . I've changed my mind." Her voice quivered, her eyes were stricken. "I can't go through with it."

His lips thinned into a narrow line and his eyes darkened with anger. "You must," he said. "Did you not understand that you have a choice between me or Buffalo Grass?"

"Y-yes. But does it have to—do we have to do it tonight? Perhaps tomorrow would be better." She knew she was only trying to buy a little more time.

His eyes softened slightly. "You will not be safe from the other warriors until we are wed," he said. "Now stop resisting. It does not look good before the others."

Still she continued to resist, her green eyes warring with his. How could she possibly go through with this?

Even with the knowledge that it wasn't legal in the white community, in the eyes of the Comanche, she would be his wife.

"Have you chosen Buffalo Grass?" Sky Walker asked harshly. "Think well before you do. Shall I tell you what to expect at his hands."

"No!" She shivered, accepting defeat. "Let's get on with it," she mumbled, feeling as though she'd sealed her own fate with her words.

Brandy's surprise mingled with dismay when, at the conclusion of the ceremony, Sky Walker slipped the ring from his finger and placed it on hers.

God! It made the ceremony seem so real!

And it wasn't! It wasn't!

She'd had no idea the Indian customs were so similar to her own. Her stomach knotted with tension, a tension that continued to build through the feast that followed the marriage rites. And all the time she was totally aware of the man beside her who seemed to be waiting as well . . . waiting for the end of the celebration.

Her hands and feet felt icy and she held her body stiffly erect as she watched the dancers whirling and gyrating, shaking their feathered lances.

She was unprepared when he rose to his feet and pulled her upright. "It is time for us to leave," he said.

She should have felt relief. But suddenly leaving was the last thing she wanted. Brandy realized she was being ridiculous, she had no reason to fear Sky Walker. But she didn't want to be alone with him.

She couldn't be alone with him!

"I'd like to stay awhile and watch the dancing," she protested, her cheeks flushing bright red.

"Custom decrees we leave now," he insisted.

119

Taking her hand, he led her toward their tepee. After they were closed inside, he removed his shirt and laid it aside. She watched him, feeling completely fascinated by his presence. His ebony hair hung loose about his shoulders, his bronze skin glistened in the soft firelight.

She sucked in a sharp breath when he turned to her, for the hunger in his eyes told her she must be wary. "Don't," she said, when he reached for her.

"Yes," he said, snagging her wrist with his fingers. He raised his other hand to her face and gently stroked her cheek. She shuddered at his touch.

"What . . . what do you mean to do?" she asked.

Pushing a golden curl away from her face, he said, "I only wish to love you."

"But . . . but, you can't mean that," she said.

"Yes. I do." He wrapped his arms around her, pulling her into his embrace. His breath flowed softly against her cheek, his lips hovering only inches away. "We are married now," he said. "You belong to me."

"But . . . it's only a marriage in name only," she said. "The ceremony meant nothing . . . to either of us."

He smiled down at her. "No?"

"No!" she said.

His lips brushed softly against hers and she shuddered at the thrilling sensation that coursed through her body. His hands slid slowly down her back and she shivered again.

"Why do you tremble so?" he asked. "It is not my intention to harm you."

Her heart raced in her breast and she felt weak with some unknown longing. His face was only inches from hers, his breath warm and caressing. He gazed deeply into her eyes. "Have no fear," he murmured. "You will come to no harm. That is the last thing I would wish."

"Then, please, please let me go!"

"Go?" His eyes held hers. "Where would you go?"

"Just . . . just out of your arms."

"Why do you protest? Don't you know I feel your heart beating against mine. So fast." He spread one hand over her left breast. "It races even faster now. You want me to teach you the ways of husband and wife. And I would deny you nothing."

"No," she protested. "I don't . . . don't want you to teach—"

"Do not protest. I can feel the way you tremble in my arms, can see the way your eyes evade mine." He lifted her chin, forcing her to look up at him. "Kiss me, sweet one. Let us remember this night forever."

"Please. You must not talk this way."

"How, would you have me speak, I wonder." His lips covered hers, gently caressing. His tongue came out and traced the outline of her lips and she shuddered with the pleasure he was bringing her.

Unconsciously, with her pulse drumming in her head, she pressed closer against him, seeking to increase the pleasure he was giving her.

Drawing her tighter against him, he pressed her soft body against the length of him. Her soft curves seemed to melt against him, forming to the shape of his body.

Then he pushed her garments aside. The drumbeat was serving to lull her, creating a magical enchantment around them. She returned his kisses and when his hand found her breast, she uttered no protest. The feelings he was arousing in her needed no interpretation. For some reason, she felt married to him, unable to object to his attentions, not even wanting to. Instead, she wound her

121

arms around his neck and returned his caresses.

"No," she whispered, when he began to remove her clothing. But he paid no heed to her protests. Soon she was divested of her clothing and he had removed his. She uttered no other protest as he laid her back and covered her body with his. It seemed fate had always planned this for her. This night, with this man.

Her husband.

His hand slid across her stomach, then glided slowly and deliberately down her leg, then up the inner side of her thigh.

"You are so beautiful," he whispered, lowering his lips to taste her neck. "From the moment I saw you I knew this night would come to pass." His head lowered to her breast, and when his mouth closed over the tautened peak, she cried out with pleasure.

"There's no need to be afraid of me," he said, looking deeply into her eyes. "Don't you know how much I need you?" His mouth returned to hers to capture her lips in a demanding kiss that left her a trembling mass of confusion and desire.

Brandy groaned and pulled him tightly against her, caressing his back, feeling the hard muscles beneath her hands. Soon he had her wild with desire, wanting more than he was giving.

As though sensing her need, he raised himself above her. She felt a momentary pain as he entered her body. A surprised gasp escaped her lips, a gasp that ended abruptly with his searing kiss.

Sky Walker was still for a moment, allowing her time to accommodate him; then he moved, slowly at first, then faster and faster, introducing her to a world of passion that she had never before even imagined.

Her body was his to do with as he pleased, fed by the fires of passion that he was building. They flamed higher and higher, burning brighter with each thrust, leading them along unexplored pathways. His thrusts became deeper and deeper, and her passion slowly built into an all-consuming desire until finally she was lifting her body, meeting each thrust of his with one of her. Then, they catapulted together through eternity, until they lay entwined, shuddering with ecstasy, experiencing the joy of their mutual release.

Chapter Twelve

When Brandy woke the next morning, Sky Walker was gone, and she was faced with the reality of what she'd done. She bolted upright on the sleeping matt, burying her face in her palms.

Remembering how she'd responded to Sky Walker's touch, she was filled with self-loathing.

My God! He was a Comanche Indian! How could her body have betrayed her in such a manner? Even now she could be carrying his child.

Instinct told her to flee! To escape before he returned. *But how?*

Without a horse she would die. If only she hadn't lost Thunder. He could have carried her away from here. If she had . . .

Suddenly she jerked her head up. She was a fool! It wasn't imperative that she have Thunder! Any horse would do. All she needed was a mount. And there were plenty to be had just outside the compound. All she had to do was get one and find a way to leave without anyone knowing.

Which was next to impossible.

The place for the Peace Council had been carefully selected so they could not be taken unawares by intruders. Only sparse vegetation covered the landscape in every direction.

Brandy's jaw set grimly. Although escape seemed out of the question, she refused to give in to defeat. Sky Walker had probably gone hunting again. If he had, then he would be gone most of the day.

She reached for her clothing, her mind made up. She would find some way to leave before he returned.

She must.

Her fingers had automatically closed over the doeskin dress. She jerked away with revulsion and looked for the torn blouse and skirt.

Someone had taken them away.

Her lips tightened grimly as she donned the doeskin dress and fastened it. At least they'd left her boots. After pulling them on, she left the tepee, intent on devising a plan of escape.

The village was a beehive of activity. Women were hard at their work, some weaving baskets out of yucca fiber, some sewing, while others were busy preparing meat again. Across the compound she saw Yellow Moon talking to another woman. Brandy turned away, unwilling to be caught in a conversation with the woman who'd befriended her.

Realizing she couldn't afford to waste time, she hurried toward the rope corral where some of the horses were kept confined. She knew there were others, hobbled farther away, but wasn't certain of the direction.

Hearing a voice raised in the distance, she looked around . . . and collided with something solid.

Whirling, she stood facing Buffalo Grass.

Brandy stepped back in fright, her hands clenching into fists. "I — I didn't see you," she stuttered.

He remained silent, his eyes cold, menacing. His very presence was ominous. Suddenly, he reached out and captured her wrist between his fingers. "Do not scream," he said with threatening quietness.

She was so frightened that it took her a minute to realize he had spoken in English. Why had he pretended not to understand her language. "Please let me go," she said, her voice quivering. "I have work to do. Sky Walker will be expecting me."

"Sky Walker has gone hunting with the others," he said. "But even had he not, he would not object. You did not please him last night and he has given you to me."

Her heart gave a painful jerk. "I don't believe you," she whispered.

His fingers dug into her wrist. "You would call me a liar?" he asked harshly.

Brandy's breath came in a harsh gasp, making it impossible for her to speak. She twisted her wrist, struggling to free herself from his grip, but her efforts were ineffectual against his greater strength.

Suddenly she became aware of someone behind her. It was his sister.

"What are you doing with Sky Walker's woman?" Although she spoke to her brother, she spoke in English and her eyes never left Brandy.

"She no longer belongs to him. He found her displeasing and gave her to me. Take her to our tepee. She will help with your work."

The girl's lips curled with contempt. "Why do you want the girl Sky Walker has thrown away? If she is not good

126

enough for a Comanche, then she will not do for a Cheyenne."

Brandy stared at them. Was it true? Had Sky Walker really given her to Buffalo Grass? He couldn't have. He had wed her to save her from the Cheyenne warrior. Hadn't he?

Or had he only told her that?

He had said it was of utmost importance to appease the Cheyenne. Perhaps he'd only been toying with her, intent on taking his own pleasure before handing her over to Buffalo Grass.

Hurt mingled with anger, making her eyes glitter like the emerald ring on her finger. Wrenching her wrist away from Buffalo Grass's grip, she tugged at the ring, but it wouldn't slide off. She wasn't going to stay here anyway. Somehow she would find a way to leave.

"Perhaps you are right," White Owl was saying. "Perhaps she will be able to help me."

"I see no reason she should not warm my bed," Buffalo Grass said.

Warm his bed? She'd kill herself first!

Where the hell was Sky Walker? How could he have done such a thing? When he returned, she would demand an explanation. But was it really necessary? Hadn't he said all along she was nothing but trouble?

Well. He didn't know what trouble was. But he'd damn well learn.

"My sister will take you to our lodge," Buffalo Grass said. "I will be along soon."

Brandy remained silent, pretending to accept defeat. "I am returning to Sky Walker's tent," she said coldly. "He will have to tell me to go."

"Very well."

She felt surprise that he didn't insist. She didn't expect him to give in so easily. White Owl followed her to Sky Walker's lodge. "I don't want you in my lodge," she said. "You will only bring disgrace to my brother."

"Don't worry," Brandy said coldly. "I have no intention of living in your lodge. I refuse to allow myself to be passed around in such a way."

"You have no choice . . . unless . . ." Her eyes became sly. "There is a way. You could leave this place."

Brandy's lips stretched tight. "A very good idea," she said. "Get me a horse and I'll just do that."

"You would be stopped."

"Not if you help me. If we had some errand outside the village. Something that required a pack animal . . ."

"We could gather buffalo chips. When we are far enough away, then you could ride off. It would take me awhile to walk back and sound the alarm."

Brandy studied the other girl. She actually sounded as though she might be persuaded to help. Why?

"You must carry some food and water," the other girl was saying. "Otherwise you will be tempted to return."

"You're going to help me?"

"I am but a foolish girl who cannot stand to see another's pain. Yes. I will help."

"And you'll tell me how to reach Taos?

"No. Taos is too far. You would be caught."

"What about Bent's Fort?"

"William Bent is married to a Cheyenne woman. He would not hide you. But there is a mining town only a day's ride from here. If you go there, the other white-eyes would protect you."

"Brandy!"

Hearing her name called, Brandy turned to see Yellow Moon approaching.

"Say nothing to her," White Owl whispered. "She would betray you."

"Get me the horse," Brandy muttered. "Make the excuses and come back for me. I'll get rid of Yellow Moon."

A deep sense of loneliness washed over Brandy as she watched the sun set in a blaze of glory. She seemed to be the only person in the world. Her eyes welled with unexplained tears and she blinked them away furiously.

She would not cry over Sky Walker.

Never.

Her green eyes chilled and her mouth compressed grimly. She had done what she had to do. Sky Walker had left her no choice when he'd given her away to another warrior.

But had he really given her away?

She'd had time to think about it since she'd left the village. Time to wonder why he would have done such a thing. Especially when he'd married her to protect her from Buffalo Grass. Why should he suddenly change his mind and give her to him? If only he'd been there when she woke up. If only they'd had a chance to talk together.

Her mount snorted, reminding her the sun was going down and it would soon be night. She must get to shelter by nightfall. Digging her heels into the flanks of her mount, she urged him into a gallop.

Sky Walker's stride lengthened as he neared the village. He could hardly wait to see his bride. Brandy. A smile tugged at the corner of his mouth at the thought of her.

Remembering how she looked last night, he felt an ache in his gut that would have to wait until night to be satisfied.

Would his pale-skinned wife be shocked to know his thoughts? Even now he visualized her lying naked on the sleeping mat. The sudden tightening in his groin had him quickly turning his thoughts in another direction. If he didn't, he wouldn't wait for night to fall before he made love to her.

Hearing footsteps beside him, he turned to see Long Knife. "You appear to be in a hurry," the warrior said. "Could the reason be waiting in your lodge?"

"Where else would my woman wait for me?"

Long Knife laughed. "Indeed. Where else?"

"You may well laugh," Sky Walker said. "But I have seen your eyes turn many times toward Yellow Moon."

"Yellow Moon is only one of many," Long Knife said. "I will take my time before I decide who is to share my lodge."

Sky Walker grinned. "Let us hope the maiden is not taken while you are deciding." He stopped before his te-pee, unwilling to invite the other man inside, wanting to greet Brandy alone.

Long Knife seemed to sense his need. Clapping Sky Walker on the shoulder, he went on his way.

Lifting the tepee flap, Sky Walker stepped eagerly inside. "Brandy," he said softly. No one answered. Disappointment flooded through him. He'd wanted her there, waiting for him. Realizing that she would come as soon as she heard he was back, he stripped off his buckskin shirt and tossed it aside. Then he settled down on the sleeping mat to wait.

Stretching his arms, he sighed with pleasure. It had been a good hunt. He had killed three antelope. Yes. A good hunt. Tomorrow Brandy's hours would be occupied helping the other women dry the meat while he talked with the council.

But tonight would be theirs.

After they had eaten . . .

Raising his head, he looked around the empty tepee. Why hadn't she started a fire? Why was there no meal cooking? A faint twinge of alarm coursed through him, but he forced it back down. Perhaps she had gone to visit Yellow Moon and had lost track of the time.

Leaving the tepee, he strode across the compound until he came to the tepee that housed Yellow Moon's family.

"I have not seen her since shortly after sunrise," Yellow Moon told him. Her dark lustrous eyes were worried. "My mother has not been feeling well and I could not leave her for any length of time. When I explained this to Brandy, she said she had made plans to gather fire chips with White Owl."

He breathed easier. "Then they are together."

"No. I saw White Owl earlier. She was washing her clothing at the river."

Sky Walker's fear for Brandy began to grow. Something had happened to her, and he must discover her whereabouts . . . quickly.

He had turned to go when Buffalo Grass hailed him. "I hear you search for your woman," he sneered. "It is useless. She is gone."

"What do you mean?"

"She took a horse and rode away. My sister, White Owl,

saw her leave." Buffalo Grass's eyes glinted with spite. "You should have let me have her. I know how to keep a woman."

Sky Walker's muscles bunched. Buffalo Grass had insulted him. They both knew it. A crowd had gathered around them . . . waiting . . . watching tensely.

Suddenly High Backed Wolf and Three Feathers joined the crowd.

"I have heard your woman has left," Three Feathers said. "That is good. The Peace Council is no place for domestic quarrels. High Backed Wolf sent a tracker to follow the woman's trail. When he finds her, he will return. You must put her out of your mind for now."

Sky Walker shut his mouth tight. Although the waiting would be hard, he would wait. The Cheyenne knew this country well and there was no place she could hide from them. He would have to stay here until the peace conference was over. . . . Then, no matter where she had gone, he would find her.

Chapter Thirteen

The shadows were lengthening and Brandy was beginning to think the Cheyenne girl had sent her to a nonexistent mining town when she heard the sound of wagon wheels against hard-packed earth . . . and beyond that, the rinky-tink sound of a piano.

She had found it!

Urging her mount forward, she passed the yawning mouth of an abandoned mine.

The mining town was little more than a small settlement laid out in a clearing. A few buildings had been built of rough logs and chinked with mud, but most of the business establishments were nothing more than tents.

Although Brandy had heard wagon wheels rolling, the street was empty.

Pulling up her mount in front of the first building, she slid to the ground, circled around a mud hole, pushed open the door, and stepped inside.

The leather-faced old man leaning against a plank counter jerked his head up and stared at her in bewilderment.

"Where'd you come from?" he asked, squinting at her

with faded blue eyes. "I ain't never seen you before."

"No," she said. "I've only just arrived in town. I'm Lady Brandy Tremayne." Brandy didn't hesitate to use her title, hoping it would help her get to Taos faster. "I desperately need some help. I must get to Taos as quickly as possible."

"Thet so?" he inquired. "Taos is two days' ride from here. Stage don't come through these parts." He stuck out a gnarled hand. "Name's Jonas," he said. When she took it briefly, he gave her hand a hard shake and let it drop.

"Can you help me?" she asked.

"I dunno," he said, scratching his grizzled head with gnarled fingers. "Reckon Jeffers is the onliest one could spare somebody to take you to Taos. But I don't knows he would put hisself out."

"I would see that he's paid for his trouble," she said. "I—I don't have any money with me, but I can get some in Taos."

His gaze dwelt on her doeskins. "Looks like you done spent a spell with the Injuns," he commented. "Thet right?"

She nodded and ran a hand through her disheveled hair. "Yes. I was with them for a short time. The caravan I was traveling on was ambushed by renegades. They killed my father, but I escaped. If a Comanche warrior hadn't found me, I'd still be lost."

He nodded, sliding his faded blue eyes past her to the horse outside. "See the Comanch ain't with you now."

"No. I'm alone." Brandy had no intention of explaining further.

He cleared his throat. "Well, I guess Jeffers is the one to ask. Like I done said, he's the onliest one could send somebody with you. Could even prob'ly put you up for a spell if 'twas needed." He looked away from her, back to his newspaper, then his eyes came back to hers, hesitantly, uncertain. "Ain't so sure you'd want to stay in his place, though."

"I'd rather not stay in town. I just need a guide to Taos. Could you tell me where I can find your Mr. . . . Jeffers, did you say?"

"Thet's his name. But Jeffers ain't nobody's man." His gaze was shrewd. "Ain't so sure I'd be doin' you a kindness by gettin' him for you, but if'n you wanta talk to him, best I bring him here."

"Please don't trouble yourself," she protested. "Just tell me where I can find him."

"Ain't no trouble," he said, headed for the door. "An' Jeffers, he's at the saloon across the way. Most everbody's at the saloon by now."

The saloon.

Now she thought she understood his reluctance for her to find Jeffers on her own. He'd only been trying to protect her delicate sensibilities from the type of man who frequented the place. A smile of gratitude curled her lips, softening her features.

"That's very kind of you," she said. "If you're certain you don't mind finding Mr. Jeffers for me, then I'll just wait here for you."

"Better all around," he muttered.

Brandy watched him hurry out of the building, wondering why Jonas still appeared nervous. Was it just because Jeffers was in the saloon, or was there another reason? It was possible she was imagining the whole thing. She'd just have to wait and see.

Jonas wasn't gone more than ten minutes. When he returned, he was followed by a lithe, deeply tanned man

135

wearing a trim black suit with an embroidered vest and a black, flat-crowned hat.

After Jonas performed the introductions, Jeffers sauntered over to Brandy and studied her beneath hooded eyes. His gaze went from the top of her head to the tip of her toes, lingering overlong on the supple figure between. As he openly appraised her, she lifted her chin and tugged at her skirt, frowning at him as a blush rode high in her cheeks. She was unused to such boldness from a man and took an instant dislike to him. But she forced herself to stay her opinion, realizing how badly she needed his help.

"Jonas tells me you want to go to Taos," he said.

"Yes. My father, Lord Tremayne, and I were traveling there at the invitation of the governor. Our caravan is long overdue and they must be searching for us." She had deliberately stressed her father's title, something she rarely did.

"A lord?" he questioned. At her nod, he stuck out his hand, affecting a friendly fashion; and after only a moment's hesitation, she held hers out to him. "How'd you come to be alone out here?"

She repeated the explanation she'd given Jonas.

"Lucky you found the town," he said. "You could have been lost for months on this mountain."

"I know," she said. "Could you find someone to take me to Taos?"

"I'm afraid that's impossible right now," he said. "We're short of people around here. Every available man is needed."

Every available man? For some reason, she didn't believe him. "Then there's nothing to do except go on alone," she said stiffly.

"You'd better stop for the night," he said. "You'd be

sure to get lost in the dark. Come morning I may be able to spare someone. Meanwhile I'll put you up for the night."

"I wouldn't think of imposing," she said. "If you'll just tell me where I can find a hotel . . ."

He gave an abrupt laugh. "No hotel in this hole of a town," he said. "But I do have rooms I rent out. You won't find anything else."

For some reason she didn't quite trust Jeffers. She gave him a polite smile. "That's very nice of you," she said. "But I think I'd like to check around first."

"Sure. You go right ahead," he said. "If you need me I'll be in the saloon." Whistling softly between his teeth, he left the store.

Brandy turned to Jonas, who'd returned to his place behind the counter. "Jonas. Is Mr. Jeffers trustworthy?"

He gave a long sigh. "Whisht you hadn't asked me thet, ma'am. Purely do whisht you hadn't."

"I take it he's not. Then why did you fetch him?"

"Ain't nobody else can help you but Jeffers," Jonas muttered.

"Surely there must be someone. Why can't you . . . ?

"This ain't much of a town we got here, ma'm. I keep this store open sixteen hours a day. Ain't much time for nuthin' else. Sure is a sorry place you come to for help."

"Mister Jeffers makes me nervous, Jonas."

"Better you stay nervous of him, miss."

"But you can see my position, can't you? I'll only be here for one night. Don't you know someone who'd be willing to let me stay with them?"

"Yes, ma'm, I surely do. But they's no women in them places. Fact is, women's as scarce as hen's teeth around here." He shook his grizzled head and looked at her sadly

137

"You couldn't a picked a worse place to come if 'n you tried."

She gave a long sigh. She was bone weary and hungry. Perhaps things would look better after she'd eaten and had a good night's sleep. "Mr. Jeffers's rooms, Jonas. Where are they?"

"In the saloon down the street."

Her lips tightened. Somehow, she'd suspected as much. "Do they have locks on the door?"

"Ain't sure, ma'am. But was I you, I'd make damn sure nobody could get in afore I bedded down."

Oh, God! she was so tired. Why did life have to be so hard. "Perhaps I'd do better to sleep in the forest," she said.

"Wouldn't do no good now," Jonas said. "By now everybody in the saloon knows you're here. There'd be no hidin' from 'em. You'd be better off behind a locked door."

"You're probably right," she said. "Thank you for your help, Jonas."

"Wasn't no help," he muttered.

Leaving the store, she made her way to the saloon — easily identified by the rinky-dink piano — pushed wide the double doors, and stepped inside. Instantly her senses were assaulted with barroom noises, sour whiskey, and stale cigarette smoke.

Fighting against the urge to back out again, Brandy squared her shoulders, lifted her chin at a defiant angle, and let her eyes travel over the room. Behind a long, ornately carved oak bar, bedecked with mirrors, a bartender polished a glass. His eyes met hers and his movements stilled. She tried to ignore the painted women in their scanty costumes being pawed by drunken men as she searched for . . . and found, Jeffers, deep in

138

conversation with a burly, heavyset man.

A hush fell over the room as the occupants became aware of her presence. Although she kept her eyes fastened on Jeffers, she was aware that everyone was watching her.

"So here you are," Jeffers said, his lips formed in a smile that managed to soften his features. Reaching out a well-manicured hand, he hooked his fingers around her forearm and drew her closer. "I was just sending Stony here to install a lock on your bedroom door. I'm sure you'll feel much safer that way."

Had she perhaps misjudged him? It certainly would seem so. She offered him a smile. "How very kind of you," she said. "I must admit a lock would make me sleep much easier."

"Consider it done," he said, steering her toward a door behind him. "We can wait in my office while Stony installs the lock."

When the door was closed between them and the saloon, he spoke again. "I must apologize about the room being in a saloon. But this is only a mining town. Barely civilized. Certainly never graced with a lady of quality before."

She began to relax, wondering why she'd been so nervous about him. He was really quite nice. "I've already made arrangements to have a meal prepared for you." His eyes traveled over her doeskin dress before returning to her face. "I forgot about clothing. We must do something about that as well."

"You've already done too much," she said. "I couldn't let you do more."

"It will be my pleasure. And I'm sure you don't want to appear in Taos wearing animal skins. You don't want to give anyone the wrong impression."

She frowned. "Surely I can be excused for wearing less than perfect clothing after the ordeal I've been through," she said.

"You'd be surprised at the gossip that abounds in these frontier towns. Many an innocent woman has actually been tarred and feathered and run out of town on a rail, for nothing more than the suspicions of the good women of the town. A beautiful woman is always suspect."

Suddenly the door swept open. "Well, lookee who's here!" The harsh voice had a familiar ring that made Brandy's heart leap with fear.

She jerked around and sucked in a sharp breath.

Franko!

God! What was he doing here?

Dread swept over her as her eyes darted from Franko to Jeffers. Had she fallen from the frying pan into the fire?

"What are you doing here?" she gasped.

Jeffers gaze swept from Franko to Brandy. "I take it you two know each other."

"Yes," she said. "We certainly do. Franko and his ruffians abducted me. He met with the renegade, Gallinos, about the purchase of some rifles."

Jeffers seemed to consider her words while he took a cigar from his breast pocket. Biting off the end, he stuck the cigar in his mouth and fired it up. Only then did he speak. "Did Gallinos buy them?"

"No. He bought me instead." Anger surged through her. Jeffers seemed unconcerned with her words, as did Franko. "Aren't you going to do anything?" she asked.

"Why? It's none of my affair."

"Perhaps it would be the sheriff's affair," she suggested boldly.

Franko laughed. "Don't have no sheriff in this town."

"I'm the law around here," Jeffers said. "I make the laws and see they are enforced."

"Then arrest this man."

"Why? He hasn't committed a crime here."

"But he is a gunrunner."

"You got any guns, Franko," Jeffers asked.

"Sure," Franko said easily. "The ones I'm wearing."

"Man's got a right to wear a gun to protect himself," Jeffers said.

Before Brandy could speak, the door opened and Stony stuck his head inside. "Lock's on the door, boss."

"Good," Jeffers said. "Looks like you're all fixed up, Brandy. Stony, send Josie to me."

"You're not really going to let this man run loose," Brandy protested.

"None of my business." Jeffers turned to the dark-haired girl who'd entered the room. "This young lady is Brandy Tremayne, Josie. She'll be using Maisie's room."

Brandy noticed he'd left off her title. She objected to it and she objected to his use of her first name. But she was indebted to the man. Perhaps she'd best remain silent. After all, she'd only be here overnight.

"My horse—"

"Will be taken care of," Jeffers inserted smoothly. "I'll send someone to take him to the stables."

"Come on, honey," said Josie. "I gotta hurry and get back to work."

Brandy allowed herself to be hustled out of the door. Franko muttered something as she was leaving. Although the words were unclear, it sounded as though he'd said he'd see her later.

Not if I see you first, she silently told herself.

Josie's red dress rustled as she hurried Brandy across the saloon toward the stairs. Ribald remarks followed them to the second floor but Brandy tried her best to ignore them. Josie opened a door at the top of the stairs and entered.

"This was Maisie's room," Josie said. "It ain't been used in a while so you may have to clean it up a little."

"That's all right," Brandy said. "I'll only be staying the night."

"You sure about this?"

"Of course. Mr. Jeffers said he'd find someone to guide me to Taos tomorrow."

"If you're leavin' depends on Jeffers, then you can forget it," Josie said. "I imagine he's gonna like havin' you around."

"Whether he does or not, matters little," Brandy said. "If he doesn't come through with the guide, then I'll find my own way there."

After Josie left, Brandy locked the door, curled up on the bed, and tried to rest. She'd only just closed her eyes when there was a knock on her door.

"Who is it?" she called.

"Josie."

Frowning, she unlocked the door and peered out. Josie carried a green satin dress over one arm. "From Jeffers," she said. "He wants you to dine with him."

Brandy sighed. "Please tell him I'm too tired," she said.

Josie shrugged. "You oughta eat."

"I know," Brandy said. "But I had some dried beef today. I'm good until morning."

"Have it your way. And honey, keep that door locked."

Brandy nodded. "Thanks Josie." After locking the door she curled up on the bed again, and despite her

142

anxiety, she was soon fast asleep.

Brandy's fury was barely held under control as she made her way to the stables. She should have known Jeffers would do something like that. When she'd presented herself at breakfast this morning expecting to be introduced to her guide, she'd been told instead that an emergency had arisen and he couldn't spare anyone.

He must think her a simpleton! Obviously he'd had no intention of helping her. Pushing wide the door to the stables, she stepped inside. Instantly she could smell hay, its biting aroma filling her nostrils as she moved deeper into the building. She could hear the noises of horses eating, blowing and bumping against the sides of the stalls, but upon moving closer, she found most of the stalls were empty.

She saw nothing of the horse she'd ridden into town the day before.

"Help you?"

Whirling, she found herself facing the stabler. "Yes," she said. "Mr. Jeffers had my horse brought here last night. I need to —"

" 'Fraid not."

"I beg your pardon."

"Wasn't no horse brought here last night."

"But there must have been. Jeffers said . . ."

"Nope. If they'd been a horse, then I'd have seen him."

Her eyes searched the shadowy interior of the barn. Her mount was nowhere to be seen. Her lips tightened grimly. This was obviously Jeffers's fault. Well, he damn well wouldn't get away with it!

Chapter Fourteen

Sky Walker chafed at the delay as the peace talks continued. High Backed Wolf's runner had returned with the news that Brandy had gone to the mining town located in the mountains to the west. When he'd learned her whereabouts, his first impulse had been to go after her. But he realized such an action would be irresponsible, because Three Feathers was right. More than his pride was at stake. There was the future of the whole Comanche nation.

Nothing must be allowed to take precedence over the peace talks.

Not even Brandy.

Jeffers wasn't in his office, so Brandy went in search of him. But he proved elusive. The saloon was empty and she had no intention of searching out his room. Instead, she went to see Josie.

Wearing a faded yellow wrapper over her nightgown, Josie opened the door to Brandy's knock. "You're up bright and early," she said with a smile. "Come on in while I find something to wear."

"Where can I find Jeffers?" Brandy asked, stepping into the room.

"You prob'ly can't," Josie said, yawning as she closed the door. After waving Brandy toward the only chair in the room, Josie sat down on the rumpled bed. "Jeffers owns three mines. He goes out and talks to his overseer every morning."

"Damn him to hell!" Brandy exclaimed, popping up from the chair she'd just sat down in. "He knew I'd be looking for him!"

"You sure know some strong words for a highbred lady," Josie laughed, her blue eyes twinkling. "I thought respectable ladies didn't swear."

"What I've been through the past few weeks would be enough to make a monk swear," Brandy fumed, crossing to the window and staring down into the empty street. "How long will Jeffers be gone?"

"He's usually back by midday, but he'll prob'ly be later today. They found a new vein of silver in the Lucky Lady last week. Talk is, the find is a big one. He's expecting it to produce a lot of ore. Some say it could prove to be the biggest find in the Territory."

Brandy wasn't the least bit interested in Jeffers's mine. Right now, her only concern was in leaving this place, on continuing her journey to Taos. "When do you think he'll be back?"

"Ummm" — Josie scratched her head and smothered a yawn. "He might be back by three. But then, again, he might not. You can't ever tell what he's gonna do."

"Three! This afternoon?"

"If you're lucky," Josie said.

Brandy swore again and ground her teeth in frustration. "Damn his hide! He knew I'd be looking for him this morning!"

"What did'ja want him for?"

"My horse seems to have disappeared."

Josie gave a short laugh. "I'm not surprised. He was bound to try keepin' you here. Jeffers never had any intention of lettin' you leave since you rode into town."

"He can't keep me here!"

"He kept me," Josie muttered.

Brandy was so intent on her problems that the words slid right on by her. "He should at least have left some word for me."

"What kinda word did'ja expect him to leave?" Josie asked. She pantomimed scribbling on a piece of paper. "Sorry Miss Tremayne . . ." Her grin became impish. "I beg your pardon, *Lady Brandy.*" Scrambling off the bed, she spread the faded yellow wrapper wide and curtsied low. Then she pretended to scribble again. "Sorry Lady Tremayne, but my saloon could use a little sprucin' up. An' I decided you're gonna be the sprucer."

Brandy watched the other girl's antics with mixed feelings. On the one hand, she felt amazed that Josie could accept a life that she obviously hated and still remain such a fun-loving girl. On the other hand, anxiety mingled with fear that Josie could be right in her estimation of Jeffers's intentions.

But what could she do?

Brandy watched Josie search through her wardrobe, thumbing through the array of gowns. "We need to find you something else to wear," she said, finally settling on a blue chambray. Tossing the gown to Brandy, she continued, "Try that on. It should fit since we're about the same size."

146

"That's very nice of you," Brandy said. "But I couldn't possibly accept the gown."

"Why not?" Josie asked, her voice suddenly harsh. "It ain't contaminated or nothin' like that. You ain't gonna catch nothin' by wearin' it."

"Josie . . . I never meant . . ." Brandy's words trailed off. She'd obviously hurt the other girl's feelings by refusing the gown. "If you really don't mind, I'd be proud to wear it," she said softly. "I only refused because I hated to deprive you of your clothing."

Josie's good humor was immediately restored. "I ain't bein' deprived," she said. "Go on, wear it. I got a whole lot more than I'll ever need."

Pulling a yellow gown from the wardrobe, she threw it across the bed and began to unfasten her wrapper. "Hurry and change clothes so's we can go out for some breakfast."

Unwilling to disappoint the other girl, Brandy changed her clothing, finishing long before Josie. Something Josie had said was worrying at her mind. Something barely heard, about Jeffers having kept her here.

"Josie?"

"Ummmm?" Josie paused in the act of pulling the gown over her head.

Brandy's lips twitched, then her expression became serious. "Did you say Jeffers kept you here?"

"Yes."

"Then—you didn't want to stay either."

"Nope," Josie said cheerfully. "Sure didn't. Raised a lotta hell about it too." She shrugged the gown over her shoulders. "Didn't matter in the end though. Jeffers was bound to get his way."

Brandy frowned at her, unable to understand how Josie could remain so cheerful. "You seem so happy here, so uncaring of what Jeffers has done to you. How can you be so accepting of the situation?"

A veil seemed to lower in Josie's eyes, and for an instant a hint of bitterness crept through, but it was only a fleeting thing, disappearing almost as quickly as it surfaced. "Come on now," Josie said, tossing her a smile. "I been here for nigh on to a year now. Finally decided this was the life I was meant to lead and I'd do better makin' the most of it, instead of cryin' about what I couldn't have." Smoothing down the skirt of her gown, she turned her back to Brandy. "Button me up, will ya?"

Brandy thought about what Josie had said as she fastened the buttons on the blue gown. No matter what her circumstances, Brandy would never accept defeat without a fight. But then, perhaps Josie hadn't either. Was all the bubbly exterior just put on? Perhaps a way to live with her circumstances?

"Tell me what it was like growing up in England," Josie said. "How does a lady of quality live?"

"How do you know I'm a lady of quality?" Brandy asked. "There. That's the last button."

Josie gave Brandy a quick smile, then moved to the dresser and began to arrange her dark hair. "I ain't stupid," she said. "Anybody can see you wasn't raised on a farm like me. Did you have lots of parties?" She paused in the act of picking up her comb, eagerly awaiting Brandy's reply.

"We had parties, but not so very many. Perhaps if Mother hadn't died so young, there'd have been more." She twisted the ring on her finger, her green eyes pensive. The stone caught the sun's rays and flashed emerald and her thoughts turned to the man who had given her the ring. Why had he done so?

"Josie." Her voice was hesitant. "Do you know anything about the Comanche wedding ceremony."

"No," Josie said. "Why?"

"I wondered if they used rings . . . you know . . . maybe exchanged them . . . or something."

"I don't think so."

Brandy had suspected as much. So why had Sky Walker given her the ring? It was almost as though he wished her to feel truly wed to him. But surely that couldn't be the case. Angrily, she pulled at the ring, trying to slide it off. Dammit! It was well and truly stuck. Perhaps if she used soap, it would slide off. She would have to try, for suddenly she knew she must get the ring off her finger.

Intending to remove the ring with soap, Brandy crossed to the washstand. The water jug was empty.

"Do you need some water?" Josie asked. "I forgot to fill the jug last night. I'll get some soon as I finish with my hair." She wound a curl around her finger and pinned it in place. "I gotta wash this stuff today. Hair gets real sweaty in my line of work."

At Josie's reference to her line of work, Brandy's cheeks flushed bright red. "How did you come to be here, Josie?"

Josie shrugged her slim shoulders. "My Ma died when I was eight. Then Pa had the raisin' of me. It's a fact he liked his liquor more than us kids. Pa was a farmer but after Ma died he got lazy. When Sophie was twelve he started bringin' men to the house." She fell silent, almost pensive. "I'd lay there in the night, listening to the bedsprings squeaking and the men grunting over Sophie, knowing the same thing was in store for me if I stayed. Reckon where I went wrong was when I trusted that

149

drummer. Shoulda known better, but I was hankerin' to get away from that farm before Pa woke up and realized I was filling out."

Brandy waited for her to go on.

"Nick, he's the drummer, decided we could get rich in the mining towns. Rich! Ha! We wound up here and he lost me in a poker game."

"He did what?"

"Lost me in a poker game," Josie repeated. "To Jeffers."

"You were put up for stakes in a poker game?"

Josie laughed. "This here is a mining town, honey. And Jeffers figgered I was worth ever penny he put up."

"Why do you stay?"

"Where else would I go?"

"Perhaps you could go back home," Brandy suggested. "You said you had a sister."

"Got more'n one. Sarah and Ruby was younger'n me."

"Perhaps Sophie is married now. If she is, then she could provide you with a home."

"Who'd marry Sophie?" Josie asked. "The whole town called her a slut for what she done. They ain't nobody there that'd marry a slut." The laughter had gone out of her eyes when she faced Brandy. "Girls like us are plentiful. It's the ones like you that men look to marry."

"Get in touch with Sophie," Brandy urged. "Don't give in to Jeffers. You're too good for this kind of life."

"That's what I been tellin' myself. But I already tried Sophie. Few months back they was a feller with book learnin' stopped here for a spell. Had himself a mine for a few months. While he was here, he wrote off a letter for me and I sent it to Sophie. Never got an answer to that letter."

"But there might have been —"

150

"Forget about it," Josie said, stepping around Brandy and opening the door. "I did a long time ago. Now let's get some breakfast."

Brandy thought it was amazing how easily the other girl could shrug away her problems and face the world with a smile. No wonder Jeffers had wanted her. She must be a favorite with the men. But they would just have to find themselves another favorite, Brandy decided. Because she was going to leave this place, and when she left, Josie was going with her.

The Peace Council was finally over and Sky Walker was free to leave. He wasted no time gathering his things together for his trip and fastening them on the horse Long Knife had given him.

Although the others would stay another night and some would extend their stay for days, his every thought had been directed toward the woman he had taken to his lodge.

The week that had passed since she'd left had provided time for his anger to build. Only his duty to his people had kept him at the gathering on the Arkansas River.

But no more.

Now he was free to go . . . free to find the woman who had made him lose face. He'd had no wish to take a wife, especially one who was a paleface, but in order to save her from Buffalo Grass, he had put his feelings aside. And she'd repaid him by running away.

All week he'd had to contend with the smirk on Buffalo Grass's face. All week, with the Cheyenne warrior laughing at him . . . telling others Sky Walker had been unable to hold his woman.

Sky Walker's face darkened with fury.

When he caught up with Brandy, he would show her what happened to those who dared shame a Comanche warrior. He would teach her a lesson she'd never forget. And she would rue the day she was ever born.

Even as his mind silently uttered the threat, the memory of her pale arms reaching out to him had his body reacting in a way that he was angry about. Her beauty was undeniable and many warriors would gladly change places with him. But he had no time or mind for such things.

"You will find you are mistaken about her," said a soft voice beside him.

He turned in the act of mounting his horse and recognized Yellow Moon. "What do you mean?" he asked gruffly.

"If she ran away there must have been a reason," the young woman said. "Before you harm her find out what the reason was."

He shrugged. "There can be no excuse for her actions. She must be taught a lesson."

"Our ways are strange to her. And she did not want to marry. Can she be blamed for running from something she did not understand? You must make allowances for the fact that she is not of our race."

"Do not worry, he said gently. "It is not my intention to harm her. But she must realize she cannot do such things to a warrior."

She searched his face for a moment, then seemed to relax. "Give her my greetings," she murmured. "Perhaps we will meet again one day."

"Perhaps," he grunted, swinging onto his mount.

Sky Walker was surprised when Long Knife appeared

leading a pinto pony. Without a word, the Kiowa warrior mounted and joined him.

Brandy's dresser stool crashed loudly against the far wall, sent hurtling there by the girl's angry kick.

"Take it easy," Josie said. "You don't want him gettin' mad and coming up here, do you?"

"I won't work in his saloon!" Brandy snapped. "There's no way he can make me."

"He says you owe him for food and rent," Josie reminded. "You don't have no choice."

"He'll get his money," Brandy snarled. "All I have to do is get to Taos. My father has friends there."

Josie put a calming hand on her arm. "Brandy, honey. Why don't you just make up your mind that you ain't going nowhere. Jeffers ain't gonna let you."

Brandy sighed. "I should never have stopped here for the night. I should have rode on out as soon as I met Jeffers. While I still had a horse to ride."

"I coulda told you he'd take the horse," Josie said. "Once Jeffers saw you, there was no way in hell he was gonna let you leave again. You're beautiful, Brandy. And you're quality. Jeffers said you don't even have to service the men. All he's wanting is for you to drink with them."

"I suspect he's saving me for himself," Brandy said.

"Yes. He is."

"Josie, help me leave."

"I can't," Josie muttered. "Jeffers would kill me."

"God! What am I going to do? I have to get away. This town isn't safe for a decent woman. Jonas would help but he doesn't dare. Those thugs of Jeffers would beat him to within an inch of his life." She sighed, crossed to the open window, leaned her arms on the sill, and stared down into the empty street. There must be something she could do. There must be!

"Franko left town this morning," Josie said from behind her.

"He did?" Thank God for small favors. At least she wouldn't be bothered by him anymore. "I guess he finally realized Jeffers wasn't going to sell me."

"Yes. It was obvious he was hanging around for nothing. He lost about all his money at Jeffers's tables." She laughed shortly. "Franko didn't leave empty-handed. He took a couple of Jeffers's men with him."

Brandy swung around to stare at the girl. "Jeffers allowed that?"

"No. He didn't know they were leaving. One of the men was guardin' the horses." Her lips twitched. "Jonas said Jeffers was fit to be tied. He went to the store ranting and raving, asking Jonas did he know about their plans."

"Did he?"

"Jonas didn't say, but likely he did. Course, he didn't let on none to Jeffers. It'd been worth his hide if he had."

"God," Brandy sighed. "I've got to get out of this place. I must!"

But how?

As the two warriors wound their way through pines and aspen trees, Sky Walker's thoughts were filled with memories of Brandy. The sound of barking in the distance jerked his head up. He had been so deep in thought that he had paid little attention to his surroundings.

Frowning, he uttered a short expletive. It was the woman's fault that he had been taken unawares. Why did he let her get under his skin in such a manner?

His gaze narrowed on the cabin only a short distance to his right. The presence of the dwelling suggested that he wasn't far from the mining town, or his bride. Excitement stirred inside him at the thought of seeing her again, but the feeling was tempered with anger. A man stepped out of the cabin and stood watching them for a moment. Turning his head, he said something to someone who stood out of Sky Walker's sight. A woman stepped out of the dwelling, followed closely by three children, all wearing dirty, ragged clothing.

Sky Walker knew they must be used to seeing Indians here, for he had been told by Long Knife that the Kiowas often traded in the mining town. He supposed that was why they expressed only a passing interest.

The two warriors continued riding toward the town.

Brandy was still at the window when she saw the warriors riding down the street. Her gaze went to the foremost warrior and froze on his long, lean form.

Sky Walker!

Her pulse quickened. What was he doing here? Surely his arrival was accidental. He looked up and she knew by the stiffness in his body that she'd been seen. Leaving the window, she moved to Josie. "Sky Walker is here," she said.

"Sky Walker? The Comanche Indian who saved your life?"

Brandy nodded.

Josie smiled. "He's come to help you," she said. Her blue eyes glittered. "Come on, I want to see Jeffers's face when he finds out the Indians come for you."

155

"I don't know why he's here," Brandy said. "But I don't think it's on my account. He wanted to get rid of me."

"You said he'd agreed to take you to Taos."

"That was before"—she paused, aware that she'd nearly mentioned their marriage, something that she intended to keep secret. "—before I ran away," she finished.

"Why else would he have come here?"

"I don't know."

"Well, we'll never find out if we stay up here," Josie said cheerfully.

Realizing the truth of Josie's words, Brandy followed the girl from the room.

There was only one man drinking at the bar when Sky Walker and his companion entered. Sky Walker knew the saloon was owned by a man named Jeffers. When a door at the far end of the room opened and a well-dressed man stepped into the saloon, Sky Walker knew he was facing him.

"Welcome, Long Knife," Jeffers said, coming forward and extending his hand. When it was ignored he let it fall to his side. "It's been a long time since you were in town. And I can't recall when you've ever been in my saloon."

"No," Long Knife agreed. "We have only visited your trading house."

Jeffers smiled. "What can I do for you?"

"I have brought my friend, Sky Walker."

"That right?" Jeffers asked, turning his attention to the warrior. "You have some furs you'd like to trade?"

"No. I've come for my woman." His eyes, hard, angry, moved to the stairway, where Brandy stood watching him.

156

"Your woman?" Jeffers's frowning gaze went to Brandy, halfway down the stairs. "Surely you aren't referring to Lady Tremayne?"

Sky Walker ignored him, concentrating his attention on Brandy, who'd come the rest of the way downstairs. He didn't know what he'd expected of her . . . but it was not her reaction to his presence.

Crossing the floor, she stopped beside him. "Yes," she told Jeffers. "He's come for me."

Chapter Fifteen

Although Sky Walker's stance seemed threatening, his dark gaze unforgiving, Brandy still preferred his company to that of Jeffers. She didn't know why, but the warrior's mere presence, the grip of his rough fingers around her forearm, gave her a sense of protection.

Jeffers's tall, black-clad figure stiffened, and his gaze narrowed on the hand gripping Brandy's arm. Lifting a dark brow, he said, "Is this some kind of joke?"

A cold sort of humor lifted the corners of Brandy's mouth. "Sky Walker doesn't appear the least bit humorous," she said softly. "I really don't think he's joking. In fact, I'm almost certain he's not." She took great pleasure in Jeffers's anger, simmering just below the surface of his seemingly polite facade.

"Would you please explain?" Jeffers said.

"Sky Walker has already done so. He came here for me." Even as she said the words, she wondered why. Later, when there was more time, she'd puzzle out the reason. At the moment, all she wanted was to hurry away from this place . . . this saloon, and the man who owned it. "I would take it kindly, Mr. Jeffers, if you would produce my mount from wherever you're keeping him."

"You won't be needing a horse," Jeffers said, dropping the veil of politeness he'd adopted up to this point. "Go back upstairs while I deal with this."

Sky Walker's grip tightened on her arm, digging into her flesh until she was certain she would have bruises. "The woman will come with me," he rasped harshly.

"You'd better think again," Jeffers said softly, his gaze sliding past them, becoming fixed on something . . . or someone across the room.

Following his gaze, Brandy saw four men step out of his office and separate, taking up positions at each side of the room. Muley, the bartender, stooped below the bar and emerged with a shotgun, laying it carefully on the counter in front of him.

"Jeffers, don't be a fool!" Josie said. "If you kill them, every Indian within a hundred miles will be after your hide." She grimaced. "Not that I'd give a damn, but they'd prob'ly kill everybody in town."

"She's right you know," Brandy announced cheerfully. "Have you ever seen what the Indians do to their enemies?" Although she wasn't sure how true the reports were, she'd derive a great deal of satisfaction from putting the fear of God into Jeffers — if that was in fact what she was doing. "I understand it's not a very pretty sight. They don't leave much to identify." A smile played around her lips. "They like to burn their victims, but first they scalp them. Then — "

"I get the picture," Jeffers said, his cold eyes studying her expression. "But I'm not so sure you do. You seem in an almighty hurry to go with them."

"Anything is preferable to staying here with you." Her

voice dripped ice. "I thought I had already made that plain enough."

Jeffers appealed to Long Knife. "We've never had any trouble with your people before. I'd kinda like to keep it that way."

Long Knife shrugged. "Neither do I wish trouble, but the woman belongs to Sky Walker. He has a right to his wife."

"His wife?" That stopped Jeffers cold. His eyes fell on Brandy with something like loathing. "All right," he agreed shortly. "Take her! She deserves everything she gets!" He clenched and unclenched his hands, his expression dark and savage. When his gaze fell on Josie, he snapped, "Josie, get upstairs! I'll deal with you later!"

A chill settled over Brandy. She couldn't leave Josie to face the consequences of her actions. "Josie is coming with us," she said.

"The hell she is!" Jeffers fury was barely contained. "Get out of my saloon before I order my men to open fire on the lot of you."

"I'm not leaving Jo —" Brandy broke off as Sky Walker's fingers clenched on her arms, squeezing tightly. She met his eyes, saw the warning in them, but chose to ignore it. "We can't leave Josie behind," she said. "She's being forced to stay here."

Instead of replying, the warrior pulled her toward the door. Brandy dug in her heels, tugging at her arm, struggling to escape his hold. "We can't leave Josie with him. There's no telling what he'll do to her."

Picking her up like a sack of meal, Sky Walker threw her over his shoulder and carried her, struggling, out the door. "Stop it!" she screamed, flailing out with her arms. "Let me go!"

He gave her rump a hard whack that sent a jolt of pain through her and tears into her eyes. The beast had actually struck her!

"Be silent," he ordered. "Did you not see the weapons pointed at us? To continue would have been useless."

"But we can't leave her there," she muttered, swiping at her tears with the back of her hand. "Don't take your anger with me out on Josie. Please . . . ummphhh."

Impatiently, he had tossed her across his horse.

"Sky Walker, please," she begged when he was mounted behind her. "We can't leave Josie there."

"The other woman is not my business. She belongs to him."

"Dammit! If you won't help her, then give me a rifle. I'll get her myself."

Ignoring her, Sky Walker waited until Long Knife was mounted; then he urged his mount away from the saloon.

Gritting her teeth, Brandy remained quiet as they left the town behind. She knew that Sky Walker was right. They could not have fought so many. I'll be back, Josie, she silently promised. I won't leave you there.

It was dark when they took shelter in an abandoned mine. The two warriors spoke in low tones for a long moment, then Long Knife rode away, leaving Brandy alone with Sky Walker.

He began to gather wood and soon had a small fire going. Keeping a wary eye on Sky Walker, Brandy leaned back against the rocky wall and ate the jerky he provided from a hide pouch. Afterward, she quenched her thirst from his water skin. Questions filled her mind; Why had he come? And how had he known where to find her? The feelings that had swamped her when she'd seen him riding down the street were feelings she refused to face, at least until she had some answers.

"Why did you come for me?"

He answered the question with one of his own. "Why did you leave?"

"Did you really expect me to stay after finding out what was in store for me?" she asked angrily. "You promised me you'd take me to Taos after the Peace Council was over."

"I broke no promise," he said. "The Peace Council was not yet over."

Her green eyes widened. "You really expected me to obey your every whim, to do whatever you said without complaint. Well, you were wrong. I'm no object to be passed around to whomever you wish. I'm a woman with a will of my own."

"That is very obvious," he said. "But you will keep silent until you are spoken to. I am tired and I have no wish to listen to your complaints."

She glared furiously at him. He had no reason to chastise her. She had done nothing wrong. She lifted her chin belligerently. "Just get me to Taos and you'll never have to listen to me again."

Sky Walker ignored her, reaching out to add another stick of wood to the fire. Sitting back on his haunches, he gazed broodingly into the flames.

The darkness outside the circle of firelight seemed to close around them, cloaking them in a shrouding blanket of intimacy while the flickering flames from the fire cast shadows across the bronzed planes of his face, giving him a satanic appearance. The tension Brandy felt emanating from his large frame disturbed her greatly. It was as though he felt he was the injured party, not she.

Her lips twisted wryly. She didn't know why he should feel she'd done him an injury. But he obviously did. Actually, she supposed she should thank him for giving her away. The emotions he'd aroused when he'd made love to her were strong enough to frighten her. Had he not given her to Buffalo Grass, the feelings might have overcome her good sense.

Sky Walker looked up, his gaze met hers.

"Sky Walker," she said softly, "you will help me free Josie, won't you?"

"Why should I?"

"Because you have compassion."

He arched a dark brow. "What is this word, compassion?"

"It means you care about others."

"Compassion has no place in my life." His mouth compressed into a thin, angry line. "When I tried to help you, you repaid me by running away. You made me lose face before my people."

"You didn't want me," she accused. "You made that plain when you gave me to Buffalo Grass."

His dark brows knitted together. "You make no sense. Why do you accuse me of giving you to another warrior?"

Confusion clouded her eyes, and her heart began a slow, irregular beat. "Didn't you?"

"No!" His dark eyes smoldered. "How could you believe such a thing?"

"But—he said—" Her green eyes widened. "I thought it was strange, especially after we made—" She broke off again. His gaze had become so intense that she couldn't continue. Anyway, how could she speak of that night together? Of the way he'd made her feel?

"After what?" he prompted.

"I — it really doesn't matter now," she muttered. "Obviously I was wrong."

"Yes," he agreed thoughtfully. "You were wrong. And I am finally making sense of things."

Brandy held her breath, waiting for him to make a move. Instead, he reached for his rifle, settled down into a cross-legged position, and began to clean it. Brandy watched him, feeling a sense of disappointment that he hadn't continued the conversation. Obviously Buffalo Grass had lied. She'd been a fool for believing him.

She sighed heavily as the silence stretched out between them, lengthening like purpling shadows at the end of the day. She felt as though she'd lost something important, something that could have changed her whole future, by her foolishness. But that in itself was foolish.

Sky Walker seemed so hard, so unapproachable. Not the least like he'd been that night. Then, he'd been loving, tender, caring. He'd had compassion.

Josie!

"Sky Walker," she said softly. "Please help her." He looked up from his work. "Josie was good to me. I can't leave her there."

"We will speak of it tomorrow," he said. "She will come to no harm overnight."

Brandy wasn't so sure about that, but she knew she couldn't free Josie alone. The fire began to diminish and she added another log, laying it on the smoldering embers, watching the sparks spew as it caught flame.

She was startled when Sky Walker rose from his cross-legged position and spread his buckskin robe on the ground.

"We must sleep now," he said. "There is much to do

tomorrow."

Feeling frozen to the spot, Brandy knew the moment she'd dreaded had arrived. Wrapping her arms around herself, she muttered, "There is only one sleeping pallet."

A muscle twitched in his jaw. "One is all that's needed," he grated harshly. "Come to bed."

"No," she said huskily, backing away from him. Her body quivered, her nerves stretched taut as bowstrings. How could she be expected to sleep with him after all that had been between them? They couldn't just take up where they'd left off.

But he refused to take no for an answer. A long arm streaked out and drew her against the muscular wall of his body. "Come here," he growled low in his throat.

Chapter Sixteen

"No!" Brandy gasped, fear coiling inside her.

"Yes," he muttered, burying his face in the side of her neck. "Yes, yes, yes."

Each word was punctuated by a sharp nip with his teeth, and Brandy's heart pounded wildly in her breast, her knees threatened to buckle, and she collapsed against him.

"How could you leave after what we shared?" he whispered. "Did it mean nothing to you?"

Lifting her head, Brandy moistened her dry lips. Sky Walker's gaze narrowed on her mouth and his head lowered, his lips capturing hers in a kiss of such intensity that she thought she would swoon. She slid her arms around his neck, winding her fingers through his dark hair. She'd come home! She'd come home.

Her will to resist had completely disappeared, as though it had never been. When his lips left hers, she traced the outline of his mouth with her tongue. His body was taut, his masculinity strengthening, pulsating against her lower body, raising needs that he'd introduced her to on the night they were wed.

Feeling his fingers on the fastenings of her gown, she worked at the lacings of his buckskin shirt, intent on removing the obstacles between them. Sky Walker stripped the gown from her body and tossed it aside, then his clothing went the same way. He pulled her down on the buckskin robe, sliding his hand over her satiny flesh.

The sensation sent her senses reeling, her stomach contracted sharply. "Sky Walker," she whispered achingly.

With a husky groan of passion, his mouth pressed eager kisses on her neck, her shoulders, her breasts, before moving to devour her mouth greedily.

A devastating hunger was building, growing stronger with each passing moment. His hands, caressing her body, stoked a fire that flamed higher and higher until she was pulling at him, trying to draw him into herself, pressing her body against him as her senses cried out for relief.

When his tongue entered the sweet moistness of her mouth she gave a moan of pleasured torment, raking his back with her nails. Animal sounds of pleasure broke from her throat as his lovemaking became rough, savage, and wild.

Her body bucked beneath him, aching for a release that only he could bring.

Suddenly he parted her thighs with his and plunged wildy into her moistness. It was so sudden, she had time for only a moment's breath before he was moving, plunging deeper, thrusting in and out, over and over again until she thought she would surely faint from the pleasure he was creating.

Brandy withheld nothing from him. She brought her body up against his, meeting thrust for thrust, reveling in his savagery until they had reached their peak and went soaring together, hovering among the clouds until they collapsed in each other's arms, too spent to move.

Time passed — Brandy wasn't sure how long. She lay there, content to be in his arms, thinking Sky Walker had fallen asleep, until he spoke.

"Never leave me again."

"No," she said softly. "I won't."

"Are you afraid of me, Brandy?"

"Of course not. Why should you think that?"

His voice sounded grave when he spoke again. "You sent fear into Jeffers when you told him what the Comanche did to their enemies. Where did you learn such things?"

"About him being scalped and burned at the stake?" Her voice was filled with mirth. "I only told him I'd heard your people did that. I didn't say I believed they did."

"Then you did not believe it?"

"Of course not!" Something in his voice sent a streak of alarm through her. "I just repeated stories I'd heard about the Indians. Poppa said that's all they were, stories. He said they were designed to make the settlers cautious in their dealings with the Indians." She looked at him. "He was right, wasn't he?"

"No. He was not. Those things do happen. You must be aware of it. The dangers do exist."

His words alarmed her, but she tried not to show it. She had thought the Indians were more civilized. And Sky Walker had done nothing to dispel that belief.

"H-have you ever killed anyone that way?" she asked.

"Yes. But only once. And I did not enjoy it."

She pulled away from him. "Then why did you do it?" she asked in a small voice.

"Because it was necessary," he said. "If we had not made

168

an example of the settler, others would have followed him and claimed our land. Even now the white-eyes push us farther and farther away from our beloved hills. They force us to leave our hunting grounds where the game is plentiful and there are many clear water creeks to be found. Already many of our tribes have taken to the plains in order to escape the white-eyes' cruelty. They show our people no mercy, killing women and children alike. And their numbers increase with each passing day. Our only defense is their fear of us.

She touched his face softly. "Don't speak of it anymore," she said. "We need to rest tonight. Tomorrow we must find a way to help Josie." When he remained silent, she said, "Sky Walker. You will help me, won't you?"

"Long Knife will return with more warriors in the morning," he said, smoothing her hair back from her face. "We will need them when we go after your friend."

Surprise widened her eyes. "You meant to help her all along, didn't you?"

"Yes. She helped you. I could not leave her there."

His softly spoken words were all that was needed to relax her body. Whatever he was, Sky Walker was no savage. Even when he was still angry with her, he had made arrangements to free her friend. A man like that could not willfully harm anyone. Closing her eyes, she relaxed against him and slept.

They waited until the men left for the mines before riding into town. It was obvious they weren't expected, for the town was almost deserted. Jonas, obviously curious about so many riders, opened the door of his general store and stepped outside. His mouth dropped open. He went inside again and slammed the door.

Although Sky Walker had told Brandy to wait outside, she was only a step behind him when he pushed open the saloon door.

Jeffers, the only occupant, swore loudly and jumped to his feet, sending his chair crashing against the floor.

"We have come for the woman," Sky Walker said.

"Dammit!" Jeffers said. "I thought we had this all settled."

"Nothing is settled until the woman is free."

Pushing past the others, Brandy hurried up the stairs, stopping at Josie's door. Her hand found the knob but the door refused to open. "Josie," she called. "Are you in there?"

"Brandy?" The voice was faint. "Is that you?"

"Yes. I'll get someone to unlock the door." But she needn't have bothered. When she turned around, Sky Walker was behind her. A swift kick sent the door crashing against the wall.

Brandy hurried across the room to the bed where Josie was lying, her hands tied to the bedposts. Purpling bruises marked her face. She'd obviously suffered a severe beating.

"Oh, Josie," Brandy whispered. "What did he do to you?"

"Boy! Am I glad to see you," Josie muttered hoarsely. Although her left eye was bruised, and swollen almost shut, her split lips stretched into a wide smile. "Brandy, honey. You're a sight for these sore eyes. And that's a fact. Didn't think I'd ever see you again."

Sky Walker busied himself freeing Josie while Brandy explained. "Long Knife went for help. I didn't want to leave you, but there were too many of them last night."

"I know. Had it come to a fight, you'da been done for."

Brandy helped Josie to her feet. "Get your things together," she said. "We'll have to hurry before Jeffers's men come back."

"Won't take me but a few minutes," the girl said, already hurrying around the room, gathering her things together and tossing them in the middle of the bed. Once she was finished, they tied them up in a bedsheet and carried it downstairs.

Jeffers's face was dark as a thundercloud. "This ain't gonna do our friendship no good," he warned Long Knife. "You've always been welcomed here to trade. Maybe next time you come you won't be so welcome."

"There are other places to trade," Long Knife said. "We have no need to come here."

Handing her bundle of supplies to a surprised Long Knife, Josie sauntered over to the gambler, stopping in front of him. "The way I figure it, you owe me for a year's worth of work." She held out her hand. "Fork it over!"

"Go to hell!" he snarled.

Her blue eyes glittered and she grinned. "How much do you think it'd cost to rebuild this saloon, Brandy?"

Letting her eyes wander around the room, Brandy pretended to think about it. "I'm not sure," she said. "Where would he get the men to rebuild? He needs them all in the mine."

Cursing bitterly, Jeffers pulled out a wad of bills and tossed them at Josie. "Take it, bitch! But you'll rue the day you ever crossed me."

Smiling, appearing not in the least concerned, she picked up the money and strolled out of the saloon. Brandy watched Long Knife hand Josie the reins of a painted pony. Although his face was expressionless,

Brandy could have sworn she saw a glint of humor in the Kiowa warrior's eyes.

Realizing Sky Walker was waiting for her to mount, Brandy climbed on the brown mare Long Knife had provided, and followed Josie down the empty street. When they reached the general store, Jonas, obviously recovered from his apprehension, stepped out the door and lifted his hand in a salute. Then, with an eye on the saloon, he worked up a spit and sent a long stream of brown tobacco juice hurtling toward the saloon. A grin spread wide his lips as he stood there, hands on hips, watching them ride out of town.

Chapter Seventeen

When they left the mining town, they rode into the forest, headed south. They'd only gone a few miles when the trees began to thin. As the morning sun made its way across the sky, Brandy felt the heat penetrate the heavy fabric of her purple velvet gown.

If only she'd taken the time to change back into her doeskin dress.

The steady clip-clop of the horses' hooves hid the sound of running water until they were already beside it. As the warriors dismounted, she realized they intended to allow the horses to drink, and gave a sigh of relief. She would take the opportunity to rest for a moment.

Sliding to the ground, she lifted the hair away from her neck, allowing the breeze to cool her skin. Moccasins crunched on pine needles and she turned to see Sky Walker approaching.

"Long Knife's friends will leave us now," he said. "They must return to their village, but Long Knife will travel with us for a while."

"You don't think Jeffers will follow us?"

"No. But we will watch. If he does, we will be ready for him."

The sun had long disappeared and night cloaked the land when they stopped and made camp in a small clearing. Nearby, a narrow river chuckled merrily as it made its way down the mountain. Brandy dismounted, sinking gratefully to the grassy earth. Her muscles were tired from the unaccustomed riding, and she sat there for a moment, regaining her equilibrium while Sky Walker hobbled the horses in a grassy glade nearby.

Long Knife had killed three rabbits earlier and Josie began to clean them. Brandy was tired, wanted nothing more than to sleep, but she couldn't leave all the work to Josie. Urging her weary muscles to cooperate, she pushed herself to her feet and went to help.

"Show me what to do," she said. "I'm afraid my education in England didn't include preparing rabbits for the cooking pot."

"I'm not surprised," laughed Josie. "I suppose the cook did that."

"I'm not sure," Brandy replied, picking up one of the rabbits and scowling at it. "I think the gamekeeper did it before taking it to cook."

"Well you're about to learn two jobs in one whack," Josie said. "Sky Walker, will you give Brandy your knife?"

Obligingly, Sky Walker handed it over, then seated himself in a cross-legged position beside the fire and across from Long Knife.

"Now watch this," Josie said, circling the rabbit's neck with the tip of her blade. Then, after making a cut down to the rabbit's shoulders, she began peeling the fur away from the carcass.

Brandy watched, fascinated until the rabbit was bare, completely stripped of his pelt. After tossing the fur aside, Josie slit the rabbit on the underside, stuck her hand into the rabbit; and pulled out its innards.

Shuddering, Brandy looked up at the other girl. "Josie, suppose I do the outer part and you do the inner one."

Josie grinned. "Squeamish?"

"Just a little. I thought if I took it a little at a time, it would be easier."

"Okay," Josie agreed. "I'm game. I'll find some sticks to skewer the rabbits on while I'm waiting."

Josie cut some long willow limbs about an inch through, then peeled the bark off and sharpened them, all while Brandy struggled with the first rabbit. The next one proved to be easier. She decided there must be a knack to the whole thing.

"Will we really need all this?" she asked, picking up the last rabbit.

"If we don't use the meat tonight, we will tomorrow," Josie said. "You don't never let any food go to waste out here."

Brandy thought of all the mountains of food left over from their meals at Tremayne Hall. What became of it?

Josie picked up one of the rabbits and began to gut it. "It did me good to see Jeffers's face when we left that place," she said, digging her fingers into the rabbit's stomach. "He'll never get over bein' outfoxed that way. It's hard to believe I finally got out of his town. I thought I was stuck there until the end of my days."

"So did Jeffers," Brandy said, turning her eyes away from the blood and entrails on Josie's hands. "I hope he doesn't take it into his head to follow us."

"It won't matter if he does," Josie said. "I feel safe enough with Sky Walker and Long Knife here to protect us."

Hearing his name spoken, Long Knife looked up at

them. "Will you return to your family now, Josie?" he asked.

"No. I'll have to find some way to earn my keep. But it sure as hell won't be the same work as Jeffers required of me. Not if I can help it."

Brandy frowned, realizing Josie would need a place to stay and a way to earn her living. She'd heard there weren't many positions available to women in the West. Josie wasn't educated enough to be a teacher, nor did she seem to have the qualifications of a lady's maid or any other kind of domestic help. Come to think of it, there probably wasn't much demand for servants in this wild, untamed land.

She studied Josie's pensive expression. The girl seemed to be worried about her future, which was a complete deviation from her usual happy-go-lucky attitude. "You could come with me to England," Brandy said, nervously twisting the emerald ring on her finger. For some reason it seemed unusually tight.

"Are you still going back?" Josie asked.

"Yes. Of course. Even though Poppa is gone, England is still my home."

"Gallinos might've lied about killin' your pa," Josie said. "Your pa might be waitin' for you in Taos."

"No," Brandy said. "I know my father is dead. Gallinos would have had no reason to lie about it. Nothing to gain."

"I heard Gallinos is mean. Maybe he told you that 'cause he wanted to hurt you. Or maybe he said it 'cause he thought you'd quit fightin' was you to think they was nobody to look for you. Could be your pa is alive, an' he wouldn't want me."

"Nonsense!" said Brandy. "If what you say is true . . . if Poppa was alive, then he would insist on you coming with us." She swallowed hard. "But I know . . . in my heart I know that he's not. Gallinos and his renegades killed Poppa."

"Maybe, an' maybe not." Josie said. "But be that as it may, I ain't so sure that I'd like livin' in England. Why don't you forget about going back and stay here?"

Brandy bent her head and twisted the ring again. She didn't know why it felt so tight. Just all of a sudden, too. Odd, how she kept experiencing that same feeling. She must do something about removing it from her hand. She looked over at Sky Walker, who was laying another piece of wood on the fire. Why had he given the ring to her anyway? She studied the emerald stone on her finger. The firelight caused it to glitter brightly.

It *was* a beautiful ring. Perhaps she'd keep it after all. Just as a memento of New Mexico . . . and Sky Walker.

Becoming aware that she hadn't answered Josie, she lifted her head and met the other girl's eyes. "There are several reasons why I couldn't stay here, Josie. Not the least is the estate itself. Tremayne Hall was built more than two hundred years ago. It was built by my forefathers and has never left the family. It will be my responsibility now that my father is . . . gone."

"Ain't there nobody else to see after it?" Josie asked.

"My father has a sister, but she wouldn't want the responsibility. Aunt Rebecca and Miranda, my cousin, are the only family I have left now." She swallowed hard. "I dread telling Aunt Rebecca about Poppa. I don't think her heart can stand up to the shock."

Suddenly, Sky Walker rose and crossed to her. "Walk with me," he said.

Josie gave them her quick smile. "Don't be long. I'm starved and when these rabbits are done cookin', me and

Long Knife are gonna eat."

The full moon lit their way as Brandy followed Sky Walker into the darkness. A sense of peace washed over her as she listened to the sounds of the night . . . the water lapping gently against the shore, the crickets chirping beneath the bushes, and the song of the nightbirds.

"You are thinking of returning to your people?" It was more a statement than a question.

She looked away from him, willing her voice to remain steady, finding his very presence almost overwhelming. "What else would I do?" she asked.

"You could stay with me." Although the words were spoken quietly, they carried a world of feeling.

Her heart beat with a slow thud as she tried to still the whirling vortex of her mind. Did he want her to stay with him? He hadn't said so. Silence stretched out between them, like ripples in a pond, spreading in ever-widening circles.

He seemed to be waiting for her reply, but she couldn't think straight. It was hard to remain coherent when he was standing so close.

"Come swim with me," he commanded.

"What?" Her head jerked up, her eyes met his.

A smile twisted his lips. He cupped her face in his hands. "I said come swim with me."

Swim with him? She stared at him in dazed exasperation. Had he or had he not asked her to stay with him? Had he only been teasing her? "Where?" she muttered.

He laughed, kissed her on the end of the nose, then put her away from him. "In the stream, of course."

Flushing, Brandy looked at her surroundings. She'd been so mesmerized by him that she hadn't even been aware that they'd left the river and were standing beside a narrow creek. And not more than twenty feet away was a small waterfall that cascaded into a deep pool, surrounded by a dense growth of ferns. The water glimmered softly in the moonlight, reflecting the stars in the night sky.

"How lovely," she exclaimed.

"Swim with me," he said again, and his voice seemed almost urgent.

Brandy's cheeks were rosy as she smiled shyly up at him. She wanted to prolong their time together, but to swim with him? It would be the height of immodesty. The thought caused her to laugh out loud. Why was she worried about modesty after the intimacy they'd shared?

"The water does look inviting," she conceded.

"Then you will do it?"

"Yes. I'll do it. But you must turn away while I disrobe."

A laugh burst from him and his lips twisted wryly, but he didn't tease her. "I'll wait for you in the water," he said, stripping his shirt off and tossing it aside. Then his fingers were hooked in the waist of his trousers. Quickly, Brandy turned away. A moment later she heard a splash.

She undressed quickly, then dove into the water, allowing him only a glimpse of high firm breasts and well-rounded hips as she plunged into the cold stream.

He was waiting for her when she surfaced. Reaching out, he wrapped an arm around her and drew her naked body against his.

Her stomach contracted with shock. "I-it's cold," she muttered, covering her reaction to the feel of his naked body against hers. The sensations she was feeling had sent her senses reeling.

Wiping the water from her eyes, she tried to pull away, but he was having none of it. He held her tightly, his eyes dark with passion; and the raw hunger she saw in them lit an answering flame deep within her body.

"Sky Walker," she whispered, wrapping her arms around his neck and turning her face up to his.

With a husky groan his lips found hers in a kiss of intense sweetness. While his right hand spanned her waist, his left slid down her back and caressed the silky flesh of her buttocks.

A devastating hunger overpowered her, a feeling of intense longing to be drawn into his very being. "Sky Walker," she moaned. "Love me."

Swinging her into his arms, he carried her from the water and laid her on a bed of grass. Then he covered her body with his and made love to her with sweet abandonment.

When it was over, he clutched her against him. "We were meant for each other," he whispered hoarsely, his face buried in her neck. "Say it is so."

She knew it was true. "Yes," she whispered. "I could never love anyone else." The very thought of anyone but Sky Walker holding her the way he was now was completely revolting.

He swept her hair back from her face and gazed into her eyes. "You know what your people would say if you stay with me?"

"I don't care," she whispered. "I've never felt this way about anyone before. Not ever."

Lowering his head, he found her lips again. After a long moment he lifted his head. "We must tell Long Knife and Josie of your decision. I am certain Long Knife can be persuaded to take Josie to Taos."

* * *

Josie and Long Knife seemed not the least bit surprised when they were told the news. "I suspected as much," Josie said. "But are you sure that's what you want?"

"Yes," Brandy said, looking up at Sky Walker.

"What about your property in England?"

"I will send a letter to my aunt. He will look after it until I decide what to do."

"The decision has already been made," Sky Walker said. "You will stay with me."

"But the estate will have to be settled. And I must notify Aunt Rebecca of my safety. There will be many things that must be attended to." Brandy looked at Sky Walker. "Perhaps you would go to England with me."

"We will speak of this later," he said. "There are reasons I cannot leave my people now."

His people. Brandy looked at him uncertainly. By going with Sky Walker she would be leaving everything that was familiar behind her. If the truth were known, she still felt uncertain about her future with him. Would it always be that way? Or would time, the great healer, make her a part of his world?

The parting next morning was fraught with uncertainties, on Josie's part as well as Brandy's.

"I feel as though I'm deserting you," Brandy said.

"Hogwash!" Josie said. "It's 'cause of you I got free of Jeffers. You don't worry none about me, honey. Just take care of yourself."

The two girls embraced and smiled through their tears. Then, they went their separate ways.

Now that they were beginning the journey to Texas and Comanche territory, Sky Walker seemed in a hurry to reach his village. The sun beat down on Brandy and Sky Walker as they traveled across the plains, across dry land dotted with small plants and lizards and snakes. They traveled from break of day until the purple shadows of night covered the land. Only then would Sky Walker allow them rest. The day they reached the Red River was a happy one for Brandy. Sky Walker had promised they'd stop early and not leave until morning. She suspected the concession was for the horses, not her. But whatever the reason, she was grateful for it.

Relief swept through her as she saw the trees growing along the banks of the river. She could hardly wait to get in the water. After they'd allowed the horses to drink, Sky Walker hobbled them in a grove of willows growing near the river where the grass was plentiful. Brandy took the opportunity to shed her garments and immerse herself in the water.

After the horses were taken care of, Sky Walker joined her in the river. They splashed and frolicked for a while and then Brandy washed herself, using some of the red sand, scooped up from the river bottom, to scrub herself with.

She had just finished wringing the excess water from her hair when she became aware of Sky Walker's stillness. His head was tilted as though he were listening to something she couldn't hear.

"What's wrong?" she asked.

"Get out!" he snapped. "Someone is coming. Take your clothing and hide in that bunch of cattails."

Aware of the urgency, Brandy waded out of the water, gathered up her clothing and hurried toward the cattails growing beside the river only a short distance away. Feeling totally vulnerable in her nakedness, she struggled to don her clothing while kneeling in her hiding place.

Hurry! Hurry! an inner voice cried, but her fingers

refused to cooperate . . . and the hoofbeats were growing louder and louder until it seemed the riders were going to ride into her place of concealment.

The creak of saddle leather and the jingle of spurs took the place of hoofbeats. Her heart gave a lurch then thudded loudly in her ears. The riders had stopped.

Sky Walker! Where was he?

With the thought came the feeling of his presence. She turned, saw him beside her and marveled at how silently he could move. He hadn't made a sound as he'd joined her.

"Who are they?" she whispered.

"Shhhhh," he said. "You must remain completely silent. They are white-eyes. It would not do for them to find us here."

Parting the cattails carefully, she peered at the horsemen.

God! One of the men was Franko!

If Sky Walker hadn't heard the riders coming, their situation would indeed be dangerous! She heard a whinny, and her breath stopped. "Was that our horses?" she asked.

"No. I took them farther up the river. They are well hidden. Unless the white-eyes become suspicious, they will be safe there. Now be silent."

Brandy settled down, waiting in an agony of suspense, crunching herself lower, afraid that at any given moment, the intruders would discover them.

How long had it been? Her muscles ached with tension, fear coiled deep inside her stomach. An eternity seemed to pass while she waited, until, finally, unable to stand it any longer, she parted the cattails and peered through them.

Franko sat on a log, not more than thirty feet away,

rolling a cigarette. He was deep in conversation with another man and seemed to have all the time in the world.

Brandy swallowed hard, realizing it was Franko's intention to stay the night. And, with the renegades only a short distance away, they were well and truly trapped.

Chapter Eighteen

Brandy's heart beat wildly against her rib cage while she strained against her father's weight, frantically trying to pull him behind the shelter of a boulder. Although it was pitch dark, she knew the others in their party were dead. She and her father were alone . . .

. . . pitted against hundreds of renegades.

Realizing her fingers were wet, sticky, from the warm blood oozing from her father's wounds, she narrowed her eyes, trying to pierce the darkness, needing to know how badly he was injured. But the dark was absolute, too thick to penetrate with her vision. . . .

. . . and out there, just a few yards away, the renegades waited to catch her unaware . . .

. . . waited in the darkness for her to stumble . . . to stop running. . . .

. . . running . . .

. . . running . . . swimming. . . . thrashing in the cold water, trying to reach her father who crouched on the bank, holding out his arms, pleading with her to help him . . .

. . . free him from the painted savages who danced

around the upright pole they had bound him to, while the flames licked at his feet . . . his clothing caught fire . . .

God! . . . the flames! The flames! He was being consumed in a blazing inferno . . . an inferno that sent out so much smoke that she couldn't breathe and her lungs were on fire from lack of oxygen, but she was cold . . .

. . . so cold.

Suddenly, Brandy's eyes snapped open and she stared up at Sky Walker. His expression was grim, concerned, and she realized his hand was responsible for her breathless state. He had covered her mouth, smothering her cries. His eyes flashed a warning as he bent closer, placing his mouth against her ear. "You are safe," he whispered. "But you must be silent."

The glow from a distant fire cast his face in sharp relief. Realizing it was Franko's campfire, awareness swept over her and her breath solidified in her throat. Slowly, holding the warrior's gaze, she nodded her head, showing him she understood. Sky Walker's tense body relaxed slightly and his hand left her mouth, allowing her to fill her lungs with air.

As Brandy became more aware of her surroundings, she became aware she was freezing. She wrapped her arms around herself, but it did little good; she could still feel the chill damp air, carried on the breeze across the river. Even the heavy fabric of her dress couldn't keep the cold from penetrating.

God! How long would they be stuck here?

A quick glance told her the renegades were still there, sleeping peacefully in their blankets while she shivered in the cattail thicket nearby. The full moon made it easy to see the renegades, made it impossible to keep from being seen by the man who sat beside the fire, a rifle held in the

186

crook of his arm, obviously left awake to guard the others.

Brandy turned her attention to Sky Walker. She wanted so desperately to talk with him, to have him reassure her with words, but they were so close to the renegades, they dare not risk conversation. Sounds carried in the night much too easily, and hopelessly outnumbered by the renegades, they dared not risk discovery.

Sky Walker was studying her expression, and something in his eyes caused her heart to leap with fear. Using sign language, he began to speak. She had little trouble understanding that he intended leaving her there and going off on his own. But why? Something to do with the horses?

She shook her head frantically, her eyes wide with fear. He couldn't leave her alone. He just couldn't! She opened her mouth, but he placed a warning finger across her lips and shook his head violently.

Stealing a quick glance toward the renegades, and the guard who had stood up and was stretching his body, she shuddered. No way would she allow Sky Walker to leave her alone.

She turned to tell him so and discovered he was gone.

Only the barest rustling of the grass told of Sky Walker's passing. He hadn't wanted to leave Brandy alone, but knew that he must. Had he brought her with him, she'd have given them away, for unlike him, who'd been trained to move so silently that he could even pass a few feet from a covey of quail without disturbing them, each time she moved, the crickets ceased their singing, the frogs their croaking. If the man who guarded the others had been Comanche, Sky Walker would be dead and his woman in the hands of the renegades.

Realizing he must hurry or her fear would cause her to give away her presence, he slipped easily through the rushes, making his way downriver to the draw, formed by high water cutting away at the riverbank, where he'd hobbled their mounts. The horses lifted their heads, satisfied their curiosity about him, then went back to their grazing.

After checking the ropes that hobbled the animals, making certain they were still secured, Sky Walker took a blanket from his pack and wrapped it around his waist tightly. He wasn't sure how long the renegades would stay and he knew Brandy was chilled, perhaps hungry as well. He searched through the pack, pulled out a parfleche, one of the small buffalo-hide bags, from the pack, and secured it beneath the blanket. His movements were swift, sure, but his thoughts were in turmoil, worried about Brandy's safety, yet realizing he might have no other chance to get the supplies, for they might find themselves completely cut off from the horses.

It was the half-light before dawn and Brandy felt stiff with cold and tension. A breeze lifted the soft tendrils of her hair, blowing it against her face, her ears, and her neck.

Sky Walker had been gone for so long . . . it seemed like hours had passed since she'd last seen him. What was taking him so long?

The renegades had begun stirring. She could hear the murmur of voices, and parted the cattails slightly. The guard was standing over a blanket-wrapped form.

"Come on, Idaho, get up," the guard said, digging

at the man's ribs with the toes of his boots.

"What's your hurry?" the man called Idaho asked. "And get your damn boots offa me." He sat up and pushed the covers away from him, holding his head in his hands. "Dammit! I was havin' a dream and you had to go and wake me."

"Franko said we was to get up at dawn," the guard said.

"Hell, Luke," Idaho said, casting a baleful look around. "Don't you know nothin'? Dawn is when the sun comes up. Not when the dark leaves. I coulda slept for another hour."

"Shut the hell up!"

Brandy's heart beat erratically as she recognized Franko's voice. Hurriedly, she let the cattails fall together again, fearing that he would see her peering from her hiding place.

Where was Sky Walker? Holding her breath, she bit her lower lip, fear settling over her like a dark mantle. Something had happened to him. God! She was trapped here alone! They'd be sure to find her and —

A hand closed over her mouth, smothering the gasp of fright, and she turned her head to see Sky Walker. She didn't know how he'd got past the renegades, and right now she didn't care. Closing her eyes, she leaned into his strength, letting it wash over her and comfort her.

It was midmorning before the renegades finally began making preparations to leave. Although Sky Walker tried to make her comfortable, Brandy was too afraid to relax. Any moment could be the one when they were discovered. At any moment one of them could decide to come this way. So she waited, her eyes wide with fear, her body

189

held tensely as the renegades had a leisurely breakfast, waited while the mouth-watering aroma of cooking bacon invaded her nostrils, made her stomach growl. The strip of jerky that Sky Walker offered did little to assuage her hunger.

Sky Walker seemed aware of everything around them, of every breath she took, of the slightest change in the breeze. She wasn't certain when she became aware his attention had turned from the renegades who were engrossed in breaking camp.

Fresh panic surged through her. Had one of the renegades left his companions? Was he, even now, circling around them, seeking out their hiding place, prepared to give the alarm to his fellow companions?

Brandy controlled a shudder. To become Franko's prisoner again was beyond thinking about.

Unable to bear the suspense, she leaned forward slightly, peering through the cattails again. Her eyes found each man in turn and she silently counted them. One, two, three, four, five . . . they were all there.

Unless she'd miscounted.

She looked at Sky Walker again. His attention had never wavered, his eyes were still fixed on a spot just beyond her right leg.

Wondering, she followed his gaze . . . and her heart skipped a beat and went flip-flop, then began beating in double time, pounding in erratic rhythm.

Near a rotted log, surrounded by wild daisies, not more than five feet away, was the biggest snake she had ever had the misfortune to lay eyes on. It was hard to tell the length, coiled as it was, but the size of the reptile sent icy fingers trailing down her spine. She sucked in a sharp breath.

"Do not move," Sky Walker commanded, his voice barely audible to her ears.

God! How could she keep still? Their guide, Pedro, had told her about this snake. The rattles on the tail and the black diamonds marking its back, told her it was a western diamondback, one of the deadliest snakes in North America.

And Sky Walker had told her to not move!

Her green eyes glittered with fright as she watched the snake weave its head back and forth, flitting its tongue in and out, its glassy eyes fixed unwaveringly on her.

The snorting of horses and the jingling of metal barely penetrated her mind. Her subconscious mind knew the renegades were leaving, but she could take little pleasure from that now. Her body seemed frozen in an eternity of terror, waiting in limbo for the horror to begin —

— then the waiting was over.

Chapter Nineteen

Sky Walker flung himself forward just as the snake struck. The reptile's fangs bit into the flesh of the warrior's upper arm, releasing the deadly venom and sending it surging through his body.

Wrapping his fingers around the snake, just behind the head, Sky Walker jerked the rattler loose, flung it away, then sent his knife *whoooshing* through the air toward the rattler. The blade buried itself in the snake's head, pinning it against the log, where it lay thrashing wildly.

Filled with horror, Brandy sat frozen, unable to move. Sky Walker had been bitten! Even though he was still on his feet, he was a dead man. But he seemed not to realize.

He flipped the bottom of her skirt up and, to her astonishment, tore a wide strip off the bottom of her petticoat. "You must help me," he muttered, busy winding the fabric above the wound. "Go get the knife."

She remained unmoving, staring in wide-eyed horror. "I said, get the knife!" he snapped.

Brandy realized she must get herself under control. He'd said she must help him. How? An inner voice cried.

Pedro said there was no hope of recovery from the bite

of the western diamondback.

Bile rose in the back of her throat and she swallowed back her nausea. It was her fault that Sky Walker had been bitten! All her fault!

"Brandy!" The warrior's voice was carefully controlled. "We must be quick. The snake is dead. It cannot harm you. We need the knife and I cannot release the pressure on the wound to get it. There is no one else to help me. You must do it."

No one else to help me. He was right. There was no one else. She would have to do it.

Forcing her frozen limbs to move, she approached the rattler. Her fingers trembled as she reached for the knife. Although the blade had gone through the rattler's head, it was still twitching.

Hurry! a silent voice commanded. Get the knife. There's no one else to help Sky Walker.

Grimly, she wrapped her fingers around the handle and pulled the blade out. The snake's tail lashed back and forth, striking her on the leg, and she stifled a frightened shriek, then scuttled backward, the knife held limply in her hand.

Her face was colorless as she held the knife out to Sky Walker. He shook his head. "You will have to cut it," he said. With his finger, he showed her where to make the incisions.

"I'll try," she whispered. "I'm so sorry. So sorry." She could not account for the pain she felt as she sliced into the coppery flesh of his arm, cutting across the fang marks. Immediately, he lifted his arm to his mouth and sucked, drawing the deadly venom out of his arm. After a moment, he lifted his head and spat blood and venom out, then bent to suck again.

When he'd finished, he lay back, looking pale and shaken. "I am sorry this has happened," he said.

"Don't," she whispered, tears brimming over and flowing down her cheeks. "Please don't apologize. The whole thing's my fault. You were bitten while trying to save me." Her lips quivered. "Are . . . are you going to die?"

"No, little green eyes. I would never do that. Not when I have so much to live for."

"Do you — do you promise?"

"I promise," he said solemnly. "You will not rid yourself of me so easily, little green eyes."

His words were her only comfort as the day slowly passed. Minutes seemed hours, and the hours were an eternity as he lapsed into unconsciousness. His arm became swollen, and fever raged through his body. Then he began to mumble incoherently.

She recalled his promise over and over again, dredging the words up from her memory as the time slowly passed and his arm began to turn a mottled purple. Oftentimes he cried out for someone called Johanna, asking her to help him. At any other time, Brandy would have been jealous of the unknown woman.

But not now! At this very moment, while she mopped the sweat from his feverish body, she would have given anything . . . anything at all, for someone who could help him get well.

More time passed and the sun went down. Brandy left Sky Walker long enough to bring the horses closer; then she prepared a pot of soup from dried vegetables she found among the supplies, hoping she could get him to drink some of it. But the hope was in vain. He remained asleep, or unconscious.

Realizing she must keep up her own strength, she ate a

small portion herself, then returned to watch over him. More time passed and the days seemed to merge together. She'd had no sleep since the snake had bitten Sky Walker. She dared not sleep, afraid he would need her. Instead, she fed wood to the fire and carried water for the pot, which she'd filled with strips of fabric torn from her bedraggled petticoat and left heating over the coals. Time and again she heated the rags and applied them to Sky Walker's arm. She could think of nothing left to do, but instead of getting better, he seemed to be drifting away from her.

"God help me!" she cried, looking up toward the heavens. "I don't know what to do for him!" Her gaze caught a fluttering movement and she narrowed them on a buzzard, floating lazily in the sky overhead. "Go away!" she shouted, shaking her fists at the vulture. "You can't have him! He's not going to die! I won't let him!" Dropping on her heels beside him, she gazed upon his face. "You said you wouldn't die," she whispered fiercely. "Damn you! You told me you wouldn't die!"

"I will not," he croaked, his eyes suddenly opening. "It will take more than a rattlesnake bite to kill me."

"Sky Walker!" she cried, throwing herself at him and scattering kisses across his face. "You aren't dead. You aren't dead."

"Not yet," he grated hoarsely. "But you are going to drown me with your tears."

Hastily, she pulled back and wiped the tears from his face. Even though she tried to stem the flow, her tear ducts wouldn't cooperate and the tears continued to rain down her face. "S-sorry," she said. "It's just . . . . that I'm so g-glad to see you awake."

He frowned. "How long has it been?"

"I don't know. T-two days I think. You haven't . . . didn't open your eyes once. I didn't know how to help you . . . what to do . . ." Her voice trailed away and she stared down at him, unable to say another word.

Until his eyes closed again.

"Sky Walker!" she cried desperately. "Don't . . . pass out. Please. Tell me what to do for you."

His eyes opened slowly, as though his eyelids were incredibly heavy. "My arm," he said weakly. "I can't seem to move it."

"It's . . . it's swollen . . . and it looks bruised, sort of black and blue all over." She studied him with anxious eyes. "What do I need to do? I heated rags and applied them, but they don't seem to help. And you've been out of your head with fever, calling out for someone named Johanna."

"Johanna," he murmured. "She would heal me."

She swallowed hard, taking his words as criticism. And she deserved them. "I'm trying," she said, swiping at her tears with the back of her hand. "I just don't know what to do. Tell me."

"Do not cry, little green eyes," he said, lifting his good hand and stroking her wet cheek. "There is some tobacco in a white beaded parfleche among our supplies. Wet some down and apply it to the wound. In another bag, decorated with yellow beads, is a powder . . ." He drew a shuddery breath and closed his eyes.

"Sky Walker," she cried, shaking him hard. "What about the powder from the bag with yellow beads? What should I do with it?" His eyes opened, dull, glazed, seemingly unaware of her. "The powder," she repeated urgently. "Do you want it applied to the wound?"

196

"The powder?" he repeated, his voice lifeless, incomprehensive.

"Yes. The powder you told me about. Remember? The powder in the little bag with yellow beads? What is it good for? I don't know how to use it."

"Need hot water," he mumbled, his eyelids closing again. "Heat some water . . . for fever."

"For the fever?" she questioned. "I don't understand. Please tell me what you mean? How will the hot water help your fever?"

"Not water," he muttered. "Powder. Must drink hot water . . . powder . . . fever. Drink . . ." His head lolled to one side as he lapsed into unconsciousness again.

"Drink hot water," she mumbled. "He must mean I'm to dissolve the powder from the bag with yellow beads in the hot water for his fever."

Scrambling to her feet, Brandy left Sky Walker and hurried to the packs. It didn't take long to find the hide bags he'd spoken of. If only she knew which remedy would be the most help. But she didn't and took a chance on the tobacco, remembering hearing that tobacco was placed on wounds for its drawing power. Perhaps it would help draw the poison from his system.

After making a poultice of the wet tobacco, she applied it directly to the wound and wrapped his arm up again. Then she heated some water and made a brew using the powders from the other bag.

Cursing herself for her ineptness, she poured the brew into a cup and lifted his head. But he was unconscious and the liquid spilled out the side of his mouth.

"Johanna," he mumbled. "Johanna."

Wrapping her arms around herself, she rocked back and forth on her heels and cried out her fear. She'd even

197

see him with the woman he cried out for . . . the one he'd called Johanna.

Lifting her gaze skyward, she saw the buzzard circling around them. She shuddered, her skin suddenly cold. Did they somehow know Sky Walker was worse? The thought was unnerving. As though confirming her suspicions, another buzzard joined the first in its never-ending circle . . . then another was there and another and another.

Suddenly the sight of the scavenger birds was too much to bear. She would leave this place . . .

Somehow . . .

She would get Sky Walker on his horse and find help for him . . .

Somehow . . .

Chapter Twenty

Even though her will was strong, Brandy could not have accomplished the task if Sky Walker hadn't regained consciousness long enough to help her. Under his instructions, she built a litter to carry him, but long before it was completed, he had lapsed into a state of unconsciousness again.

After she had rolled his limp body onto the hide-covered litter, she fastened it behind his horse and they set out in the hope of finding help for him.

They had been wandering for days when she saw a band of Indians top a rise. Only moments later the warriors were swooping down on them.

Brandy didn't even try to escape them. She realized she needed their help and would have to take the chance that the warriors would give it. Sky Walker was out of his head with fever; his arm, where the snake had bitten him, was purplish in color, swollen twice its size. She felt certain he didn't have long to live, not without some kind of medical help.

Surely the Indians would know what to do.

Dust boiled up around her as the Indians surrounded

them. Their faces were slashed with paint, their expressions hostile. Although fear sent icy fingers across her flesh, chilling her bones, Brandy forced herself to face them bravely. Lifting her chin boldly, she tried her best to appear unafraid.

A squat, thick-set warrior, with red-and-black paint streaked across his nose and down both cheeks, pointed his scalp-hung lance at her and spoke in a harsh guttural voice. She had no idea what he was saying, only that he didn't sound very friendly.

Brandy pointed at the limp body of Sky Walker, fastened with ropes to the litter behind his mount. "A rattlesnake bit him," she said, managing to keep her voice steady. "He needs help, but I don't know what to do. Do you know how to help him?"

A young warrior had already leapt lightly off his horse and was examining Sky Walker. Lifting the affected arm, the warrior spoke to his companions in the guttural language they used. Several Indians dismounted and worked at the ropes holding Sky Walker on the litter. When he was free, they pulled him to the ground.

"Be careful!" Brandy cried. "Don't hurt him!"

The squat warrior beside Brandy dismounted and pulled her from her mount. She hit the ground with a heavy thud that left her breathless. Fear tightened her stomach into a knot. Judging from the hostile looks she was receiving from the warriors, it was unlikely they were going to help her.

Suddenly the warrior kneeling beside Sky Walker drew his knife.

"No!" Brandy cried, scrambling toward them on all fours. "Don't hurt him!"

Before she could reach them, the warrior plunged the

knife downward, slicing into Sky Walker's arm. Curling her fingers into talons, she leapt forward, reaching for the warrior's eyes. He jerked his head back and her fingernails scraped a path down his cheek. Blood welled from the scratches and the other warriors made a grab for her. Strong hands fastened on her upper arms, holding her back.

"Turn me loose!" she shouted. "Let me go!"

Aiming a kick at the nearest warrior, she connected with the soft place between his legs. Grunting with pain, he released her, but another warrior took his place. Brandy continued to fight, struggling against the warriors' greater strength as she sought to reach the man who was tormenting Sky Walker.

But it was no use.

She was like a lamb trying to fight a grizzly bear as they dragged her away and blocked her view of Sky Walker and the Indians surrounding him.

Too late! She'd been too late to save him!

Despairing tears streamed unheeded down her face. Sky Walker had depended on her . . . the one time he'd needed her help, she'd let him down.

Burying her head in her palms, she gave way to her tears. She didn't know what they were doing to him, didn't know what was going to become of Sky Walker, let alone herself. She only knew whatever the Indians had planned for them, she could do nothing to prevent it. Her shoulders shook as she continued to sob, until finally, there were no more tears left to shed.

Brandy gave a long shudder and lifted her head. The warriors were all staring at her. One of the Indians, obviously the leader, spoke in a harsh voice.

"I don't understand you," she said in a shaky voice.

The sun was relentless as it beat down from above, but she paid it little heed. The pain she was feeling inside left little room for other concerns. She crept closer to Sky Walker, and this time they didn't stop her. A bulge beneath the cloth that had been wrapped around his arm, indicated a potion of some kind had been applied.

Perhaps she'd been wrong and they were trying to help him. Hope flooded through her and she held tightly to it.

Although she'd thought she'd shed all her tears, when she smoothed his hair back from his face, they welled into her eyes again. Quickly, she blinked the brimming tears away, trying to stop their flow. She'd already shown the Indians her weakness. She had to control her emotions. She couldn't give way to her tears again.

The warriors lifted Sky Walker and bound his limp body to the litter.

A hand gripped Brandy's arm, shoving her toward her horse. Realizing they wanted her to mount, she did so. Apparently the Indians were going to help Sky Walker. What they would do to her, she didn't know.

A chill shook Sky Walker, and he shuddered with the cold. Was it winter? For some reason he couldn't remember, couldn't even open his eyes to see, because his lids were incredibly heavy, seeming almost to be stuck together.

He groaned, and a voice, seeming to come from an incredible distance, told him to be still. But how could he? His arm was on fire. What had happened? And why was it so cold? Why couldn't he remember?

Feeling a cool soft hand on his face, he gave a relieved sigh. "Johanna," he muttered. "I knew you'd come."

202

Instantly, the hand left his face. "No," he protested. "Don't go, Johanna." He reached for her with both hands and felt a jolt of agony through his left arm. The cry of pain left his lips before he could stop it; then the soft hand was back, stroking his forehead, murmuring soothing words to him.

He allowed his mind to rise above his body, to look down on the dark-haired woman kneeling beside his wounded body. He recognized her immediately. It was Johanna, the healer. As he watched, she placed her palms around his upper arm, focusing on the snake bite. Closing her eyes, she let her head drop forward and he knew she was releasing the energy.

Sky Walker took the time to thank the Great Spirit for sending Johanna to his tribe, then he allowed his mind to float away, to drift along with the breeze intent on searching for the woman who'd captured his heart. But instead of cooperating with him, the breeze stilled, his mind entered his body again, and he slept.

When Sky Walker woke again he was immediately conscious of the stillness. Opening his eyes cautiously, he peered through narrowed lids at Johanna.

"So you're finally back with us," she said cheerfully. "You've had everyone worried."

"What happened?" he croaked, his eyes traveling around the lodge . . . Johanna and Hawkeye's lodge.

"You were bitten by a snake," she said. "A rattler. I was afraid you were already too far gone when they brought you to me."

"Bitten by a rattler?" He searched his mind for his memory, found it stuck away in a little corner — and his eyes widened. "Brandy!" He pushed himself to his elbows. "Johanna! There was a girl with me . . .

my woman. What happened to her?"

"Little Wolf took her to your lodge. He thought that was what you would want done. She seemed terribly upset about you. Now I understand why. So you have finally found yourself a woman. I'd say it's about time."

Suddenly he felt weary beyond belief. Since Brandy had been taken care of, he could afford to relax for a while and allow his body time to recover. His eyelids closed. "Will you see that she's taken care of?"

"Of course," Johanna said. "Now don't worry about her. Just go back to sleep and concentrate on getting well."

Sky Walker thought her suggestion seemed a very good one. Slowly, his body relaxed and he drifted off to sleep again.

Brandy paced back and forth in the confines of the lodge. She didn't have to open the flap to know the guard was still outside the tepee — she could *feel* his presence there. How long had it been since the Indians had brought them to the village? And, even more important, where was Sky Walker?

It seemed an eternity had passed since they'd reached the Indian village located beside the Brazos River. And although Brandy had wanted to stay with Sky Walker, the warriors had left him with a dark-haired girl.

Could she be the one? The girl he called Johanna? The one that Sky Walker had cried out for in his delirium?

Brandy had never once thought Sky Walker might have a woman here in the village. Why hadn't he told her?

Raking a hand through her disheveled hair, Brandy continued her pacing. How long had it been since the Indians had left her? Hours had passed . . . but how many?

Suddenly, Brandy heard something . . . a sound . . . like someone scratching on the hide covering. Her gaze flew to the entrance flap and she held her breath.

Scratch, scratch, scratch. The sound was raspy, like nails being dragged over the hide entrance flap.

Suddenly there was silence. As Brandy watched, the flap was pushed aside. Her heart beat an erratic rhythm while she waited . . . waited, until she was staring at a young girl with soft doe eyes . . . eyes that were wide with fright as they fastened on Brandy.

When the girl spoke, it was in a soft voice, but the guttural language she used made the words sound harsh. Brandy opened her mouth to speak but the girl backed away from her a few steps. Then, as though suspecting Brandy would do her some mischief, the girl turned and fled, leaving Brandy staring after her in consternation, wondering why she had come.

Brandy spent a restless night and her eyes felt swollen when she woke. Her guard had departed, leaving her free to leave if she wanted. And she did. She must find Sky Walker, but she didn't know where to start looking.

When she stepped outside, she saw several women deep in conversation. Among them was a white woman with a babe in her arms. Could she be Johanna?

As though becoming aware of her presence, the young woman looked up and saw her. "Good morning," she called, leaving the other women.

Brandy was relieved to hear someone speaking English, and she studied the other woman who was approaching. The firm set of her chin suggested strength of character and the sun had provided a golden tint to her smooth unblemished skin. Her startling green eyes were accentuated by high cheekbones and thin, arched brows. She had the look of a woman of quality. Was the babe she held so close to her breast a half-breed?

"So you're Brandy!" the woman exclaimed. "I've heard so much about you already that I could hardly wait to meet you. I didn't catch you at a bad time, did I?"

"Catch me at a bad time?" Brandy parroted.

"Yes. I thought you might be busy."

Doing what? Brandy silently wondered. Aloud, she said, "I was going to look for Sky Walker."

"I've just come from him," the girl said. "He's sleeping right now." The woman shifted the baby in her arms and held out a suntanned hand. "I'm Johanna. Sky Walker has probably told you about me."

"No," Brandy said stiffly, her gaze falling on the baby, taking in his cherubic features. "I'm afraid he hasn't. Could you tell me where to find him?"

Johanna frowned. "Didn't Night Owl tell you he was with me?"

"No one told me anything," Brandy said stiffly.

"That's strange. I sent her to you yesterday because I knew you'd be worried."

"I have seen no one—" She broke off. "There was a young girl who came. But I couldn't understand what she was saying."

"I'm sorry," Johanna said. "She was probably nervous of you. Believe me when I say her English is very good."

Brandy didn't care one whit about Night Owl's English. "Where *is* Sky Walker?" she asked.

"He spent the night in my lodge," Johanna said. "The fever is gone and he's doing quite nicely now. When he wakes up, he should be good as new."

That fast! But he'd been so ill! Snake bites must heal

fast when treated properly. Thank God she'd found someone to help him. Even as relief washed over Brandy, leaving her almost weak, she wondered why the warriors had taken Sky Walker to Johanna's lodge. And why had Sky Walker kept calling for her in his delirium. What would Johanna say when she was told the warrior had taken a wife?

Perhaps it would make no difference to her, Brandy silently told herself. After all, the woman was incredibly beautiful, with her sun-kissed skin and midnight dark hair.

"How long have you lived with the Indians?" Brandy asked, finding herself unable to contain her curiosity.

"Two years," Johanna replied. "I hope you'll like it here as much as I do."

"How old is your baby?"

Johanna smiled down at the baby in her arms. "Just two months. And he's the dearest, sweetest baby that ever lived." Her fingers gently caressed the baby's dark, silky curls. "Aren't you, my little precious boy." Glancing up at Brandy, she added, "He's so much like his father. He's going to grow up to be just like him." Her gaze went back to the baby. "Aren't you, my pet? You'll be so handsome all the girls will swoon when you walk by."

Johanna kept crooning to the babe while Brandy searched for signs of the baby's father. The baby's hair was black, like Sky Walker's. But so was Johanna's — and every other Indian's, too. The baby *could* be Sky Walker's baby, but then, he could belong to any of the other warriors. As bad as Brandy wanted to know, she couldn't bring herself to ask Johanna who had fathered the child.

Suddenly, the baby opened his eyes . . . green eyes, so like his mother's . . . and stared up at Brandy. His lips twitched and his eyes seemed to focus on Brandy's hair, shining like a golden halo beneath the sun.

The corners of the baby's mouth curved up in a smile and a knot formed in the pit of Brandy's midsection.

"Did you see that?" Johanna asked. "He smiled at you. Didn't you, my little love."

Yes. Brandy had seen the baby's smile and it tore at her heartstrings. "What did you name him?" she asked softly.

"Brazos."

"After the river?"

"Yes. Would you like to hold him?" Johanna asked.

"I—"

Taking her acceptance for granted, Johanna shoved the squirming baby at Brandy. She swallowed hard and looked down at the warm bundle in her arms. Yes, she silently agreed. The baby was a precious little boy and he could not be blamed for his father's actions.

"Is something wrong?" Johanna asked gently.

"Of course not," Brandy said, lifting blurred eyes to the other girl. "He's a lovely child and I know you must be very proud of him."

"Yes," said Johanna. "But no more so than his father. It's still hard for me to believe how much he dotes on little Brazos."

Brandy swallowed again. "I shouldn't wonder. Any man would be proud to have such a beautiful baby."

Yes. Any man would be proud. And how could she possibly compete with Johanna and little Brazos? Suddenly, pain stabbed through her. She had to get the child out of her arms. She felt as though her heart were breaking, knew that she was going to break down and cry at any moment, and she wanted to be alone when she did.

"I—I—" She stopped and tried to control the shaking

in her voice. "Johanna, I don't want to be rude, but I have things to do." She held the child out to his mother. "Please, t-take him. I must—I feel suddenly—" She broke off and hurried toward the cover of the forest, aware of the curious eyes that followed her.

Tears streamed down her face, blinding her, making her stumble in her mad dash to be away from the mother and her child, the cause of her heartbreak. In the dense forest, Brandy paused, grabbing a limb to support her trembling legs. Why did she feel as though her heart were breaking? Why had she allowed herself to fall in love with a man who did not return her love?

Yes, she silently admitted to herself. Even though he had deceived her, she still loved him!

God! What had she let herself in for? Why had she allowed her heart to override her good sense? She should have returned to England.

She didn't know how long she was there . . . perhaps minutes, perhaps hours. She didn't hear the sound of approaching footsteps, had no idea that anyone was there until a hand gripped her shoulder.

"Why do you weep?" asked a gentle voice.

She spun around, staring in disbelief at Sky Walker. Even though Johanna had said he was well, Brandy hadn't expected him to look so healthy. His recovery was amazing.

"Y-you recovered quickly," she stuttered.

"Yes. It was Johanna's doing. Now tell me why you are weeping?"

"I'm not weeping!" she denied.

"Then it must be raining," he said gently, brushing a tear away with his finger.

Although she wanted to throw herself into his arms,

her mind would not allow it. She chided her foolish heart for still wanting him, even though he'd deceived her.

Setting her jaw firmly, she refused to allow the tenderness in his voice to persuade her to forget the way he'd betrayed both her and Johanna, not to mention the helpless child. He was an unfeeling brute . . . an ignorant savage who cared for no one, who thought only of his own basic needs.

God! She hated him! Hated him!

Obviously unaware of her thoughts, he tried to pull her into his embrace. "Don't touch me," she snapped, slapping at his hands and stepping backward.

His dark brows drew together, his eyes puzzled. "What is wrong?" he asked. "Are you angry with me?"

"You're damn right I'm angry with you!" she snapped. "How did you think you could possibly get away with such a deception? Did you actually think I would put up with such actions?"

His expression darkened, became grim. "What are you talking about?"

"If you don't know, then I'm certainly not going to tell you!"

To her amazement, the hard lines on his face relaxed and he laughed.

He actually laughed!

"Hawkeye warned me this would happen," he said. "But I did not believe him. I guess it is the way of all white women. But still you surprise me."

"Don't you laugh at me!" she snarled, deliberately stoking the fires of fury to keep her tears at bay. "You black-hearted devil! Do you think you can keep both of us? Well, you can just think again. I refuse to live here with you. I will not be a spare wife to you. Someone you can come to when you feel like it. There's no way in hell I'm going to put up with anything like that."

His eyes darkened, became stormy. "Enough, woman!" he growled. "I do not like this side of you. I come to you expecting to find comfort and instead I am attacked with words. It is something I will not allow."

"Allow? You won't allow it?" Her eyes were flashing emerald green. "Well, that's quite unfortunate! You have no say over what I do!"

"Be careful," he said. "Your tongue is too sharp. If I were an Apache, then I would cut it out."

"You try to lay a hand on me, and see what happens!" she hissed. "I don't have to accept whatever you do just because you call yourself a man —"

Apparently he'd had enough.

Reaching out, he grabbed her with both hands, dug his fingers into her upper arms, and shook her until her teeth rattled. When she was breathless and trembling, he released her and she crumpled to the ground.

Sky Walker's body was tense, angry, as he stood above her, breathing heavily, his expression hard and unbending. Then, spinning on his heels, he stalked away into the forest, leaving her where she had fallen . . .

. . . breathless and alone.

Chapter Twenty-one

With the memory of Sky Walker's face, dissolved in a mask of rage, foremost in her mind, Brandy sprang from the ground and sprinted toward the woods, away from the village and the man who had caused her so much pain. Her breath came in harsh gasps, her heart pounded loudly in unison with her feet as she crashed through the forest.

She didn't even slow down when she reached the narrow trail beside a deep ravine. Finding the path overgrown with saplings, Brandy crossed her arms to deflect the branches from her face.

Suddenly a rabbit leapt from beneath the underbrush and Brandy's footsteps faltered, her eyes fastening on the small animal that sought shelter from the intruder. The rabbit darted in front of her, making for the opposite side of the path. With her head turned away, her eyes on the rabbit, she didn't see the fallen tree. Not until she had stumbled over it.

Flailing out with both arms, she fought desperately to regain her balance.

At first she thought she'd imagined the ground moving

beneath her feet . . . until the rocky shale began to slide down the ravine. And with the loose shale went Brandy, slipping and sliding down the slope, her breath whooshing out of her lungs while her fingers clawed at the rocky shale in an effort to stop her plummeting body.

Despite her efforts to stop her fall, Brandy continued to slip and slide and bump toward the bottom of the gully, scraping her arms and legs until the earth finally stopped moving and she lay in a heap, covered with dirt, loose shale and debris.

Groaning with pain, Brandy brushed her tumbled hair back from her eyes, pushed herself to her elbows, tilted her head, and slid her gaze back up the hill.

How had she tumbled so far without serious bodily injury?

She shifted her weight, then wished she hadn't, because her backside was sore, more than likely bruised.

Brandy flexed her shoulder muscles and winced with pain. She wondered if there was a part of her body she hadn't managed to bruise.

"Damn!" she gritted.

Pulling one leg up until it was beneath her, she tried to stand. Instantly a cry escaped her lips and the color drained from her face. The pain that shot through her ankle was so bad that she sank down again, nausea rising in her throat.

Bending over, she removed her moccasin and examined her foot. Although there was a large bruise already forming midway down her foot, she didn't think there were any broken bones.

Turning her attention to her ankle, she felt a surge of panic. The flesh around the ankle bone was swelling fast, already almost doubling its original size.

God! Had she broken it?

Perhaps not. Maybe it was only a sprained ankle. But whichever it was, she certainly needed help.

Swiveling her head around, her gaze swept the ravine, searching for some means of support. She was hoping to find a thick round stick at least three feet in length, something strong enough to support her weight, but it was too much to hope for. There was nothing but a skeletal log the termites had been at, nothing to suit her purpose.

Realizing she'd never be able to climb either side of the ravine without some kind of aid, Brandy began searching for another way out. The ravine came to a dead end at the upper end, but when she turned her gaze on the lower end, she saw a glint of silver in the distance.

Hope swelled strong in her breast as she narrowed her eyes, bringing the ribbon of silver into sharper focus.

Water! She was certain of it. And it could only be the river. Her pulse picked up speed. She was in luck, because the river flowed by the village. All she had to do was find some means to keep afloat, then she could let the river carry her to the village.

Her lips tightened grimly. She hated the idea of everyone knowing she'd been so foolish and careless, but there seemed to be no alternative. She knew she must have help. And at this time of day someone was certain to be at the river.

But getting to the water was not as simple as she'd thought. It took her an hour of half walking, half hopping, and half crawling to accomplish the trip. But when she had done so, it seemed lady luck was on her side. Bobbing gently in the curve of the river was a log, substantial enough to keep her afloat.

Muttering a silent thank you, Brandy pushed the log

farther into the river until the water was waist high and she felt the pull of the current. Then, breathing a sigh of relief, she pulled herself across the log, arranged her limbs in the most comfortable position allowed and rested her head on her arms as she was pulled down the river.

Slowly, the water lapping against the log, combined with the heat of the sun, caused her tense muscles to relax. Brandy drifted with the current, waiting for the sound of voices that would announce the presence of the village. She didn't know how long she'd been drifting when the movements of the log ceased.

Lifting her head, Brandy uttered a frightened cry, her green eyes widening with terror.

Facing her was the biggest bear she had ever laid eyes on.

A black bear!

The fiercest animal she had yet seen. Probably the last she would ever see, for he must be at least ten feet tall and weigh upwards of six hundred pounds. These thoughts crowded her mind, leaving it silently screaming as the bear reared up on his hind legs.

Hovering over her, he opened his mouth wide and exposed dripping fangs . . . just before he uttered a roar that sent a chill through her bones.

Sky Walker opened the flap of the tepee and stepped outside. He was tired of waiting for Brandy. Perhaps he had been harsh with her, but she was being childish, staying in the forest so long. It would soon be dark and she hadn't even started his evening meal.

Why had she attacked him in such a way? And why had she refused to tell him the reason for her anger? Did all paleface women behave in such a manner? Well, he wouldn't stand for it. At first he'd been amused, but his amusement had turned to anger when she'd lashed him so fiercely with her tongue. He refused to put up with such childish actions from her.

The wise ones had always said a warrior must demand obedience from his woman. Never once had she obeyed him. From the first time they'd met she had been willful, demanding that he forget everything and take her to Taos. He'd even taken her as wife to save her from Buffalo Grass. Now she berated him for some imagined something or other. As if that weren't enough, she even refused to tell him why she was angry.

Perhaps he'd made a big mistake bringing her here. Another wife, one of his tribe, would have been sympathetic, would have had compassion for him. After all, hadn't he just come through an ordeal? Hadn't he nearly died? If she hadn't been able to get help for him. . . .

His anger slowly died as reason took its place. She *had* got help for him. She could have left him behind; instead, she had kept riding until his Comanche brothers had found them.

His stomach knotted with fear. Why hadn't she come back? What had happened to upset her? Had someone been cruel to her while he was in the lodge of She-Who-Heals.

Narrowing his gaze on the dense growth of cedars, he loped toward them. There were dangers in the woods . . . especially at night. There were coyotes, black bears, mountain lions, panthers, and snakes. Did she even know they were there? He hadn't told her.

Suddenly, he knew it was imperative he find her.

Something was wrong. He knew it was. Deep down

inside, fear clutched at his innards, twisting and turning, tying them into a knot of anxiety.

Yes. Something was wrong. Brandy must be found, and she must be found at once.

Brandy lay stricken with terror, staring up at the bear facing her, expecting the creature to attack at any given moment.

But instead of attacking, the large black beast twitched his nostrils vigorously, seeming to test the air for danger as he continued to watch her, his massive body erect, unmoving.

Sky Walker! she silently screamed. Help me!

The water lapped gently against the log where Brandy lay, her heart beating in erratic rhythm, her thoughts whirling madly as she held the gaze of the monster before her.

It was a nightmare and she was living it, afraid to look away from the beast, afraid if she did, he would swoop down on her and crush her with one bite from those monstrous, slathering jaws.

God! Why had the log stopped moving?

She felt helpless, caught in limbo, drifting in time while the bear took his time about charging. And the log still wouldn't move!

Dipping her body lower, she felt her knees scrape against the gravel river bottom. Obviously, the log was stuck on a gravel shoal that fingered out into the stream.

Her heart pounded loudly in her ears. Thrum . . . thrum . . . thrum . . . She tried to shove the log back into the current.

The bear gave a mighty roar and lumbered closer, his

gaze still fixed unwaveringly on hers.

Realizing she could not run, nor push the log mid-stream fast enough to escape the bear, Brandy raised a hand and waved at the huge beast. "Sh-shooo," she whispered hoarsely.

She stifled a hysterical giggle when she realized the bear could not have heard her. But, for some reason, he had stopped moving toward her. "Shoooo," she said, raising her voice slightly and waving both arms at him. "Go away! Do you hear me? Go away!"

Opening his mouth wider, the bear lot out a mighty roar, then lumbered backward a step.

Feeling encouraged, Brandy raised her voice even higher. "Shooo! Go away! Shoo!" She punctuated each of her words with a splash of water.

The bear dropped on all fours and a growl began building, starting low in his throat. The beast started toward her again and Brandy sucked in a sharp breath. "N-never mind," she said hastily. "I'll just—just—" She strained with her one good foot, trying her best to push the log off the sandbar. The log moved slightly . . . and so did the bear. Closer to her. "N-nice bear," she said, twisting her lips in a grimace, hoping he would think it was a smile. "Good bear. I'm going away. You don't want to eat me."

The beast roared again, swatting his paw in the air toward her.

Was he going to attack?

Desperately, Brandy pushed harder against the river bottom. The log moved a little deeper into the river. But the bear was still coming . . . faster, having apparently grown tired of waiting.

Brandy's green eyes were wide with fear, and although her nostrils were dilated in terror, still she was aware of the odor of the beast's wet fur.

Then, suddenly, almost miraculously, the current grabbed the log and sent it spinning downstream with its passenger clinging tightly to the rough bark.

But was it moving fast enough to escape the bear? She was afraid not. The water thrashed violently behind her and she knew the beast was following her.

Hurry!

Hurry!

Hurry!

The words echoed in her mind, beating in time with her heart as she thrashed the water with her hands and feet, attempting to escape the wrath of the bear.

Snarls and roars punctuated the air, accompanied by loud splashing and Brandy's knuckles whitened where she gripped the log.

The guttural growl behind her was almost deafening. Something nudged her leg and she screamed and lost her grip on the log. "God, help . . ." Brandy's voice disappeared into gurgles as she went under.

A red haze clouded her vision but she knew she must not give in to it. She had to keep her wits about her, must reach the log again, must escape the bear.

She struggled upward and her head struck a solid object. Feeling the rough bark, she wrapped her fingers around the log and pulled herself up again. Somewhere behind her, she could hear the bear bellowing out its rage. She could only hope he'd given up the chase, because she was too exhausted to fight anymore.

Chapter Twenty-two

Before Sky Walker reached the woods he was joined by Little Wolf. The other warrior asked no questions; instead, he loped along beside his friend, willing to do whatever was necessary to take the troubled look from Sky Walker's face.

Upon reaching the place where he had last seen Brandy, Sky Walker knelt and studied the tracks. It didn't take long, because she'd made no effort to cover her trail. She'd headed toward the distant hills.

But why would she do such a thing? She knew nothing of the area. Why hadn't she returned to the village?

The answer eluded him but the questions persisted, even as he rose to his feet, searching the distance with narrowed eyes, looking for any sign of movement. But there was nothing.

Swallowing around his disappointment, Sky Walker followed Brandy's trail. It took them through the dense woods, where her moccasin prints, embedded in soft, mossy ground, were easily followed. Then they encountered rocky ground and lost the trail. By the time they'd found it again, the sun had set and purple shadows covered the land, making the trail difficult to follow.

But Sky Walker would not stop searching. He couldn't. Brandy was somewhere in these woods . . . and he must find her, however long it took. It would be unthinkable to return to the village without her. He must find her!

He must!

The bear had seemed disinclined to follow Brandy after all, a fact that she was very thankful for. And although she'd seen no sign of the beast since she'd rounded a bend in the river, she was still afraid he would change his mind and appear at any given moment. As though that weren't enough, darkness was falling fast. And she was afraid to leave the dubious safety of the water.

Sky Walker! she silently cried. Help me!

Why had she run away? Even as she asked the question, she knew the answer. She'd run away because she was jealous of Johanna and her baby.

Suddenly, a movement in the distance caught her attention. Her gaze narrowed on the spot . . . someone . . . perhaps a man, was standing beside the river bank.

Raising her arms, she waved at him. "Help me!" she cried, but her voice was only a croaking whisper; there was no way he could hear her. Tears of fear and frustration filled her eyes.

When she realized she was going to float past her only means of help, she thrashed wildly at the water, trying to push the log toward the shore, but she made no headway against the current at all.

She couldn't pass him by. She needed his help.

Releasing her hold on the log, she swam toward the shore. She was only halfway there when she floundered and went under.

Brandy struggled upward, her lungs burning with the need for oxygen. When she finally broke surface, she had only a glimpse of a head, covered with shaggy white hair, before submerging again.

It seemed forever before she felt rough hands on her, gripping the neck of her dress and pulling her upright. She broke surface, gasping for air, trying to relieve her burning lungs.

"Hold still," a gruff voice said close to her ear. "I ain't near as young as I used to be."

Although Brandy's instinct was to struggle, she forced herself to remain still, realizing she'd only impede the man's progress if she tried to help.

When they scraped against the gravel river bottom he released her. Brandy tried to stand, forgetting her injured ankle until she was reminded by a jolt of pain. A cry escaped her lips and she sank back into the water.

"You okay?" The words were spoken almost grudgingly.

"It's my ankle," she said. "I've injured it."

She turned to face her rescuer and her heart gave a wild leap of recognition. Ben! God! What was he doing here? Her gaze darted frantically around. Was Franko with him?

"Let me see that foot." Wrapping an arm around her shoulders, Ben helped her out of the water and lowered her to the sandbar. He seemed unaware of her fear as he examined her ankle. "Looks like a sprain," he muttered. "Wait until I get my mount. Guess you'll have to ride him."

Meeting her eyes for the first time, his gaze narrowed. "You got no call to be worryin'. I ain't gonna hurt you."

"W-what are you doing here?" she whispered.

"Live here," he said. "My cabin's only a little piece from back yonder." He nodded toward the woods.

"Does . . . does Franko live with you?"

"Nope. Ain't seen him since thet Injun got you away from him. Reckon he's still back in New Mexico. Might even be tryin' to sell rifles to the Comanches. Decided I didn't want no more part of him." He shuffled his feet, as though slightly uncomfortable. "Warn't no idea of mine to take you in the first place. I got me no use for women."

"You could have helped me," she accused.

"Don't pay to go up against Franko. Anyway, wasn't none of my business."

Her lips tightened. Neither was it Sky Walker's but he'd attempted to help her. She thought about that as she watched the old man enter the willows growing beside the river. If the old man, one of her own people, had felt that way, it made it even more remarkable that Sky Walker had helped her.

When the old man returned with the horse, she managed to mount, although it proved painful. Ben seemed in no hurry to return to his cabin, stopping to check his traps on the way. Since her ankle no longer had the support of the water, it had begun to throb with a vengeance.

It seemed she had been riding for hours, traveling along a narrow path leading through the cedars, before they came into a clearing where a rough log cabin was nestled. Ben found a thick limb that would hold her weight and helped her hobble into the cabin.

Pushing a chair at her, he said, "Set yourself down. Best soak thet ankle before I wrap it up." Crossing the room, he poured water into a dishpan and set it at her feet. "Stick your foot in there. It oughta help some."

When she had her foot soaking, she looked at him. "Thank you," she said. "That does help some."

"Thought it would," he said. "How'd you come to be in thet river anyways?"

"I fell down a gully. I thought the river would take me to the Comanche village since it's located on the water." Her brows drew together. "I can't understand why it didn't."

"Maybe you went in the river below the village. Ever think of that?"

"No," she admitted. "I didn't. It would explain why I never found it. What I did find though, was a bear. One of the biggest I've ever seen. I just barely escaped being his dinner."

"What color was he?" Ben asked.

"Black. And he had the biggest teeth." She shuddered. "I just barely escaped with my life."

He seemed unimpressed. "Prob'ly just George."

"George? It wasn't a man, Ben. It was a bear. The fiercest, biggest . . ."

"His name's George. Named him after a partner of mine. Mean old devil. The man, not the bear. Bear just growls a lot. Wouldn't hurt a fly."

"Not the bear I saw!" she snapped. "I just barely escaped with my —"

"George is the only black bear left around these parts," Ben interrupted. "Raised him from a cub myself. He comes around once in a while when he's after company."

"That bear comes here? He's dangerous Ben! I don't care what you've named him. He nearly killed me."

"And George ain't so big neither. Not more'n four feet tall. Weighs no more'n a hundred pounds or so."

"Then we certainly aren't talking about the same bear. I'm telling you, the bear nearly killed me."

His eyes slid over her. "Didn't seem to hurt you none."

"That's only because I escaped before he could reach me."

"He'd awanted you, you wouldn't'a got away." He nodded his head. "It was George, all right." He abruptly changed the subject. "Was thet Injun you was with back in New Mexico from the village upstream?"

"Yes. His name is Sky Walker."

"Sky Walker." His dark brows drew together. "I know him. Could be bad news." His gray eyes were shrewd. "Does he know I was with Franko?"

"I don't know. He didn't mention knowing anyone. But then, I'm not certain he saw all of you."

"You gonna tell him I was there?"

"I won't be seeing him again," she said stiffly. "I'd like to be taken to the nearest settlement as soon as possible."

"He won't be looking for you?"

"Why should he? He has other things and other people to occupy his mind. I'm sure I'm of no consequence to him. He's probably glad to be rid of me."

"Hmmmm. We'll see." When she shivered, he began to lay a fire, and soon, flames were leaping and sending off heat waves.

While he began preparations for a meal, Brandy examined the room. It had been designed for comfort. Shelves had been built on the wall behind the stove. Stored there were canned goods and dishes. A table and three chairs occupied the center of the room; one of the chairs was occupied by Brandy. Against the far wall was a bed covered with a patchwork quilt. And beside the bed was a dresser. There, Brandy's eyes stopped, widening in astonishment.

"Ben? Is that a rosewood dresser?"

He recognized her astonishment and chuckled. "Gotta admit thet dresser does look kinder funny in this cabin. It belonged to my wife. She brought it all the way from the East. Said it came over from England on the *Mayflower*. Been in the family for years."

His wife. Curiously, she studied his face. "I didn't know you'd been married, Ben. You claim to have no use for women."

"I don't," he said abruptly. "Not since Sarah died. She's been gone nigh on to twenty year now. Since then I been livin' here alone."

"I'm sorry," she said softly, wondering how his wife had died, but not wanting to ask him.

"Ain't no fault of your'n," he said. "Guess it was mine for bringing her out here. Shoulda stayed back east with her."

She didn't know what to say, so she kept silent.

"You want to go back to the village? I could take you back in the morning."

She thought about what he'd said. Thought as well about Johanna and little Brazos, Sky Walker's baby. He'd been so indignant, so angry with her, as though she were being unreasonable by questioning his right to have another woman. But then, to his way of thinking, perhaps she was. She'd heard that some of the Indians had more wives than one. But she'd never stand for sharing her man.

No. She couldn't go back. She'd stay here until Ben could take her to the nearest town where she could make arrangements to return to England.

Yes. Perhaps that would be best for all concerned.

When Sky Walker and Little Wolf stopped for the night, they found shelter beneath a cliff overhang beside the Brazos River. Sky Walker didn't want to stop, felt he must go on, but the sky was full of angry gray clouds and without the moon to light his way, he knew he would never be able to see where Brandy left the river. If she left it at all.

Although his mind was in turmoil, he forced himself to sleep, to rest his mind and body. He would do Brandy no good at all if the time he was forced to stay here through the darkness was completely wasted. He was wakened in the half light before dawn by a light drizzle. His spirits plummeted. The trail would be wiped out.

But he refused to give up. At least now he could see. If she were dead. . . . No. He would not even allow the thought in his head. She was not dead. And somewhere, perhaps just around the next bend, he would find her.

Brandy woke to gray skies and the rattle of pots and pans. Realizing she had slept longer than she'd intended, she pushed back the covers and slipped out of bed. She tried putting her weight on her foot and pain shot through it, making her gasp.

"Better stay off that ankle," the old man said without turning around. "Give it time to mend."

"But I can't sit here and let you do all the work," she protested. "I'll use the limb you brought me to get around."

"If you're gonna insist, then set yourself at the table. You can slice the salt pork for me whilst I make some coffee."

After hobbling to the table, Brandy slid into the cane-bottomed chair and reached for the butcher knife. "How thin do you want the slices?" she asked.

"I like 'em thick," he answered, turning long enough to measure between thumb and forefinger. "Don't like skinny slices. Ain't got enough taste to 'em." The coffee-pot clanked against the potbellied stove as he set it down, added water and coffee, then left it to boil. "You want the bacon boiled first?" he asked.

"Whatever you like is fine with me." She'd seen the guide boil the salt pork in water to get some of the salt out of it.

"Ain't never too salty for me," he said, busy with another pan and a canister. "But it does make the gravy a mite salty. Lotta folks say all thet salt ain't so good for you. But a man's gotta have some pleasures outta this life."

Brandy cut into the salt pork, listening with only a portion of her mind to the old man talking, the other part going over those last few minutes alone with Sky Walker. He'd been so angry with her. Was he the least bit sorry she'd gone? Did he even wonder what had happened to her?

". . . leastways up to now," the old man was saying. "But you cain't never tell, one of these days I might just go back and see how they was doin'. You think I orta?"

"I beg your pardon," she said. "I'm afraid I missed what you were saying."

"Just sayin' I been happy here but was wonderin' should I go and see how my two younguns was doin'."

"You have children?"

"Reckon how they ain't rightly children no more," he said. "They was when I sent 'em back east to stay with their ma's sister. Boy was five and the girl was three. Maybe I did wrong to send 'em back. Hard to say. But they wouldn't got no schoolin' here with me. And their ma's folks had plenty of money. Wanted the kids. Said I couldn't give 'em nothin' but hardships out here. They was right." He poured a cup of coffee and brought it to her. "What do you think I should do?"

"I don't know," she said.

"Was you my girl, would you want to be raised in a place like this when you had folks that could give you everthing you ever wanted?"

"Even a father?" she asked softly. "My mother died when I was a baby. My father was the most important thing in my life."

"But you was raised with money," he said.

"The money didn't matter," she told him. "My father did."

He studied her for a long moment, then looked out the window. "Maybe I was wrong to send 'em away. But I thought I was doing the right thing."

229

"Have you heard from them since they went away?"

"No. But didn't expect to. The family didn't like me none. Said 'twas my fault Sarah was dead. They'd be sure and turn my kids against me." He looked at her. "You ain't much younger'n my girl, Rosie." His eyes darkened and he cleared his throat. "Drink thet coffee up whilst I get breakfast."

Sipping the strong brew, she thought about what the old man had told her. The story was tragic. Perhaps he was right and his wife's family had turned his children against him. Then again, perhaps not.

Soon the smell of cooking bacon filled the cabin and her mouth watered. When he put a plate of food in front of her, she set to eagerly, unmindful of the falling rain outside.

Thunder sounded in the distance and the rain fell with a vengeance, seeming intent on wiping every trace of the girl away. But Sky Walker didn't let it stop him from the search. Although there were no tracks, if she had washed up on shore, he would surely find her. His heart was heavy as he continued to run along the bank, detouring where he had to but always keeping his eyes out for any sign of the girl. By midafternoon the rain finally stopped. He was nearing the old man's cabin. Hope lived strong in his breast. Perhaps the old man had seen her. He would stop and ask.

The old man was on the river fishing. When Sky Walker stepped out of the woods, Ben automatically reached for his rifle until he recognized his visitor. Sky Walker explained that he was looking for a white woman and asked the old man if he'd seen her. The old man shook his head, dashing what hope Sky Walker had to the ground.

Feeling completely defeated, Sky Walker turned away and began to retrace his steps.

Chapter Twenty-three

When Brandy woke next morning, the gray skies reflected her mood. She hadn't slept well, having been plagued most of the night with nightmares. Although she couldn't remember them upon waking, she suspected the dreams were about Sky Walker, for he was uppermost in her mind.

After they had breakfasted, Ben took himself off fishing. Brandy decided to earn her keep by cleaning the cabin, a chore that, from the looks of it, wasn't done very often.

Before Ben left, he'd wrapped her ankle tightly and cut a stout stick that would serve as a walking cane, and although she managed to get around with it, she had to move slowly. And that created a problem, because it left her with too much time to think.

And she did.

While she washed the dishes they'd used, she thought about her last meeting with Sky Walker. Was it her imagination, or had he looked puzzled, seeming completely unaware of the reason for her anger.

"He may not have been aware," she muttered angrily.

"He isn't like any other man I know. Perhaps he expected me to be grateful he had another woman. Johanna said that's the way it was with the Indians. One man takes the sister of his wife as another wife when it's needed."

Sky Walker would not do that, an inner voice cried. He loves you.

"He never said so," she mumbled. "He never said it."

Anger swamped the incredible hurt she was feeling and she grabbed the coffeepot and began scrubbing briskly at it. She couldn't stop thinking about his betrayal.

"I would have been better off if he'd died," she said. Tears started to her eyes, clouding her vision. "He couldn't have helped that . . . But another woman!"

Tears trickled down her face and she wiped them away with her forearm. God! She needed to get out of this cabin, away from her thoughts. Perhaps the water buckets were empty. She felt disappointed to find one of the buckets full and the other down only to the halfway mark.

She'd fill it anyway.

After emptying the dishpan, she dumped the rest of the water in the pan and set off for the spring that Ben had pointed out on their journey from the river to the cabin.

Sliding the handle of the bucket over her forearm, Brandy left the cabin and followed the well-worn path leading back into the woods. She'd only gone a short distance when she knew she was near, for the breeze carried a hint of cool dampness and the fragrance of fresh mint on the air.

Then she saw it. Set in a bed of limestone, it measured at least three feet across. Fresh mint and watercress grew in and around it, and as she drew closer, a small green frog leaped with a splash into the spring, sending a spray of water over the moss-covered ground around it.

Laying aside her cane, Brandy knelt and dipped the bucket in the spring, allowing the vessel to fill to the brim while she breathed in the fresh minty air.

Brandy didn't know what warned her — perhaps it was some sixth sense — but suddenly her skin chilled, an involuntary tremor ignited deep inside, and her head jerked up.

The bear wasn't more than two hundred yards away, his bulky, shaggy body poised in rigid attention, his eyes fastened on her.

Air rasped through her dry throat, erupting in terrified emotion. "Ben!" she screamed, dropping the bucket and sending water splashing over the ground. "Ben! It's him! It's the bear, Ben!"

The beast dropped on all fours and loped toward her, his heavy paws falling on the moss-covered ground. And despite everything Ben had said, she knew he was wrong.

The bear that was charging her, his mouth open just enough to show his slathering jaws, his big teeth . . . this bear was not friendly.

This bear could not be the bear Ben had called George . . . this monstrous beast had blood in his eyes . . .

. . . eyes that were riveted on her.

Uttering a terrified shriek, Brandy grabbed up her walking stick and took off as fast as she could at a hobble — skip — jump pace, ignoring the jolt of pain shooting through her injured ankle each time her foot struck the ground. Although she knew in her heart she was doomed to failure, she knew also that she could do no less than try.

Tripping over a fallen limb, Brandy struggled to her feet and hurried toward the nearest tree. Her breath came in harsh gasps as she tried her best to outrun the beast pursuing her.

God. She'd never make it! The trees were too small, the bear could easily snap them in two.

"Ben!" she screamed. "Help me, Ben!"

Her heart beat in rhythm with the bear's heavy thuds as it crashed nearer . . . nearer . . .

There! There was a cottonwood, bigger than the others . . . Perhaps she could find safety there. But could she reach it in time? Closer the bear thudded . . . closer . . . and closer.

Even when she felt the bark against her skin, she didn't stop. Hearing a deep-throated growl just behind her, she made a leap for the nearest limb, latching her fingers around the lower branch and digging her feet into the rough bark of the tree trunk.

With a strength born of desperation, she scrambled up the tree and climbed upward, higher and higher, until she was curled into a tight ball in the uppermost branches of the cottonwood.

Down below, the massive beast, furious at being thwarted, beat the tree with his hairy paws.

Brandy felt as though the earth was moving beneath her and wondered how long the tree could stand against such an onslaught. Her teeth chattered as shock set in, and she laid her cheek against the rough bark in despair.

Aeons seemed to pass as she huddled there. She wasn't sure how long it had been when she became aware of the silence. She lifted her head. Had the bear gone away?

Parting the limbs, she looked down through the leafy branches.

No! He was still there. Waiting. For me to come down? Suddenly she noticed his head was turned away, his attention directed toward the forest.

Ben? Was Ben returning? God! The bear would eat

him!

"Ben!" she screamed. "Watch out! the bear's here!"

"What'n hell are you doin', George?" Ben stepped out of the woods and moved toward the tree. "You orta be ashamed of yourself. Now get away from there and leave her alone."

Brandy watched in astonishment as the bear rolled over on its back and exposed its stomach, a growl rumbling low in his throat.

"Come on down, miss," Ben said, looking up into the tree. "It's only George. He was just playin' with you."

"M-make him g-go away, Ben," she stuttered. "I—I don't think he l-likes me."

Ben pointed toward the forest. "Go on, George. Get out of here. You've caused enough trouble already."

The bear lumbered up on all fours and, putting his head in Ben's midsection, gave him a shove that sent him sprawling to the ground. Brandy uttered a terrified shriek. The bear was out of control.

"Just calm down, miss," Ben growled. "You're scaring George."

Scaring George? Brandy stifled a hysterical giggle. What did he think George was doing to her?

"Come on, George," Ben coaxed. "Don't be so stubborn. Come away from thet tree." When the bear didn't move, Ben scratched his head and peered up at her. "He don't appear to wanta leave," he said. "Guess you could wait up there if you've a mind to. I got some fish back yonder, an' ol' George, he likes fish. When he sees thet stringer-full I've got, he'll likely leave you alone."

When he turned to go, she stopped him.

"Ben! You're not going to leave me here alone?"

"How else will I get the fish?" Ben growled. "You was

236

yellin' so loud that I dropped 'em back in the woods. Thought you was in some kind of danger." His voice was disapproving.

"Well I am!" she snapped. "I don't care what you say about the bear. He doesn't feel the least bit friendly toward me." Her fingers tightened around the limb as Ben went for the stringer of fish.

He was only gone a few minutes, and she watched the bear lope toward him at the sight of the fish he was being offered. Still, she was unable to relax until she had reached the safety of the cabin with the door shut firmly between her and the bear.

It was only after the crisis had passed that she became aware of the throbbing in her ankle again. Each beat of her heart sent a jolt of pain through the injured member. Seating herself in a cane-bottomed chair, she lifted her foot into another, attempting to ease the painful throbbing.

She gave a startled jerk when the door was flung open and Ben stepped inside, carrying the bucket of water. "All thet runnin' didn't do your ankle any good," he growled. "Better you soak it again."

"Did the bear leave?" she asked.

"Yep! He's gone. Prob'ly had his feelin's hurt too." He began filling the dishpan with water from the bucket. "He didn't mean you no harm."

Feeling thoroughly chastised, Brandy lowered her foot into the pan of water he placed on the floor in front of her.

The old man stayed close to the cabin for the rest of the day. He seemed content with her company, but Brandy knew, after her ankle had mended, that she would have him take her to the nearest town. It was past time she went home to England.

The next morning, after they'd breakfasted, Ben sat on the front stoop, whittling on a chunk of cedar, while she swept the cabin with the broom he'd made from broomweeds. When she'd finished, she leaned against the broom handle, taking her weight off her throbbing ankle.

Ben worked up a spit and let it fly. "Your ankle's hurtin', ain't it? Told you it was too soon to be up and aroun'."

"I know," she sighed. "But I've felt so useless sitting around watching you do all the work."

"You been restless too," he growled. "Don't think I ain't noticed."

Her lips twitched. "Yes. I'm certain you have." She sat down beside him. "I just keep thinking about England. And my family there." And Sky Walker, she silently added. "There are so many things to be done now that my father's gone."

"Cain't go nowhere until thet ankle mends."

"I know. But it's been so long." So long. She uttered a depressed sigh as Sky Walker's face surfaced in her mind's eye. She'd thought he might search for her. . . . perhaps had even hoped so. But there'd been no sign of him. Apparently she'd been right in thinking he cared nothing for her. Since he'd returned to his people, and Johanna and the baby, he was probably relieved she was gone. Another long sigh escaped her lips and the old man looked at her.

"Ain't just England you're thinkin' about."

She lowered her eyes, hiding her expression from him. "Perhaps not." Her green eyes clouded over. "Ben. Have you ever met Johanna?"

"Yep. Sure have. Lots of times. She's a mighty nice little lady."

Picking up a wood shaving, she twirled it idly between

238

her fingers. "She seemed very nice," she said quietly. "Although I didn't have much time to really get acquainted with her."

"Take it from me, she's the nicest lady I know. 'Ceptin' yourself, that is. Since my woman died I ain't had much use for women."

"That's because you've been faithful. Even to her memory." Her voice was slightly bitter. "Sarah must have been a very special woman for you to have loved her so much."

His gaze was shrewd as he studied her bent head. "I'd say you're pretty special too."

She shook her head. "No," she denied. "I couldn't be. I'm one of the most ordinary people around."

He frowned down at her. "Sounds mighty like you're feelin' sorry for yourself. An' I wouldn't be surprised to find a man behind it."

She swallowed hard. "Isn't there always?"

"You ain't makin' a whole lotta sense."

"I guess not." She lapsed into silence.

"If'n you wanta—" He broke off and looked up. Something in his face warned Brandy. She followed the direction of his gaze and her heart gave a lurch. Sky Walker, his expression dark, had just stepped into the clearing, followed by three other warriors.

Brandy's emotions were mixed as she watched him approach . . . joy mingled with apprehension.

Ignoring Brandy, Sky Walker addressed the old man. "I have come for my woman."

"Your woman," the old man began, looking from Brandy to the warrior. "You mean Miss Brandy?"

"I see no other woman!" Sky Walker snapped.

"No," she protested, glaring up at him. "I won't go back with you."

Grabbing her around the wrist, he pulled her forward and she cried aloud with pain.

The old man stood up. "The girl's hurt," he said. "Leave her be!"

Sky Walker looked at the bandage around Brandy's ankle. "How is she hurt?" he demanded.

"Sprained her ankle," Ben said. "She can't walk."

"Nevertheless, she will come!" Sky Walker growled, picking her up and slinging her across his shoulder, sending the breath whooshing from Brandy's body. "I will deal with you later, old man."

"Now hold on," Ben protested. "She don't wanta go with you."

Sky Walker spoke in a guttural language and the old man's path was blocked by the other warriors.

"Put me down," Brandy cried, pounding her fists against the warrior. "You can't get away with this. If you take me back you'll be sorry."

But even as she screamed at him, she knew her protests were useless, as ineffectual as they'd been when he carried her out of Jeffers's mining town in New Mexico.

Twisting her head, she saw Ben watching her abduction with a concerned expression, but he was unable to stop Sky Walker. At this point, with the fury that possessed the Indian, she didn't think anyone or anything could stop him.

Chapter Twenty-four

Brandy wondered if Sky Walker intended to carry her all the way to the village. But she didn't have long to wonder. The horses had been left with a guard only a short distance from the cabin.

Flinging her on his horse, Sky Walker mounted behind Brandy and urged his mount into a gallop. The steady rhythm of the horse beneath her and the warmth of his body against hers caused a curious sense of longing . . . mingled with an undeniable sense of hurt . . . to burn within. When he pulled her against him, she stiffened. She couldn't so easily forget Johanna and the baby, Brazos.

The journey back to the village was necessarily silent, for Sky Walker set a swift pace, seeming to be driven by the devil himself. Not until they neared the village did Sky Walker finally slow his mount.

The sound of the horses' hoof beats brought the Indians out of the tepees in force and when Sky Walker pulled his horse up, the villagers surrounded them.

Feeling their condemning eyes on her, Brandy shivered and shrank back against Sky Walker. The Indians' expressions were hostile. Because of Johanna and her baby? Didn't they realize Sky Walker had told her nothing about the baby and his mother?

The warrior held his body stiffly erect. "Lift your eyes and face my people," he said sharply. "Do not shame me further by showing cowardice."

His words stiffened her backbone and brought her chin up sharply. She wouldn't be accused of cowardice. And she had no reason to feel shame. She had done nothing wrong. Nothing!

Her chin lifted defiantly and she faced the villagers, her eyes holding a challenge as it swept the crowd, silently daring anyone there to accuse her.

"Get down!" Sky Walker grated between clenched teeth. "And greet my people properly."

As Brandy slid off the horse, her gaze fell on Johanna, saw the sympathy in the young woman's eyes. Why should Johanna feel sympathy for her rival? If Brandy were in Johanna's place, she would be resentful. The girl's attitude made what Sky Walker was doing to her even more horrid.

Contact with the hard ground sent a jolt of pain through Brandy's ankle, but she refused to let it show on her face.

Unwilling to give anyone the satisfaction of knowing her discomfort, Brandy was tempted to shrug away Sky Walker's hand when it fastened around her upper arm. But she knew by doing so, she would only be cutting off her nose to spite her face, because she needed the support his grip offered.

Clenching her jaws tightly, she limped along beside Sky Walker, managing the few feet that separated her from the lodge she'd slept in without giving vent to the pain she was feeling.

Brandy remained bitterly silent, refusing to even look at Sky Walker even after they'd entered the privacy of the lodge.

"Twice you have made me lose face by running away," he said harshly.

The unfairness of his accusation had her spinning around to face him. "What do I care about your face?" she snapped.

"In the future you will not leave the village without my permission," he said coldly, his face a hard mask of anger. The tension was so thick between them that it could be cut with a knife.

Her hands clenched into fists and her green eyes glittered brightly. "I won't be your plaything any longer," she snapped. "And neither will I have my freedom restricted. I'll go where I please whenever I please. And as soon as my ankle is healed and I can travel, then I'll go back to my people."

A muscle twitched in his jaw but his voice was emotionless. "You promised to stay with me, Brandy. I have not released you from that promise, nor is it my intention to do so."

"Other promises were made," she said harshly. "Promises that . . ." Suddenly she couldn't go on. She felt weary beyond belief, unable to continue to fight. Her shoulders slumped and her voice, when she spoke, was raw with pain. "How could you treat her that way, Sky Walker? I thought you were so kind . . . so unselfish. You had me completely fooled." She turned away, wincing as pain jabbed through her ankle. She felt sick to her stomach, her face blanched, became colorless. Swallowing hard, she hobbled to the buckskin pallet and sank down on it, curling herself into a fetal position. "Go away," she muttered. "Leave me alone."

"Are you in pain?" His voice, so near, actually sounded concerned.

Damn him! Why did he have to pretend?

"Of course I'm in pain!" she snapped, straightening her body out and glaring up at him. "My ankle feels like hell! You've just dragged me at a breakneck speed through miles of rough countryside, intent on your own selfish needs, caring nothing for the little baby that depends on you, never mind Johanna! My God! Have you no feelings at all?"

His expression hardened. "You make no sense, woman. We will speak no more of this. I am tired. I have searched for you with no food in my belly and very little rest. You have given me no reason for leaving the village in the first place. Instead, you speak in riddles, going on about Johanna and her baby." He began unlacing his buckskin shirt. "Perhaps you will make more sense after you have slept." Pulling the shirt over his head, he tossed it aside and untied the lacings on his trousers. "I am willing to forgive you for running away." Hooking his thumbs in the top of his trousers, he began peeling them down his hips.

Anger turned to rage as Brandy stared at him. "Forgive me? You're willing to forgive me?" Her voice rose with hysteria.

"Yes." He paused in the act of shedding his trousers. "Do you find fault with forgiveness?"

"You're damn right I do," she snapped, struggling to

244

her feet, wincing as the pain struck her again. "Where do find the nerve to say *you* forgive *me?* Dammit! I've done nothing to be forgiven for." Snatching up one of the buffalo furs, she hobbled to the other side of the lodge and threw it down on the ground. "I refuse to sleep with you," she said. "I could never allow you to touch me again. Every time I think about what you're doing to Johanna and that little baby it makes me sick to my stomach. I want nothing to do with you. Nothing at all!"

"You make no sense, woman!" he snapped. "What do Johanna and her baby have to do with us?"

Her green eyes blazed emerald. "I should have expected you to think that way," she snapped. "But you had the wool pulled over my eyes. Little Brazos needs his father and Johanna needs a husband. How can you deny them that?"

"I deny them nothing," he grated.

"Nothing?" she raged. "How can you call it nothing?"

His eyes were dark with fury. "Enough!" he snarled. "I am tired and I wish to sleep. Is that too much to ask?"

Tears filled her eyes and she blinked rapidly, trying to stop them from overflowing. But the battle was useless. One lone tear found its way down her cheek, then another followed, and another, until they were flooding her face.

Instantly, he took her in his arms, pulling her against him. She pushed against his chest, trying to break free, unable to bear the pain his touch was causing her. "I d-don't want you to touch me," she said. "I can't forget you betrayed me. Please leave me alone." Her lower lip quivered and she swiped her face against her forearm. She sniffled, then straightened up and returned his gaze. "Leave me alone," she pleaded. "I

245

trusted you and you b-betrayed me."

His hand caressed her hair, pushing the damp tendrils away from her face. "Speak to me," he muttered. "How did I betray you? Tell me what I am being accused of."

"Y-you don't even feel guilty about what you've done. I s-suppose you think it's normal to have two women. To have a baby when. . . ."

Sky Walker's brows drew into a frown as he studied her face. He wiped the tears away with his palm and, when he spoke, his voice was incredibly gentle. "Another woman? Is that what this is all about? You think I have another woman? And a baby?" His dark brow lifted, his expression became incredulous. "There is no other woman, Brandy. And there is no baby. At least not mine."

"No woman?" What was he saying? What about Johanna? What about her baby, little Brazos? She put the question to him. "Don't they matter at all?"

"They matter very much to Hawkeye," he said. "But what has that to do with us?"

She gasped. "Is Hawkeye involved with Johanna too? Oh, the poor girl."

With a disgusted sound, he set her free and stalked out of the tepee. "Where are you going?" she demanded.

But silence was her only answer.

246

Chapter Twenty-five

Sky Walker strode across the compound, headed for Hawkeye and Johanna's lodge. He was halfway there when Little Wolf left his father's dwelling and fell into step beside him.

"Where are you going?" Little Wolf asked. "I did not expect to see you away from your lodge for a while since your woman is back. A woman such as she would be hard to leave behind."

"Not if she talked in riddles that you could not understand."

"She is doing that?"

"Yes. Paleface women are hard to understand."

"Perhaps you would have done better to select your wife from the maidens in our tribe. They are not as independent as the paleface women."

Sky Walker remained silent as he continued toward Hawkeye's lodge.

"I have been speaking to the elders. While we were searching for your woman, visitors came to our village."

Sky Walker cared little about the visitors. At the moment he was totally absorbed with his own problem. But there was something about Little Wolf's voice, some lilt that revealed his pleasure — or was it satisfaction? — with the news he had to impart, that made Sky Walker turn a questioning gaze on the other warrior.

"Are you going to tell me who the visitors were?"

"They were traders."

"What makes them different from other traders?"

"The goods they are trading makes them different," Little Wolf said. "The raid on the Texans will be made with new rifles in our hand, brother."

"The trader brought us rifles?"

"Not yet. A price was agreed on. Hawkeye goes tomorrow to the town to get the gold from his bank. The traders will return in two risings of the sun with the rifles."

The news gave Sky Walker a lot to think about as he left Little Wolf and continued on to Hawkeye's lodge. With new rifles there would be fewer of his people killed when they went about the business of teaching the Texans a lesson they would not easily forget.

Putting the coming battle out of his mind, Sky Walker focused his thoughts on his problems with Brandy. He must get things smoothed out with her, discover what was troubling her. And he pinned his hopes on Johanna's help.

When Sky Walker left her alone, Brandy threw herself face down on the hide pallet. Muffling her sobs against her crossed arms, she gave release to her pain. She cried for the mother she'd never known and she cried for the father who'd been so disappointed in her.

248

Then she cried for the love she'd imagined was hers . . . the love that had never existed . . . and when she was done, she cried for herself.

The sobs had finally ceased, and she lay on her back staring with glassy eyes at the buffalo hide above her when the entrance flap was flung aside.

Brandy's pulse gave a wild leap, her heart began an erratic pounding as she turned to look at Sky Walker.

Despite everything that had gone before, she loved him. The knowledge was followed by a quick stab of agony as she recognized the woman who followed behind him.

Johanna!

Sky Walker had returned, but he'd brought his other woman with him.

Grimly, Brandy wiped her face with the back of her hand, trying to erase all signs of her weakness.

Hurrying across the lodge, Johanna dropped to her knees beside the sleeping mat and put a comforting arm around Brandy's shoulders. "What's wrong?" she asked gently.

"Nothing," Brandy said, her voice wobbling slightly despite her efforts at control. "Sky Walker shouldn't have brought you here."

"He said you were upset and wouldn't tell him why."

Brandy shrank away from Johanna's touch. "I'd rather not talk about it," she muttered.

"You'd rather not talk at all? Or just in front of Sky Walker?"

Brandy threw an anguished look at Sky Walker. Hadn't he done enough to her? His face was set in harsh lines, his expression completely unreadable.

Johanna followed her gaze to the warrior. "Go outside," she commanded. "Leave us alone." When Sky Walker had done her bidding, Johanna spoke again. "Now tell me why you're so miserable." She studied the other girl's face. "You are miserable, aren't you?"

Brandy looked at Johanna with tear-drenched eyes and nodded her head. "Didn't you have trouble accepting the Indian way of life?"

"A little," Johanna admitted. "But things were so bad for me in my world that I was glad to leave it behind. I found acceptance here with the Comanches." Her lips curled into a curious half-smile. "Acceptance and love."

"But . . . but, doesn't this part bother you?"

"What part?"

"The . . . you know. The men . . . the warriors having more than one wife."

Johanna frowned. "That bothers you? It shouldn't. It has nothing to do with you. I know it seems odd since it isn't your way, but there are many beliefs in this world, Brandy. Even among our people. The Mormons, for instance. They have more than one wife."

"That doesn't make it right."

"According to the way we were raised it isn't right. But who's to say what's right or wrong? Sometimes it's a necessity. Take the Indians, for example. The settlers keep coming, pushing the Indians farther and farther west, away from their hunting grounds. Civilization, as we know it, has brought death to the Comanches. Death in the form of disease as well as superior weapons. The Comanche tribes grow smaller and smaller with each passing year. Soon there will not be enough of them to defend their land."

"But they have children. I know because I've seen them playing in the village."

"Yes. But with the buffalo herds being depleted so fast, with the game so scarce in the winter, the diseases brought by the white men, smallpox, to name just one, fewer children are growing up to be adults. Did you know that six out of ten babies die before reaching their first birthday? The future of the Comanche depends on the strength of their warriors, Brandy. If one wife proves barren, the men often take another wife so they may help the growth of the tribe."

"But you aren't barren, Johanna. You have little Brazos!"

"Yes," Johanna said softly. "I am one of the lucky ones."

"Then the reason for another wife isn't always children," Brandy said.

"No. Sometimes when a woman has lost her husband, through sickness, or battle, or any other reason, then her sister's husband will marry her in order to take care of her. Would you have it not so? Would you have a woman's sister suffer, perhaps even starve because there is no man to hunt for her?"

"But I'm not your sister."

"No. But what difference does that make?"

"Johanna! I don't understand how you can be so calm about sharing your husband with another woman!"

Johanna drew back in astonishment. "Share my husband? Of course not! I would tear another woman's hair out."

"But . . . but what about Sky Walker? Would you absolve him of all guilt in the matter?"

Johanna's frown deepened. "We seem to be talking at cross purposes here. What exactly is Sky Walker guilty of?"

"Well . . . of having two . . ." She gulped. Didn't Johanna know that Sky Walker was bedding her?

"Two what?" Johanna asked gently. "Honey, I really want to get to the bottom of what's bothering you, but I'm afraid little Brazos is going to want to be fed soon and Hawkeye will be getting impatient for me."

"Hawkeye?" Brandy's expression was clearly puzzled.

"Yes." Johanna watched the other girl closely. "I guess you haven't met my husband yet."

"Husband?" Brandy stared up at the dark-haired girl, her eyes astonished. Had she heard correctly?

"Yes. My husband is Hawkeye. Surely Sky Walker told you."

Brandy felt subdued. She hung her head in shame. "I'm sorry," she whispered. "I seem to have mixed everything up."

"Do you want to tell me about it?"

"No. Not yet. You go on back to the baby . . . and your husband. I'm sorry for bothering you."

Johanna squeezed her shoulders gently. "It was no bother," she said. "We'll talk in the morning."

Brandy listened to her leave. Then Sky Walker came in and stared down at her. She couldn't look at him. What could she say? How could she even begin to tell him what she'd imagined?

But one look at his face told her she could do nothing else.

"I—I'm sorry," she whispered shakily. "I misunderstood. Please forgive me."

"Are you going to tell me what you misunderstood?" he asked, his voice sounding incredibly gentle as he took her into his arms.

"I thought you and Johanna . . . that the baby was yours."

"Brazos? Johanna and Hawkeye's son?"

"Yes. You stayed in her lodge. . . . You cried out for her when you were out of your head with fever. . . . It seemed to explain why they took you to her lodge and why you kept calling out for her. At least I thought it did."

"Johanna is our healer," he said. "They would have taken me nowhere else."

Now she understood and she felt shame that she had been so quick to judge. "I should have trusted you," she murmured. "I have done you a disservice, not to mention Johanna. What must she think of me."

"She did not blame you."

"She said things were bad for her in our world. Do you know anything about it?"

"They did not understand the healing touch she possesses and things the white-eyes do not understand, they try to rid themselves of."

"So she found safety among your people."

"Yes. The elders have taught us there are things we are not meant to understand. The Great Spirit gave Johanna the gift of healing and then he sent her to us. She is happy here."

"As I shall be," she murmured, sliding her arms around his neck and lifting her face to his. Although she was curious about Johanna and her healing touch, uppermost in her mind was the need to know Sky

253

Walker had forgiven her.

Slowly, as if testing her response, his mouth closed over hers with tantalizing gentleness. Her heartbeat quickened as the pressure of his lips increased and his mouth coaxed hers to open.

Brandy felt the sudden intrusion of his tongue as it pierced her lips and, at the same time, his rough hands found the ripe fullness of her breast. Desire consumed her, spreading like wildfire through her veins.

Needing to get closer to him, hating the clothing that separated them, Brandy struggled with his buckskin shirt. But it wouldn't budge.

Sky Walker's hands were eager, caressing, and she felt his heart beating in rhythm with her own. His body was hard, his masculinity throbbing against her lower body, driving her wild with passion.

Melting against him, she arched her body against his lean hardness, her fingers giving up their struggle to remove his shirt and twining, instead, in the thick darkness of his hair.

"Sky Walker," she murmured, her voice full of longing as his lips left hers to trail a path of fire down her neck, stopping only when they reached the neckline of her gown. Brandy felt light, boneless, ecstatic with longing.

His fingers worked at the fastenings of her gown; then it was slithering over satin-smooth skin as Sky Walker skillfully removed it. Her undergarments followed the trail of the gown. When her breasts were freed, she felt the moistness of his mouth as it teased first one nipple and then moved to give the other one satisfaction.

Moaning low in her throat, Brandy felt delicious shudders quivering through her as Sky Walker continued the tactile stimulation with his lips while his hands moved downward, stroking her body to a fever pitch, inviting the rhythmic movement of her hips against him.

But it wasn't enough.

God! She wanted more.

His caresses offered a vague satisfaction, but not the complete kind she wanted, needed, craved.

Her fingers tightened in his hair, applying pressure to express the urgent needs of her flesh. She felt his body weight shift, and he raised his head as though to withdraw.

"No, Sky Walker," she said urgently. "Please." She wanted him so desperately, she was willing to beg in her need for him to make love to her. "Don't stop now. I couldn't bear it."

"I have no intention of stopping, my little green eyes. I could not even if I felt I should." Sky Walker's voice was husky with passion.

Stripping his clothing off, he tossed the garments aside, careless of where they fell. Then he joined her on the bed of buffalo hides again. As his lips returned to hers in hard possession, her mouth opened to him, like a flower to the sun.

When Sky Walker's hands slid down to her hips, lifting her slightly and coaxing her thighs apart with the burning heat of his own, she could feel the excitement racing through her body at the intimate contact with his. She was mindless with pleasure, filled with an aching need that must be satisfied, caught in a raging tide that she had no need to fight, because this man was hers. In the eyes of the Comanche as well as her own, she was wed to him.

His possession of her was swift and left her gasping as incredible pleasure swept over her. Even though they'd made love before, this time was different, incredibly so. She had no time to wonder why, because when Sky Walker began to move, the pleasure he was creating beat at her in ever-increasing waves until she was moaning involuntarily beneath the burning demand of his mouth.

With her arms locked around his neck, her body arched with instinctive need to prolong the pleasure that he was giving her. They rode the waves of passion, cresting higher and higher until they reached their peak together.

The exquisite fulfillment of their lovemaking stayed locked inside Brandy's mind, even when her body had relaxed into exhausted satisfaction.

Neither of them was inclined to leave the dwelling that afternoon, both being content to savor the sweetness of their reunion. He wanted to know how she'd come to be at the old man's cabin, and in the telling, she told him about the black bear Ben had called George.

He laughed. "Ben was right. George likes to frighten people, but he would not harm you."

"You didn't see him trying to shake me out of that tree," she said, barely controlling a shudder. I swear I almost died of fright."

"You didn't," he teased. "Not my brave little green-eyed woman who stands unafraid before the fiercest warrior in Hawkeye's camp.

"Fiercest warrior? You wouldn't happen to be bragging, now would you?"

"Do you not agree I am the bravest man you have ever met? Did I not ride into Jeffers's mining town and take you out when all his men would have killed me had they been able?"

"Yeeesss," she agreed, drawing the word out teasingly. "I suppose you did do all that, but—"

Becoming aware that Sky Walker wasn't listening to her anymore, she stopped her teasing and looked at him. His expression looked distant, as though he were listening to something . . . some sound . . . coming, perhaps, from far away, remaining just below her range of hearing.

Cocking her head, Brandy strained to hear. But there was nothing.

"Sky Walker . . ."

"Hush," he cautioned.

Then she heard it, distant, but drawing closer. The sound of hoofbeats, drumming against the hard-packed earth on the far side of the river.

Brandy held her breath, realizing there was something about the sound that chilled her. Suddenly, she realized it was the creaking of saddle leather, the jingling of metal on leather harnesses that told her the horses didn't belong to Indians. She heard water splashing . . . the riders were obviously crossing the river.

Leaping to his feet, Sky Walker flung the buffalo hide flap aside. Then his face became an expressionless mask, his muscles tensed, and his body froze.

Chapter Twenty-six

"What's wrong?" Even as she asked the question, Brandy felt almost certain she wasn't going to like the answer. When she peered past Sky Walker's shoulder, she saw that several riders had entered the village. White men. She counted eight in all.

Her gaze fell on the grizzled rider nearest them and relief flowed through her. It was Ben. She should have known. The man who claimed to have no use for women had been worried about her. He'd probably found the other men at the nearest settlement. She'd better go to him before there was trouble.

With that in mind, she started around Sky Walker, but found her way blocked by his arm. "Sky Walker," she protested. "It's only Ben."

"Stay inside!" he rasped harshly, blocking her view with his body. "The white-eyes must not see you."

"But Ben already knows I'm here. He probably thinks you're holding me prisoner and he's come to rescue me."

"Do not argue with me!" Sky Walker snapped. "Remain inside the lodge, and whatever happens, do not leave it."

"But Be—" Her protest died abruptly when Sky Walker fixed her with his heated gaze. "All right," she said in a subdued voice.

Stepping outside, he closed the entrance flap on her. Brandy realized he was only trying to protect her, knew as well that there was no reason for his caution. Ben would never deliberately harm her. Neither would he leave the village until he was convinced she wanted to remain there. Eventually, she would have to face him.

She began to pace back and forth. It might save hard feelings if she showed herself now and explained to Ben. She paused before the entrance flap.

Sky Walker said wait, a silent voice warned.

Reluctantly, she turned away and began to pace again. Outside, she could hear the murmur of voices, but the usual sounds, children playing, dogs barking, were absent.

She found the waiting hard, but realized if she disobeyed Sky Walker, he was sure to be furious, and she couldn't go through the strain of another argument or misunderstanding, not when they'd just smoothed out their problems.

She would have to wait.

Sky Walker joined the other warriors who faced the mounted men. His gaze narrowed on the man farthest from Ben, the man he'd recognized the moment he had raised the entrance flap. It was Franko.

Sky Walker worked his way through the crowd of

people until he was standing beside Hawkeye. Franko's gaze was fastened on Hawkeye, who was chief of the small band, and he had not become aware of Sky Walker's presence . . . but Ben had.

"Ben tells me you got one of our women here," Franko said. "We're here to see about buying her from you."

"Ben was wrong," Hawkeye said. "There is nothing in our village that belongs to any of you."

Franko's face flushed with anger. "Dammit, Hawkeye," he growled. "Yesterday we made a deal on a whole wagonload of rifles."

"For which you will be well paid."

"That ain't neither here nor there," Franko said. "Civilized men protect their womenfolk. Now, Ben here, saw Lady Brandy throwed across one of your buck's shoulders and carried off while she was screaming for help. Are you sayin' she ain't here?"

"You mistake my words," Hawkeye said. "I made no such claim. I said we have nothing here that belongs to any of you."

"It's true she don't belong to us. But I can't just hardly ride off and forget you got her. Now can I?"

"My advice would be to do so. As you can see, we number sixty to your eight. I wouldn't give much for your chance of taking anyone out of here without our agreement."

Franko's tense body relaxed and his face broke into a smile. "That's just what I'm after, Hawkeye. Your agreement." He looked well satisfied with himself. "Now I mean to pay for her. And I mean to pay dearly. Suppose I give you half that wagonload of rifles. Absolutely free. You won't have to pay a cent. Now how does that sound?"

Sky Walker's fists clenched and unclenched. He longed to wrap his hands around Franko's neck and squeeze the breath of life out of him. Instead, he made himself stand there while the renegade who thought to use his Brandy so badly tried to deal for her life.

"Your offer would sound better if I had a woman to bargain with."

"Dammit, Hawkeye!" Franko exploded. "I know she's here." He turned to Ben. "Do you see the buck that carried her off?"

Ben took his time replying, first working up a spit while he scanned the crowd, then moving his gaze back to Sky Walker. Letting fly with the tobacco juice, straight toward the ground at Sky Walker's feet, he said, "I'd know him anywheres. It was Sky Walker that rode off with her and he's standing there. Right next to Hawkeye."

Franko looked at Sky Walker for the first time, and recognition was instant. "So you're the one," he muttered. "Shoulda known." He turned back to Ben. "Why didn't you say he was the buck who gave us so much . . . who was with her in New Mexico?"

Ben's eyes narrowed and he studied Sky Walker thoughtfully for a long moment. "Guess because I didn't know he was the one," he said gruffly. "Never did lay eyes on the Comanch in New Mexico. If'n I had, then I wouldn't'a worried so much about Lady Brandy."

Franko directed his attention to Sky Walker. "I suppose you're the one I shoulda been talkin' to all along, the one laying claim to her. I'm willing to pay in gold for her. Gold, or rifles and ammunition, or whatever else you want."

Although Sky Walker wanted to smash the man's face in, he fought to keep his emotions under control and his voice expressionless. "She's not for sale."

Franko gripped the pommel of his saddle and his knuckles showed white. He seemed to be fighting his rage. Finally, he shrugged his shoulders. "Suit yourself. But it ain't reasonable that we can't at least see she's not hurt. Unless you're afraid she'll beg us to take her with us."

"My woman is not a prisoner. It is her wish to stay with me."

"That's all we want to know," Franko said. "Me an' the boys will leave willingly with no hard feelings between us if you'll bring her out so she can tell us that she's happy here."

Sky Walker tried to keep the rage he felt from showing as he met the eyes of his friend and chief, Hawkeye. Since Hawkeye was a white man raised by the Comanches, he could have purchased the rifles himself—if he could have found a wagonload, but there was no time to search for other weapons.

The rifles Franko had were readily available and Sky Walker's people needed them badly for the coming battle with the Texans. Sky Walker knew without question what Hawkeye wished him to do, but that didn't make him like it any better.

Spinning on his heels, he went back to his lodge to get his woman.

* * *

Brandy was startled to see Franko. Startled, and uneasy. When he asked to speak to her alone, she started to decline; then, deciding he could do her no harm with Sky Walker so near, changed her mind. Franko dismounted and they moved a short distance from the others.

"I'm glad to see you unharmed, Lady Brandy," he said.

"You could have told me so before Sky Walker and the others."

His lips thinned and he came to the point. "I saw your father a few days ago."

Brandy felt as though she'd been kicked in the stomach. Whatever she'd expected, it wasn't that. "My father is dead," she whispered. "You heard Gallinos tell me so."

"He obviously lied, because I saw your father myself. Not only did I see him, but I spoke to him as well."

"You are lying."

"No. He was in San Antone looking for you."

"Why would he be in San Antone?"

"He met Josie in Taos. She told him you were with the Comanches. Since everbody knows Texas is their stomping grounds, he came searching for you. He put an advertisement in the paper offering a reward to anyone who brought you to him. It was pure luck that I saw the advertisement." When he saw she still wasn't convinced, he reached into an inner pocket and pulled out a piece of paper. He waited while she read the advertisement.

Hope flared through her, but still she was afraid to believe. "Anyone could have put this in the paper," she said. "Even you."

His lips thinned, his eyes darkened with anger. "Dammit, woman. Use some sense. Why the hell would I want to do a thing like that?"

"To convince me to leave here," she said coldly.

His hands tightened into fists and he looked as though he would strike her; then, as though exerting an extreme effort, he slowly relaxed. "Suit yourself," he gritted. "But I can't see you living with a bunch of redskins when you got something better to go back to. If you're worried about your reputation, then forget it. Nobody in England would know what you been up to."

"I suggest you leave before I scream with rage," she said coldly. "I don't think Sky Walker and his friends would take kindly to that. They might think you were hurting me and you'd likely be dead before they discovered any different."

Muttering a string of curses, he spun on his heel and rejoined his companions. After a word with Hawkeye, they mounted and rode away.

Brandy had been thoughtful since the white men had left. But she hadn't yet told Sky Walker what Franko had said to her. Somehow, that made him uneasy, but he didn't want to ask. He meant to show he had faith in her.

That night Sky Walker woke in a cold sweat. He wasn't sure what woke him, perhaps the wind soughing through the trees, whistling around the lodges, moaning and whipping the hide flaps like rugs shifting beneath a broom. For a moment he lay unmoving, breathing harshly in the darkness, afraid he would wake the woman who lay sleeping beside him, then suddenly afraid he wouldn't.

Although he could feel the warmth of her flesh against his own, he couldn't hear her breathing. He was beset by a curious uneasiness, a vague anxiety that he could not identify. The shrouding darkness seemed suddenly oppressive, the air almost too thick to breathe, and he was stricken by the crazy notion that something . . . or someone was out there, just waiting to whisk her away from him, to steal her away and take her forever beyond his reach.

No! he silently protested. Suddenly he became aware of her stillness. Had she stopped breathing? Had death come to steal her away from him?

Leaning over, he placed his lips close to hers, felt the stirring of air, ever so slightly, that proved she was still alive.

With his heart pounding loudly at his foolish, childish fears, he lay on his back and stared up into the darkness. He couldn't bear the thought of losing her. Although he hadn't intended it to happen, he had fallen in love with this woman. And by doing so, he had made himself vulnerable to fear and pain.

It was a long time before he fell asleep, and when he woke, she was gone.

In the half light before dawn Brandy had risen early and left the lodge, turning her steps toward the river. Dreams of her father—nightmares, really—had plagued her during the night, and she felt restless.

Just a few steps away, the Brazos River flowed slowly on its way downstream. The frogs croaked, splashing into the water, and across the river she heard the sound of the whippoorwill. Although her surroundings were peaceful, her thoughts were in turmoil. Was it possible Franko had been telling the truth? Could her father really be alive?

If he was alive, then she must go to him, let him know she was safe. But that would present problems. How could she tell him she wanted to stay with Sky Walker? Would he understand? She had a feeling he wouldn't.

Sighing, she pushed thoughts of her father away, letting the peace of the morning wash over her as she watched the sun rise over the eastern horizon.

It was a lovely day. A fine day to be outside. Her skin felt warmed by the rays of the sun, by the gentle breeze blowing across the river, whipping through her golden hair, blowing it against her cheeks.

Robins flitted from limb to limb, chirping, celebrating the dawn of a new day. As she watched, a squirrel darted down the trunk of a spreading oak tree and hurried across the grass, stopping momentarily to nibble on an acorn, but keeping a wary eye on Brandy.

Stooping to one knee, Brandy made a clucking sound at the squirrel and held out her hand, absently running thumb and forefinger together. But the squirrel wasn't having any part of her. Although it hadn't stopped its nibbling, it was giving Brandy a suspicious eye.

Rising to a half crouch, Brandy moved toward the squirrel, still making the clucking noise, still working thumb and forefinger together.

The squirrel allowed her to get within six feet before turning and darting up a cottonwood tree, the morsel still in its mouth. Halfway up the tree, it stopped, leaned out, held only by its remarkable claws, and looked down. It made a sudden chittering sound, then was gone, a brown flash lost among the branches.

Disappointed, Brandy turned away and bumped into Sky Walker.

"You startled me!" she said, stifling her shriek. "I didn't think anyone was here."

He gathered her into his arms. "I woke and you were gone," he said. "Why did you leave?"

"I was restless. I couldn't sleep."

He lifted her chin. "Perhaps it is time to tell me what Franko had to say."

She nodded her head. "It's time," she agreed.

Then she told him.

Chapter Twenty-seven

Three days had passed since Franko and his men came to the village, and Brandy had learned much about the Comanche during that time. While Sky Walker stayed busy hunting and repairing his weapons, she learned how to make moccasins, how to tan hide, how to pulverize dried meat and berries, mix it with bear grease, and make the pemmican.

Now, as night cloaked the land with a blanket of darkness, while the full moon glimmered softly above, she lay on the pallet of buffalo hides, locked in Sky Walker's embrace, blissful in the aftermath of their loving.

Sighing contentedly, she opened her mouth and placed a moist kiss on Sky Walker's naked chest. His arms tightened convulsively around her.

"Brandy. There is something I must tell you."

His voice was curiously gruff, and apprehension trailed chill fingers down her spine. Something was seriously wrong. Brandy's movements stilled. Her body tensed as anxiety spurted through her and she felt a curious dread as she waited for him to continue.

"I have been thinking about your father."

His words, although totally unexpected, caused her tense muscles to relax. Expelling an audible sigh of relief, she raised her eyes to his. "Is that all?" she whispered. When he started to speak again, she placed a silencing finger against his lips. "Sky Walker. Listen to me. Since Franko was here, I've thought a lot about Poppa. But I've thought about us too. These last few days with you have been the happiest of my life. I know I could never be happy without you. And I know Poppa would never understand the way I feel. That's why I've decided that I won't see him. He must be allowed to think me dead."

"No, dear one. It would be—"

"It's the best way," she interrupted.

"Little one . . ." His voice was coaxing. "Do not close your ears to my words. You must see your father. It would be cruel to allow him to believe you are dead."

"I don't want to leave you."

"I am leaving at sunrise," he said. "The journey I make will be long. I do not know when I will return."

He was leaving her? Panic washed over her. "Where are you going?" Brandy whispered, hearing the catch in her voice.

Sky Walker smoothed her hair back from her face. "It is better not to know."

His words had an ominous ring to them. "Why? Will you be in danger?"

Instead of answering her question, he cupped her face in his hands and studied her intently. "I went to the old man's cabin today and asked him to take you to San Antonio. He will stay with you until you find your father."

Shoving him away, Brandy sat up abruptly. "Why are you insisting I go? Have you already grown tired of me?"

"Of course not!" Pulling her back into his embrace, he whispered, "Trust me, little green eyes. Go with the old man to San Antonio. When I return from my journey then I will come for you there."

Brandy searched his eyes, trying to understand his reason for sending her away, but they remained dark and unfathomable. "You don't know my father," she said, trying to reason with him. "He's used to having his way in all things. He'll want me to return to England with him."

"Do you not love your father?"

"Of course I love him."

"Then you must go to him. See him one last time, for when he returns to his own land, he will be lost to you forever. Surely you owe him that much."

Yes, she silently agreed. She did owe him that, and she did love him. Before she met Sky Walker, he was the most important thing in her life. Perhaps she could make her father see how much the Comanche warrior meant to her. But whether he could understand or not, she would never return to England with him. Never.

She wound her arms around Sky Walker's neck and twined her fingers through his hair. "You are such a sweet, thoughtful man, and I don't want us to be apart."

"Neither do I. But this is something I must do." His gaze held hers. "Promise me you'll go with the old man."

"I promise," she said, wondering why it was so important to him.

Pushing back her golden hair, he scattered kisses across her forehead, her eyes, her nose and cheeks. Then his lips captured hers, fastening there, seeming intent on drawing her very soul into his body.

Brandy was breathless when he finally lifted his head.

"Love me," she whispered achingly. "Love me, Sky Walker . . . my husband."

He needed no further urging.

Sky Walker left her in the half light before dawn. Brandy controlled the tears threatening to fall and watched until she could no longer see him. Only then did she return to their lodge and allow the tears to fall.

The old man arrived midmorning. His shrewd gaze searched the village, seeming to dwell overlong on the few warriors left in the compound.

"Will they let you leave?" he asked, nodding his head at the villagers who watched them.

"Yes," she said. "Sky Walker said I'm free to leave whenever I wish. Will Franko give us any trouble?"

"No. He and the rest of his bunch will be down in Mexico spending the money they got for the rifles they sold Hawkeye." His brows were drawn together thoughtfully. "Where's the rest of the warriors?"

She shrugged her shoulders. "I really don't know. They all left with Hawkeye. Sky Walker wouldn't tell me where they were going."

"Kinda odd, wouldn't you say?"

Brandy shrugged again. "Not really. They often go hunting together." But even as she spoke, she realized she was only trying to convince herself. Something *was*

271

different this time. She'd have to think more about it later, when there was more time.

Gathering her things together, Brandy said her good-byes to Johanna and the villagers she'd become acquainted with, then joined Ben where he waited with the horses.

After helping her to mount, he spoke in a voice too low to be overheard by the villagers. "I think they's something mighty peculiar goin' on here. Looks like durn near all the warriors left the village at the same time. Didn't leave nobody to guard the womenfolk, 'ceptin' a bunch of old men and young boys."

Brandy frowned. "Is that so unusual?"

"I'd say so." He mounted and urged his horse out of the Indian village.

His words kept nagging at her while she followed him across the river. When they reached the other side, she turned to him. "Why are you worrying so? Couldn't the warriors have gone on a buffalo hunt?"

"Not likely. They'd have taken the women along to skin the critters, not left 'em alone in the village with no protection except them ol' men."

"What are you suggesting?"

"Ain't suggesting nothing," growled the old man. "But I ain't so sure I'd feel much better was I to know the reason behind them all leavin'."

Her troubled mind worried about Ben's cryptic words, but only for a short while. As they left the Brazos River and headed south, she began to think about her father. She was so glad he was alive, yet she had to wonder how wise it was to see him again. Lord Tremayne would never be able to comprehend her need to stay with Sky Walker, but she would try her best to make him understand.

San Antonio, once the capital of Spanish Texas, was more than a century old when it became part of the Republic of Texas in 1836. Wood and brick homes, general stores, and saloons had been built among the adobe structures of an earlier era.

It was to the American-built hotel dominating the north side of the plaza that Ben rode. Although Brandy was excited at the prospect of seeing her father again, she felt curious about the people who populated the town. The women wearing American clothing seemed to be in a great hurry as they bustled about, hurrying in and out of the stores, while their Mexican counterparts seemed to have all the time in the world.

When her mount stopped at the hotel's hitching rail, Brandy slid from the saddle and handed the reins to Ben. "I hadn't realized San Antonio was so big," she said.

"Hear tell they's more'n two thousand people livin' here," Ben said.

"Do you think it will be hard to find my father?"

"Franko said he was in this hotel. If he ain't, then they should know where he's at."

Brandy felt curiously fearful and wondered why. She should be happy she was here, happy to see her father again. But somehow, she feared the step she was taking wasn't the right one.

She followed Ben inside the hotel, totally unprepared for the sight of her father standing near the registration desk. He was unaware of her presence, deep in conversation with two men.

Slowly, Brandy walked across the lobby toward him, her heart pounding in erratic rhythm. Now that the time was here, she didn't know what to say, how to act.

Although there were several people in the lobby, they each fell silent as they became aware of her presence. She had no idea why she excited such interest, didn't know that even though San Antonio was a frontier town, the presence of a buckskin-clad girl with golden blond hair flowing down her back was highly unusual.

The two men her father was speaking with became aware of the silence first. They looked up simultaneously, searching for the reason . . . their eyes found her and remained fixed, staring.

Then Lord Tremayne lifted his head and his jaw hung slack as his disbelieving gaze fastened on her.

An unfathomable expression crossed his face. Then, he spoke. "Brandy! Brandy, my dear!" He crossed the distance between them in two long strides, gathering her so tightly in his arms that she thought she would surely suffocate. "I thought I'd never see you again," he muttered. "Are you all right?"

"Yes," she said, tears of happiness coursing down her cheeks. Their meeting was everything she could have possibly wished. "Gallinos said you were dead. And I believed him. Otherwise, I would have gone on to Taos."

Lord Tremayne stretched out a hand to Ben. "I must have you to thank for bringing my daughter back to me. Won't you dine with us tonight?" After Ben declined the invitation, Lord Tremayne said, "I know Brandy must be worn out. She's bound to have been through a terrible ordeal. If you gentlemen will excuse me then I'll take her upstairs to my room."

He hurried Brandy up the stairs and into his room. "You mentioned Gallinos, my dear. You spoke with him?"

"He captured me," she said, then went on to tell him everything that had happened, leaving out nothing except her relationship with Sky Walker. She'd get to that later. "Franko said Josie told you where to find me."

"The waitress in Taos? Yes. Thank God I went to that hotel to dine or I never would have known you were alive."

"Is Josie well? I want to help her, Poppa. She was so good to me."

He was silently thoughtful. "I'll send the girl some money," he said.

Brandy knew money wasn't the answer and told him so. "Josie must be found a good situation . . . perhaps we could finance a business. We can decide later. Right now I want to hear what happened after I left you."

"Pedro and I managed to get away when the renegades followed you. We found a hiding place and stayed there all night. The next morning Pedro found three of the horses they'd run off. One of them was your mount. We looked for you but found nothing." He patted her hand. "We wouldn't have gone on, but my wound became infected and Pedro was afraid I would die without medical attention. It was more than a week before he could organize a search party. They found no trace of you. I thought you were dead until I ran into that waitress — that Josie person — in the hotel." He hugged her against him. "God! It's good to see you. I'll arrange for another room and have a maid sent to you.

We'll get you a bath and some food and decent clothes to wear."

She smiled. "I'm used to doing for myself these days, Poppa. But I can use the bath and clean clothes. Somehow, I doubt if my deerskin garments will go over very well in the hotel."

Lord Tremayne glanced distastefully at her dress, then his gaze flitted away from her. "We won't speak of your ordeal again," he said. "It's over and we're together again. That's all that matters now. The rest we'll put behind us." He turned to leave the room.

His words echoed in her mind: *That's all that matters now. The rest we'll put behind us.* She couldn't put it behind her, didn't even want to do so. Her father had no idea what really mattered to her now. But in time, she would tell him about Sky Walker. Somehow, she'd make him understand her feelings . . . at least she hoped she could.

Brandy tried to still the thought that she could never make her father understand.

Sky Walker, Hawkeye, and their Comanche brothers met at Comanche Peak. Horses and more than five hundred warriors, all with the same mission . . . to make the treacherous Texans pay for their sins against the Comanche tribes.

Even while Sky Walker listened to the plan, his mind was on Brandy. Had she found her father yet? He hadn't wanted to send her away from the village, but he couldn't help feeling concerned there would be repercussions from this raid on the white settlements. He certainly didn't want his woman caught in the middle of this war. His mind told him he had done right to send Brandy to her father. Only there would she be safe until he returned for her.

If he returned. Some of them would not return, and he could be one of those who died.

Becoming aware that another warrior had joined him, he turned to see his friend and blood brother, Hawkeye.

"Are you troubled?" Hawkeye asked.

"I was thinking of Brandy, wondering if I would ever see her again."

"As I wonder about my woman and child."

"Would it not have been better to have sent Johanna and little Brazos away from the village until this is all over?"

"I tried. She refused to leave."

"Did she know what we are about?"

"She knew. And she begged me not to go. She said it would accomplish nothing."

"Perhaps she was right."

Hawkeye's face was grim. "If we are to live in peace, then we must fight for the right to do so. You know that."

"The Texans are greedy, set on having our land for themselves. Each day more and more settlers arrive and their numbers keep increasing. I fear they will surely win the fight for our land and there will be no place left for the Comanche."

"I know," Hawkeye said, a faraway look coming into his eyes. "One day the Comanche will be herded like cattle to a place of the white-eyes' choosing. But let us hope that day will not come in our lifetime. Let us hope that we can live free and our children after us."

"The Texans will retaliate for this raid."

"They will retaliate," Hawkeye agreed. "But we will have taught them the Comanche will not be deceived. They will know our strength, will know we are a people to be reckoned with."

Realizing the line of warriors had started moving, Sky Walker swallowed his doubts and raised his lance toward the sky. "Are you ready, my brother?"

"I am ready."

Chapter Twenty-eight

Brandy had just finished bathing when she heard a knock on her door.

"Who's there?" she called.

"Clarice, miss," a woman's voice answered. "Your pa sent me."

Unlatching the door, Brandy peered out at the wiry woman standing in the hallway. She carried several gowns, carefully folded, over one arm.

"Your pa said you'd be needin' these," she said.

"My goodness!" Brandy's eyes glittered with excitement as she opened the door wide enough to allow the woman to pass through. "Has Poppa bought every gown in San Antonio?"

Clarice seemed almost as excited as Brandy. "Your pa . . . that is to say, *Lord* Tremayne, said you was to meet him in the dining room when you was ready." Clarice had put special emphasis on the title. "It ain't usual for me to work so late, but your pa, Lord Tremayne, paid me to stay and be your maid." She spread the gowns out across the bed, then turned back to Brandy. "A lady's maid, your pa called it. I ain't never done nothin' like that before. Ain't so sure I know how neither. What's a lady's maid do?"

"She does things of a more personal nature," Brandy explained. "For instance, she helps her mistress dress." When the woman's eyes widened, Brandy's lips quirked slightly. "I know it sounds ridiculous, Clarice. But you'll have to admit there are a lot of buttons on those gowns. And the hairstyles of today often call for skilled hands."

"I don't know, miss," Clarice said, eyeing Brandy's hair doubtfully. "I don't know much about fixing hair." She smoothed a hand over her own dark hair, tucked a few strands into the bun at the back of her head. "I could put it in a bun like mine was you a mind to wear it up."

"No," Brandy said. "I've become used to managing on my own these past few months. I'm afraid I really have no need for a maid."

"You sayin' you don't want no help?" Clarice asked. "Mighta knowed that'd happen. The whole thing sounded too good to be true. Sure coulda used the money your pa give me."

Brandy could almost feel the woman's disappointment. "I wouldn't dream of asking you to return the money," she said, running her hands over a pale green satin gown.

Clarice shook her head. "Mr. Johnson, he's the hotel manager, wouldn't let me keep money I ain't earned. Says it's not good business."

"I see." Brandy lifted an embroidered camisole with tiny buttons sewn down the back. "I suppose I could use some help with these buttons. There certainly does seem to be quite a lot of them."

"That's good," Clarice said. "I'd be proud to do for you, though there's them that would think they's too good with all that talk going around town."

"What talk?"

"Talk about you livin' with the Comanches. That true?"

"Yes. It is." Brandy felt no need to elaborate. Reaching into her bag, she pulled out her porcupine quill brush and worked the tangles from her hair. How had word spread so quickly? she wondered.

"Musta been real hard on you." The woman gave an exaggerated shudder. "Reckon if it'd been me, I'da prob'ly killed myself. Wouldn'ta been able to stand them dirty savages puttin' their hands . . . and all . . . on me."

Feeling a flush darkening her cheeks, Brandy quickly lowered her lashes to hide the anger her expressive eyes must surely reveal. "The Indians I came in contact with were just as clean as the white race. They bathe and wash their clothing the same as we do."

"Can't hardly believe that," Clarice said. "You gonna wear this green dress?"

Brandy tightened her lips, but allowed the change of subject. It was either that or give in to the urge to yank the other woman's hair out. "Yes," she said. "I have decided on the green."

She donned the undergarments, pulled the gown over her head, then allowed Clarice to fasten it up the back. After brushing her hair, she tied it back with a ribbon that matched the color of the gown. A quick glance in the mirror assured her she looked presentable, so she made her way downstairs to join her father.

When she entered the dining room she saw him sitting alone at a corner table, his body stiff and unbending as he restlessly scanned the new arrivals coming through the door. Brandy had never seen him look so ill at ease before.

Smiling, she wound her way across the room to her father's table, aware of the interest she was arousing in the other patrons.

"There you are, my dear," her father said. "I was wondering when you'd appear." After she was seated, he flicked a quick look around, then muttered in a low voice, "Word seems to have spread already. I should have thought of that. We could have eaten in your room."

Brandy raised an eyebrow. "Why in the world would you want to do that?"

"I—I don't want you made uncomfortable." He met her eyes briefly and there was something in his that she'd never seen before. She'd almost swear her father was ashamed of her. His gaze dropped suddenly, became fixed on the silver setting on the table. "We could leave if I hadn't already ordered our meal, but I'm afraid to leave would create more talk than remaining would."

"I have no wish to leave, Poppa," Brandy said, her gaze sweeping the room, stopping on a richly dressed woman at the nearest table. The woman flinched as though Brandy had physically touched her. "We seem to be the center of attention. If it bothers you, we can leave."

At that moment the waitress arrived with a tray. "Our meal is here," he said gruffly. "We might just as well eat it." He reached for his silverware.

Although Brandy had said she wasn't bothered by the stares of the other patrons, it wasn't so, because her appetite had vanished and the hair at the nape of her neck prickled. Trying to ignore the reason for the feeling, the attention of the other patrons, she picked up her fork and scooped up a bite of scalloped potatoes. She could hear the murmur of voices as the occupants of the nearby table resumed their conversation.

"I hadn't expected San Antonio to be such a large town," Brandy said conversationally. Her father grunted and cut into his steak.

Brandy studied his bent head as silence stretched out between them. Finally, she was unable to stand it any longer. "Poppa, are you ashamed of me?"

His head jerked up, his eyes darkened. "Of course not!" he snapped. "That is . . . not ashamed *of* you, but maybe *for* you."

"There's no need to be."

"Then you didn't . . . they didn't . . . you are still . . . untouched?" A flush crept up his cheeks while he waited for her answer.

Slowly, Brandy put down her fork and studied him with eyes that had gone cold. "I think you are inquiring if I am still a virgin," she gritted. "The answer is no."

A shocked silence followed her words. "No? But you said . . ."

"I said I have nothing to be ashamed of. And I haven't. But I have known love, Father. And the man I love is Comanche. Although I fail to see what difference that should make." Suddenly, the anger drained away. She leaned forward, intent on making him understand. "Poppa, I can't wait for you to meet Sky Walker. He's the most handsome man I have ever known. And so gentle and kind that—"

"No!" His voice was harsh, his face red with anger. "Have you no shame, daughter? How can you say such things to me? I refuse to listen to any more."

283

"Please, Poppa," she said. "Come to the village with me. Meet Sky Walker. Talk with him and—"

"No!" He hit the table with his fist, beyond worrying about what the other diners would think. The force of his blow sent the dishes crashing over the table, spilling their contents onto the white tablecloth. "Don't speak to me of such things," he roared. "You'll never go there again. You'll put the whole thing behind you."

Slowly, Brandy pushed her chair back and stood up. "I believe I've lost my appetite," she said, her voice quivering. "Please excuse me."

Hurrying from the room, from the prying eyes of the other diners, she went to her room and locked the door behind her. She would have to wait until her father calmed down. Then she would talk to him, make him understand the way she felt. It was obvious he needed time to adjust. But she couldn't give him a lot of it. She wasn't certain how long Sky Walker would be gone, but she intended to be at the village when he returned. She had given herself a week with her father. No more. Whether or not her father accepted her wishes would make no difference in the end, because she would return to the village alone if she must.

But she would return.

A whisper of feathered fletching sliced through the air, sending a whooshing sound across the clearing. Sky Walker watched the flaming arrow strike the cabin, saw the flames licking hungrily at the logs, heard the sound of rifles booming from inside the dwelling.

Screams filled the air, sounding from inside the cabin, while bullets buzzed like angry wasps around the war-painted Comanches.

The flames licked higher and higher at the logs.

Suddenly the cabin door was flung open and a man hurtled outward, hitting the ground and rolling, leaping to his feet while he brought his rifle up to bear on the warriors. An arrow slammed into his chest, sending him reeling to the ground.

"Poppa!" the shout came from the cabin. A young man, not more than twenty summers, leapt from the cabin and raced toward the man on the ground.

"Run, Josh!" the man screamed. "Get to the—" His words turned into a rattle as an arrow pierced his throat.

The young man, Josh, grabbed up the rifle and turned with it, but he didn't have a chance to fire. A flint war ax sailed through the air and caught him in the chest. Without uttering a sound he fell beside his father.

Upon determining there was no one else in the cabin, the warriors drove their moccasined heels into their ponies' flanks and rode away from the burning cabin, the slaughtered livestock, and the dead white man and his son.

As they left, Sky Walker felt the bile rising in the back of his throat. He had no taste for such slaughter, was only taking part in the raid because he felt it was necessary for the survival of his race. The Texans must feel the strength of the Comanche, must learn they could not slaughter them like cattle, nor could they drive his people from the land that was rightfully theirs.

Even knowing what he was doing was necessary, it was still not easy. How could he forget the father and son he'd just left behind?

The Texans were told what would happen if they did not vacate Comanche land, a silent voice said. There is nothing left to be done except show them what happens to those who trespass. Even so, he did not like what he was forced to do.

Brandy had been at the hotel for two days when she decided it was time to leave. She was accomplishing nothing, for her father seemed to avoid her presence, appearing uneasy when he was around her. At the moment, he stood at her bedroom window, his hands shoved deep into his pockets, staring down into the street.

"It is past time we left this place," he muttered. "Things will be different in England. No one there will know what happened. We'll leave as soon as possible."

"Poppa!" Her voice was exasperated. "Haven't you heard a word I've been saying? I am not returning to England with you."

"I heard you," he said harshly, spinning on his heels to glare at her. "But I'm assuming what you've been through has affected your mind. You are no longer capable of making your own decisions."

"When did you ever think I was capable of making my own decisions?"

He began to pace across the room, pausing beside her dressing table to pick up a statue he'd bought for her. He turned it over and over in his hands, as though searching for flaws, but she knew he was only intent on avoiding her gaze. "You are a child, Brandy. . . . You've never—"

"I am eighteen years old, Poppa. I am a grown woman."

"You are my charge until you reach the age of twenty-one, daughter. I think I know what is best for you."

"You think returning to England is best for me?"

"Yes. I certainly do. And I'm not prepared to argue the point. I want you to be ready to leave this afternoon."

"No!"

The word stopped him at the door. He looked around at her. "Are you defying me?"

"If I am defying you by staying here with the man I love, then, yes, Father. I *am* defying you."

The air seemed to leave him, whooshing out as his shoulders slumped. Amazingly, he passed a trembling hand across his eyes. "Brandy, my dear. What have I ever done to deserve this from you?"

Brandy had never seen her father express such sorrow. He looked almost broken. Did he care for her after all? Perhaps she had judged him too harshly. "Poppa," she said softly. "Please try to understand. I love Sky Walker so very much. I couldn't bear to live apart from him. Can't you understand that?"

"If it means so much to you, then of course I will," he said. "Just give me a little time, my dear. Come with me to Galveston and see me off?"

"See you off?"

"Yes. On the boat to England. It wouldn't take much more than a week or so."

"I couldn't do that. It's too far away. How would I ever find my way back to the Comanche village?"

"I could make arrangements for a guide."

"I don't know."

"Think about it. Grant your old father this one last wish." His voice actually trembled as he turned away.

Brandy felt troubled. She'd never known she meant so much to her father. His voice had actually trembled. If she didn't know he'd never stoop so low, she might believe he was only trying to make her feel too guilty to leave him.

No! Her father would never do that. He was more likely to have her guarded day and night to see she obeyed him, if he hadn't actually had a change of heart.

"Perhaps we could have a few more days together here, Poppa, in San Antonio," she said.

"Don't refuse to accompany me yet," he said. "Think about it for a few days. That's all I ask." Bending over, he kissed her gently on the cheek. "Just think about it," he repeated.

"All right," she agreed.

"Thank you." He reached for the door, opened it, then stepped into the hallway. "We'll eat in my room as usual," he reminded, then closed the door behind him.

Her lips twisted grimly. His last words were enough to let her know that his feelings had not altered the least bit. He was still ashamed to be seen in public with her.

Darn it! Why had she consented to wait around here for several more days? She wanted to return to the village and she wanted to return now.

Chapter Twenty-nine

The vast ebony sky was cloudy and a few shafts of pale moonlight shone down on Sky Walker as he kept his solitary vigil. He had been there more than an hour now, waiting in the shadowy darkness beneath the stairway, his dark eyes fixed intently on a window in the hotel across the street.

The window wasn't just any window. Sky Walker knew that somewhere beyond that pane of glass, behind the drawn curtains, he would find his woman . . . Lady Brandy Tremayne.

Sky Walker knew it was so, because he had seen her at the window.

Nearly an hour had passed since she'd drawn the curtains and it had been at least half that long since her darkened window suggested she'd retired for the night, but still he dared not go to her. He must continue to wait until the town had settled down, until the other patrons in the hotel had retired and there was no danger of him running into them, because no one, not another soul, must know he'd ever been here.

A warm breeze lifted a lock of dark hair, blowing it

across his face, and he pushed it away impatiently, his gaze never leaving the window. He remained motionless, so still that his presence did not even disturb the crickets chirruping in the rubble that had been carelessly thrown beneath the stairway.

Suddenly a stealthy movement in the alley behind him caught his attention. He spun around, his wary gaze probing the shadowy corners, finding nothing to alarm him.

But there had been something there. He had heard it. Had the white-eyes somehow learned of his presence in their town and were even now trying to sneak up on him, hoping to catch him unaware?

Footsteps crunched on gravel, then came the sound of boots thudding against the boardwalk. His heart picked up speed, but he remained motionless, waiting . . . crouching beneath the shadowy stairway with his back against the building. Only in that way could he be certain of safety from that direction.

The footsteps were closer now and Sky Walker's hands gripped his rifle, lifted it, preparing to aim.

The boots left the boardwalk, crunched on gravel again . . . the intruder had reached the alleyway. The bulky figure of a man appeared, illuminated by the pale light of the moon. He stopped between the buildings, not more than six feet away from Sky Walker. The warrior's fingers tightened on the rifle and he lifted it to his shoulder.

"Bill!"

The harsh, gravelly voice caught Sky Walker by surprise. He spun around quickly, almost positive that another man, a man called Bill, was approaching from the alley. His narrowed gaze searched the shadowy darkness, but all in vain. There was no one there.

"Bill!" the man repeated harshly. "I know damn well you're at that garbage again! Now you git on out here. We gotta get home before Mamie throws us both outta the house."

The man's words didn't make any sense. Who was he talking to? And why would the unseen man be at the garbage?

The faintest stirring came from the alley behind Sky Walker, but whoever or whatever was there, still remained hidden.

"I know you're in there, Bill! Now get out here before I get my dander up. I ain't gonna wait here all night for you."

Having decided the unknown man, Bill, obviously offered more danger than the man only a few feet from him, Sky Walker directed all his efforts toward piercing the darkness with his gaze. Finally he was rewarded by a slight movement, just a smaller shadow among the larger ones, but. . . . *yes.* It was definitely a movement.

His hands tightened on his rifle as he watched the shadow move closer, then detach itself from the darkness. His eyes widened slightly and his lips twitched as a gray cat ambled slowly up to the man and rubbed against his leg. Kneeling, the man scooped the cat into the crook of his arm.

"It's about time, you mangy critter," he grumbled. "Don't know why Mamie wants you around noway. Far as I can see you ain't nothing but a nuisance. And I'm gettin' plumb tired of havin' to fetch you outta that alley ever night before I can go home." He was still mumbling at the cat as he went on down the boardwalk, obviously headed for home and the woman he called Mamie.

Sky Walker slowly relaxed his body and turned his attention back to the hotel. Except for the light in the lobby, all the windows were dark.

It was time.

Sleep had been long coming to Brandy and now she tossed restlessly beneath the patchwork quilt, caught in the grip of a nightmare.

"No," she moaned, pushing fretfully at the coverlet that seemed to be stifling her. "No . . . no."

The rattlesnake was the biggest one she'd ever seen, measuring at least fifteen feet long and coiled to a height of more than ten. She knew the reptile would have no trouble catching her, even as she ran . . . and ran . . . and . . . ran.

"No, no, no," she moaned, thrashing back and forth on the bed as she tried to get her legs to move faster.

Casting a quick look behind, she saw the snake sliding after her, its jaws open, slavering . . . the beast's black fur was almost smothering her . . . and . . . she was in the water, unable to move because her right leg was swollen from snakebite . . . she was unable to see anything but the bear, drawing closer and closer through the foggy darkness surrounding her.

"Come to me, little green eyes."

"I can't," she cried. "I can't move . . . the bear . . . the bear . . ."

"The bear won't hurt you," Sky Walker soothed, pulling her into his embrace. And although she was blind, completely blind, unable to see anything except the gray shadows around her, Brandy knew she was safe in his arms.

"Don't leave me," she cried hysterically, her arms slipping around his neck. "I can't see. I can't walk."

"Shh," he whispered against her ear. "It is not real, little green eyes. It is only a dream."

A dream? Brandy's tense body relaxed and she melted against her lover. She was safe in his arms. Sky Walker had invaded her nightmare to quiet her fears, and although she was still blind, she could feel his dear lips on her eyelids, on her neck and . . . she smiled and whispered sweet nothings until she could no longer speak because his lips had taken possession of hers.

The nightmare had faded, leaving behind only this sweet dream . . . a dream where his hands were everywhere, touching her body in ways that she remembered very well, seeming intent on learning all its secret places. When his lips left hers, he whispered in her ear, but she couldn't understand what he was saying.

It didn't really matter, she decided, because his hands were telling her everything she needed to know, awakening a fire that had lain dormant since she'd last seen him.

His lips brushed against hers again, then moved across her jaw, below her ear, then down to her neck, leaving a trail of fire everywhere they touched. Moaning low in her throat, Brandy turned her head back and forth, trying to capture the lips that so carefully eluded hers.

When his hands pushed aside the neck of her nightgown, her breasts swelled eagerly, thrusting into the palm of his hands, seeming to beg for his touch while her nipples tautened, eager for his possession.

Brandy's moans became intense, and his mouth quickly smothered the sounds. His kiss, tender at first, deepened until she found it hard to catch her breath.

With her head spinning, her senses reeling, she opened

her eyes and stared up at Sky Walker.

"Sky Walker?" Her dazed eyes widened, then began to glitter brightly. "I thought I was dreaming," she whispered. "But I wasn't." Her hands felt his sinewy upper arms, moved around to caress the back of his neck. "You are real. Aren't you? Have you finally come for me?"

"No," he said gruffly. "I have only come to warn you."

Alarm flickered through her. "You came to warn me?"

"Yes." His expression was wary, as though he was uncertain how she would react to his words. "Before I left the village you asked me where I was going and I would not answer."

Brandy's movements stilled. There was something about him, perhaps the wary look in his eyes or the grim set of his jaw, that told her she might not like what he was going to say. "You're going to tell me now?"

"Yes. But first I must explain. Only then will you be able to understand. Last spring my people, the Comanche, were lured to this town by the Texans. They claimed they wanted to sign a peace treaty with us. Our chiefs came, some of them bringing their families, their women and children. But the Texans spoke with false tongues."

Even as he spoke, Brandy realized he had told her this before. On the way to the Peace Council, he had said these very words. But at the time her own problems had seemed overwhelming and his of little concern.

Now the words had the impact of a knife, cutting into her flesh, slicing away little pieces, probing deep, as though searching for the very heart of her.

"Do you understand, little green eyes?" Sky Walker continued, and she wondered how he could use the endearment with such cold rage in his voice. "Do you not see what they have done? When our people were here, they

294

shot them down like dogs. Only a few escaped this place to reveal the treachery of the Texans."

Brandy hardly dared breathe as she waited for him to reveal the reason for his presence. She watched his mouth move, wondering when the words would come that would mean the end for them . . . because somehow, some way, she felt certain that would be the final result.

Something was going to happen here tonight, and it would have such an impact on her that she would never be able to deal with it.

God! If only she could stop his words. Instead, she waited quietly for him to continue.

"The Texans must be stopped before they kill my Comanche brothers . . . before they slaughter our women and children. They must be stopped before they destroy us."

"What are you going to do?" She didn't want to ask the question, but knew she must have the answer and could not bear to wait any longer for it.

His fingers dug into her shoulders. "I only do what must be done," he said fiercely. "But I could not take the chance that you would be killed when we attack this place."

Attack! She felt ice spreading through her stomach. "No. You can't attack San Antonio. What about the people? The women and children. And Ben is still here. You can't do it. It would be a massacre."

"No," he said grimly. "The white-eyes will call it that. But it is war. The only way to drive the Texans from our land. The choice is theirs: leave or be destroyed."

"If you do this you will be a murderer." She didn't want to believe he would take part in such a thing, but he stood before her, telling her he was going to kill the inhabitants of San Antonio . . . and wanting her to condone his actions.

"Have you not understood a word I have said? They attacked our villages, killed our women and children, stole our livestock, burned our lodges, and destroyed our food supplies. We cannot allow such actions to continue. They must be taught a lesson, must learn to fear our strength. Only then will we be able to live peacefully."

She had never taken her eyes off him. "You speak of peace after saying you are going to drive them out of Texas? You talk of killing them, of burning their towns . . ." She shook her head in denial. "I don't know you. I thought I did, thought I loved you, but I don't know you."

"Do you know another way to make them leave our lands?"

"But what about the cost of innocent lives?"

"What about the innocent Comanche who suffered because of the Texans? Do they not count?"

"But if you all get together . . . like you did with the Cheyenne, then perhaps you could work something out."

"Did you not hear me?" he asked harshly. "We tried to effect a peace treaty. They killed our emissaries. Is it only the white-eyes you have compassion for? How would you feel if the soldiers took little Brazos and bashed his head against a rock. How would you feel if they raped Johanna?"

"They wouldn't do that," she whispered raggedly, lowering her head.

Lifting her chin, he forced her to meet his gaze. "They *have* done it, over and over again. We know of no other way to stop them. We have a right to live in peace. This is our land. It was the land of our fathers and their fathers before them."

She jerked her chin away from him. "Don't do this to me," she cried, tears blurring her vision. "How can you expect me to stand aside and say nothing while you attack the town?" Her eyes blazed as she stared up at him bitterly. "Why did you have to come here anyway?"

He rose from the bed. "The answer should be obvious. I did not want to see you dead."

"Well, I don't intend to see my father dead, either. Or anyone else in this town." She scrambled out of the bed. "If you don't want them to find you here, then you'd better leave now."

"It is your intention to warn them?"

"Yes! It most certainly is." Crossing the room, she snatched up her wrapper and jerked it on. "There's no way I could—" She broke off, realizing there was no one to hear her. Except for herself, the room was empty.

Chapter Thirty

Sky Walker left the hotel by the window, dropping lightly to the ground with a soft thud. He had started across the street when he heard a door slam against a plank building only a few doors down the street. A quick glance found the burly figure of the man who'd left the saloon.

Fading into the darkened shadows of the nearest building, Sky Walker saw a match flare, recognized Ben's face as he bent to light his cigarette. A moment later he shook the flame out; then, except for the red glow marking the end of the lit cigarette, there was only darkness.

The crunch of boots against gravel sounded, becoming more distant with each passing moment as the old man moved off down the street.

Sky Walker's wary gaze scanned the darkened street and boardwalk. There was nothing there to prevent his leaving, yet still, he hesitated. His gaze returned to the window that marked Brandy's room. He didn't want to leave her, wanted to hurry back and snatch her into his arms, wanted to ride into the wilderness with her and forget what he had to do. But he could not. He must ride with his brothers on their trail of vengeance.

But in coming to San Antonio, at least he had saved

Brandy. He had saved her by making a successful raid on this town impossible. Now that the alarm would be raised, San Antonio would have to be spared. He had known this might happen, but he'd had to take the chance. He would die before allowing harm to come to his woman.

Feeling as though he was leaving the best part of him behind, he made his way to the far end of town, where he'd left his mount.

Brandy hurried out the door to her father's room and beat on the door. "Poppa," she called. "Wake up! Poppa! You must let me in!"

It seemed forever before the door was flung open and her father stood facing her. He blinked against the hall light. "What on earth is the matter?" he asked.

"The Comanches—" She stopped abruptly, staring in silence at her father. Fear for the man she loved had halted her voice, stopping the flow of words. How could she tell her father about the attack?

But then, how could she not?

She couldn't let the Indians attack San Antonio, couldn't allow people to be killed, not when it was in her power to stop it.

What about Sky Walker, an inner voice whispered. Won't he be killed if the people of San Antonio are warned? The thought caused a heaviness in her chest.

"What is it, Brandy?" Lord Tremayne asked. "Have you lost your voice?"

Suddenly a door opened down the hall and a man wearing a scruffy robe peered out into the passageway. "What is the trouble, Señor Tremayne?"

"No trouble, Señor Lopez. Please accept my apologies for disturbing your rest. My daughter's been having bad dreams. She just needed someone to talk with."

Wrapping his fingers around Brandy's arm, Lord Tremayne pulled her into the darkened interior of his room and shut the door. After lighting a lamp, he turned to stare at her. "Have you lost all sense of decency?" he asked. "If you found it necessary to speak to me now, then you should have dressed first. What is so important it couldn't wait until the morning?"

His harshness, coming so soon after he'd extracted a promise from her to stay with him a few more days, was totally unexpected. "I am sorry to wake you, Poppa. But what I have to say is of utmost importance. The life of everyone in this town is at stake."

"What the devil do you mean? Don't beat around the bush. If you have something to say, than spit it out."

"The Comanches are going to attack San Antonio," she said bluntly.

"They're going to—" He broke off, his gaze narrowing on her face. "How do you know? Who told you?"

"Sky Walker."

"Sky Walker!" He made the name sound more like a curse. "That Indian! He is here in this hotel?" He opened the door and looked out into the hall as though expecting the warrior to be waiting there.

"He was here," she said. "But he has already gone."

"How long ago?" Stepping back inside the room, he crossed to the window and stared down into the street, obviously hoping to catch a glimpse of him there. "How long has it been since he left?"

"Only a few minutes." She swallowed around an

obstruction in her throat. "I came straight to your room, Poppa."

"Damn him! Daughter! Go back to your room and get dressed while I wake the proprietor of the hotel."

Feeling as though her world was coming to an end, Brandy left her father's room and returned to her own. Her thoughts were in turmoil. Where had Sky Walker gone when he'd left her? She had placed him in terrible danger by revealing his visit to her room.

Run! her heart silently cried. Hide, my love! Don't let them find you!

Numbly, she donned her clothing and gathered her things together, supposing that her father meant for them to flee the town. But where would they go?

Her question was answered when her father came to her and said the townsfolk were gathering at the Alamo — even though it still bore the old battle scars, the fort remained the only sensible place to make their defense. But first, the men were gathering in the saloon across the street. He was to take her there because they wanted to question her about the Indian who'd told her about the attack.

"Why?" she cried. "I told you all I knew."

"Nevertheless, you'll speak to them. It's the only way they will believe you had nothing to do with this."

"They actually think I had something to do with it?" she whispered, the color leaving her face. This was a turn of events that shocked her. She'd never expected her motives for informing them of the raid would become suspect.

"What are they expected to believe?" he asked. "You lived with that Indian. You told me yourself that you stayed with him gladly. This whole thing could be a lie . . . a ruse to get the citizens of San Antonio to abandon the town and leave it open to those thieving redskins."

She stared up at him bitterly. "It didn't take long for you to start thinking like the rest of them, did it, Father?"

His lips twisted angrily. "What else am I to think? Do you even comprehend how much you have cost me? Just giving birth to you weakened your mother and in the end caused her death. But I did the best I could by you. I spent a fortune on you . . . on governesses, on clothes, horses, everything you ever wanted. I denied you nothing, saw you had the very best life had to offer. It was even at your insistence that I allowed you to accompany me to this god-forsaken wilderness — and you repay me by forming an alliance with ignorant savages. How can I be expected to believe you?"

"So now the truth is out, isn't it, Father. You finally admit how you really feel about me. You never wanted me. Not from the day I was born."

"Nevertheless, you are my blood and I will stand by you. I can do no less." He turned away from her. "I'll be down in the lobby. Don't keep me waiting." With that he stalked away from her, slamming the door behind her with enough force to shake the frame.

Brandy sank down on the bed, tears misting her eyes. She finally had the truth before her. Her father had never loved her. Any concern he'd ever shown for her welfare had been pretense . . . acted out for the benefit of others.

Sky Walker! her heart cried out. Come back! Take me with you!

Her eyes went to the window and she stared out into the empty street . . . to the darkness beyond, but there was no sign of movement to be found. He was gone.

Despairing, Brandy picked up her carpetbag and opened the door. She didn't know if she'd be returning to her room, wasn't sure what lay ahead . . . at the moment she could only see pain and misery. But whatever was to be her fate, she would be suitably dressed. Her father had at least seen to that.

She entered the lobby expecting to see her father, but Lord Tremayne was nowhere in sight. Hearing shouts from outside the hotel, she opened the door and stepped outside. Her father stood on the other side of the street, talking to a man who looked vaguely familiar. A sense of uneasiness fell over her. Where had she seen him before?

"Father!"

The words had no sooner left her lips when she was suddenly pulled back against a hard, masculine chest. A rough palm covered her mouth, muffling her cries. Terrified, she turned her head, lashing out with her bag, hearing a hoarse curse as it connected with her attacker's shoulder before glancing off. Losing her grip on the bag, she had time for one glimpse of Franko, the man holding her captive, before his fingers pinched her nostrils together, making it impossible for her to breathe.

A red haze swirled around her head, blackness closed in, and she lost her senses.

The clip-clop of horses' hooves caught Sky Walker's attention as he entered the alley where he'd left his mount. He faded into the shadows, waiting silently for the riders to pass. Something about the foremost figure seemed familiar. Although he knew he must leave quickly, he felt the need to identify the rider before he went.

He made his way back through the shadows, reaching the saloon in time to see one of Franko's men enter.

Hatred surged through him. Where were the man's

companions? Sky Walker felt almost certain Franko was the rider who had captured his attention. But where had he and his companions gone?

A big man emerged from the hotel and crossed the street. He was joined by another man who stepped from the shadows. "There is a meeting taking place in the saloon," the first man said. "The sheriff is asking every able-bodied man to attend."

Sky Walker realized his time had run out, for the meeting that was taking place must have been called because of the information he had given Brandy. He must leave before he was discovered.

"Father!"

Recognizing Brandy's voice, Sky Walker spun around . . . just in time to see his woman attacked. He sprang forward, drawing his knife at the same instant.

A bellow of rage told of his discovery and he turned to face the man who sprang at him.

Although in his middle years, the man was strong. His foot came up and landed a hard kick on Sky Walker's wrist, sending a jolt of pain through his bones and causing him to lose his grip on his knife. The weapon fell from his numb fingers, clattering against the boardwalk.

Doubling up his fists, Sky Walker delivered a hard blow to his opponent's chin, sending the man reeling to his knees. Realizing the noise of the fight was attracting the attention of others, Sky Walker took advantage of the other man's temporary plight and sent a kick into his belly. He heard the man's breath whoosh out of his lungs, and followed with another kick.

From the corner of his eyes, he saw Franko struggling to put Brandy's limp body on his horse. He turned swiftly, intending to go to her aid, but a bullet whizzed past him, barely missing his head. Shouts from nearby told him others had joined the fray and he made a dash for the alley. He couldn't help his woman if he were dead.

He ran swiftly through the night until he reached his mount. His only chance for Brandy and himself was to flee, but Franko would never keep her. No matter where he went, Sky Walker would find him. . . .

And he would take his woman and his revenge.

When Brandy regained consciousness, they had left San Antonio far behind. Although her wrists were bound together, she fought against the arm holding her upright in the saddle before her captor.

"Be still!" Franko growled, tightening the arm around her waist until she thought he would surely squeeze her in half.

As though her waking was the signal for speed, he dug his spurs into the flank of his mount, sending it bounding forward, and throwing Brandy against his chest.

Realizing she could not free herself, that fighting would be useless and only waste energy that could be put to better use at a more opportune moment, Brandy subsided, but continued to hold her body stiffly erect.

Her sullen eyes swept the band of renegades, counting the numbers. There were six, counting Franko. Six against her. Not exactly what she'd call even odds. But she'd managed to escape them twice before and she would do it again.

They rode hard throughout the night, covering a distance of perhaps fifty miles. Dawn found them on a bluff overlooking the Brazos River. Down below, on the opposite bank of the river, was a small Comanche village, not more than two dozen tepees in all.

Smoke from a single campfire curled skyward and the only sound that could be heard was the barking of a camp dog. A few horses were corralled in a rope enclosure near a grassy meadow. It was to them the renegades looked.

The rider nearest Brandy spoke. "Looks like we're in luck, boss. They ain't many horses in that corral. Not for the size of the village. Most of the warriors must be gone. Them horses is just setting there waiting for us to come take 'em."

"It sure seems that way, Idaho," Franko said. "Way it looks from here, they ain't nobody much to object to whatever we've a mind to do."

"Reckon them braves is off on a huntin' party?" Idaho asked.

"Don't matter to me where they're at," Franko said. "So long as they don't come back until we've gone." He grinned down at Brandy. "Me an' you got us a little business to tend to when we get in the clear."

"You reckon that sheriff can round up a posse, Franko? Seemed like they was something mighty important going on back yonder in San Antone for them not to notice us robbing that general store."

"Don't much matter if they do come. With fresh horses under us, they ain't no way they're gonna catch us. And no way they could follow us last night. Not with all them clouds in the sky. Made it next to impossible for anybody . . . except an Injun . . . or maybe old Ben . . . to track us." He pulled at the reins. "Let's get moving, boys."

Brandy wondered if she could warn the villagers the renegades were coming; but then, there would probably be less bloodshed if Franko and his bunch were able to take the horses without trouble.

They obviously didn't know what was occurring with the Comanche Indians. And although Brandy knew, the knowledge did her little good.

The villagers had no warning before the attack. Neither did Brandy. One minute the mount she was on was crossing the river amid the soft swish of water, the creaking of saddle leather, and the jingle of metal harnesses. The next minute the air was filled with sounds of violence—gunfire, whistling bullets, yelling, harsh laughter—the screams of women and children, wounded, ravaged, and dying.

Brandy swallowed the bile rising in the back of her throat as the noise beat at her ears. Sickened by the brutality, she twisted and turned, struggling against Franko, tears raining down her face as the renegades mutilated the Indians and smashed the babies' skulls. Her mind refused to accept what was happening and her brain screamed over and over again, *no, no, no*.

Sky Walker sat on his mount and watched the posse down below. The sight of the dead bodies, the blackened ruins of the tepees that were still smoking, sickened him. Obviously Franko and his bunch had been busy. Just the thought of Brandy in the hands of such a man sent chills racing down his spine. He must hurry and find them before Franko could do her harm.

A numbness had taken possession of Brandy, still clinging even after they'd left the Indian village behind. The cruelty the outlaws had displayed was hard for her to deal with. How could such men call the Indians savages?

307

Now she understood what Sky Walker had been trying to tell her. But comprehension had come too late.

Franko had obviously decided the trauma of seeing the Indians slaughtered in such a way had made her docile, because when they stopped to water the horses in a narrow stream, he pulled her off the chestnut and cut the ropes binding her wrists.

"Riding double slows our pace," he said by way of explanation. "I know a cave where we can hole up for a few weeks until the heat dies down. Then we'll head for Mexico and have us a fine time."

She remained silent, accepting the canteen he offered, lifting it to her mouth and quenching her thirst with the tepid liquid before handing the container back to him. It suited her purpose for Franko to believe she'd given up all hope. Perhaps he would become lax in his guard, allowing her to escape.

"Hey, boss," shouted the man they'd left for lookout. "Riders coming in the distance. We'd better get outta here before they spot us."

Franko frowned. "How'd they get on our trail so fast?"

"Beats me," Idaho said. "Less they got a tracker to read sign."

"Which is probably what they did," Franko said, turning to Brandy. "You ride my horse since it's got the saddle and I'll take the Indian pony. But don't try nothing. I wouldn't hesitate to kill you."

Brandy put her foot in the stirrup and swung up on the chestnut horse. Franko kept the reins of her mount in his hands and mounted. Then the renegades made for the cover of the trees. They'd only gone a short distance when a shout told them they'd been discovered. Realizing the dense growth of cedars would only slow them down, the renegades left the woods.

Brandy's horse seemed eager to gallop and Franko had fallen back until he was riding beside her. A quick glance told her that her mount's reins were held loosely in his hand while he was studying the area, obviously trying to decide their best route of escape.

Now was the time.

Reaching for the reins, she gave them a hard yank, at the same time digging her heels into her mount's flanks. Bending low over the chestnut, she urged him toward the riders.

She heard Franko's shout, felt a bullet whizzing by her head, and knew that someone was shooting at her.

"Go! Go!" she shouted at her mount, urging him to even greater speed.

He was running all-out and she felt him drawing away from her pursuers. Then the chestnut broke his stride, stumbled, and she realized he'd been shot. She only had time to kick her feet from the stirrups before he was falling.

Brandy went sailing through the air and landed with a thud on the grassy meadow. For a moment she lay stunned, unable to breathe. And then she rolled over, crawled to her knees, and stared at the horse and rider thundering toward her.

It was Franko. And even at this distance she could see the fury darkening his face.

A swift glance told her the riders that had been pursuing them were coming closer. She could make out her father riding beside another man. Was it Ben? Moving stiffly, she got to her feet and began to stumble toward them.

A quick glance behind told her Franko was gaining on

her. He'd reach her before her father did. Suddenly, as she watched, Franko swayed in the saddle, righted himself, then doubled over and fell from his mount.

Suddenly the riders surrounded her. She was vaguely conscious of her father gathering her into his arms. "Daughter," he rasped. "I didn't think I would ever see you again. Forgive me, my dear. I didn't mean a word of what I said."

Brandy looked into his shamed eyes, realizing he meant what he said. "I didn't think you would either," she said huskily. "How did you know where to find me?"

"The hotel clerk saw the outlaws leave with you. The sheriff happened to know that Ben was a good tracker and went for him. Luckily, he hadn't left town. If it hadn't been for him, we'd never have been able to follow your trail."

As though only now becoming aware they were not alone, he turned to the sheriff. "Is the man who abducted her dead?"

"Yes," the sheriff said grimly. "And I've sent my men after the one that killed him."

"Whatever for?" Lord Tremayne asked. "The man was a scoundrel. He didn't deserve to live."

"I agree he had it coming," the sheriff said. "In other circumstances, and if'n he'd been killed with a bullet, then I'd forget about the man who done the killing."

"He wasn't killed with a bullet?" Lord Tremayne questioned. "Then what did kill him?"

"An arrow."

Brandy's heart gave a lurch as she heard the sheriff's words. She barely heard her father asking questions; instead, her gaze was searching the horizon. Tears filmed her eyes when she saw him . . . for just one moment . . .

at the edge of the woods.

It was Sky Walker. Although he had faded into the forest, she knew the man she'd seen was her love. Brandy leapt to her feet and ran toward the woods where she'd last seen him.

"Brandy!" her father shouted. "Where are you going?"

The sound of more shouting and boots thudding against the ground told her she was being pursued. Her breath came in short bursts as she continued to run. Even though she knew she couldn't make it before they caught her, and even though Sky Walker might no longer want her, she had to go to him.

Because her choice had been made.

The civilized world had nothing to offer her, nothing that was equal to one infinitesimal moment in Sky Walker's arms.

She was vaguely aware of shots behind her, wondered momentarily if they were shooting at her, and then the thundering of hooves drowned out everything else and she was swept up into the arms of her lover.

Chapter Thirty-one

Realizing he couldn't outrun the posse with his mount carrying double, Sky Walker headed for the cedar brakes, intent on eluding the men who pursued them. Although he was greatly outnumbered by the sheriff and his posse, he had a distinct advantage over them in this area. He knew every rock, every stream in these mountains. But what was even more important, he knew about the network of caverns that existed throughout the hill country; caverns and sinkholes and tunnels which carried underground streams. Although he had no idea of the number, more than two thousand existed, formed by water cutting into rock for millions of years, some of them dark and hard to explore, others light and airy, capable of providing permanent living quarters for an entire tribe. It was to one of these caves that Sky Walker directed his mount.

Brandy didn't know the cave was there until Sky Walker dismounted and led his mount through the dense cedars growing at the entrance.

"They will not find us here," he said, lifting her from his mount.

Locking her arms around his neck, she gazed lovingly into his eyes. "I was never so glad to see anyone in my life," she murmured. "I could hardly believe it when I realized who you were." Her hands clung tightly as she pressed her body hard against his. "I thought I had lost you forever."

"You could never do that," he muttered, his lips claiming hers in a hard kiss that was over much too fast. When she would have clung to him, he set her aside. "No, little green eyes. There is no time. The white-eyes know nothing of this cave, but we must take no chances. Wait here until I return."

Alarm streaked through her and she caught his arm with desperate fingers. "Wait. Where are you going?"

"To cover our tracks." The words were no sooner spoken before he disappeared back into the cedar thicket.

Brandy stared at the cavern entrance, trying to still her fears. Suppose the men who pursued them saw Sky Walker? She was almost certain they wouldn't hesitate to kill him. Although her father had apologized to her, that didn't mean his feelings for the warrior had changed. In fact, she was certain they had not.

Oh, God! How would she be able to stand it if her father was responsible for the death of the man she loved? Aeons seemed to have passed, but still Sky Walker had not returned. She tried to get her thoughts off him, turned her attention instead to her surroundings.

The cave was big, hollowed out of creamy limestone, and although the air felt cooler than it did outside, she didn't find it uncomfortable. It wasn't the air that was responsible for the chill that had settled over her.

Her gaze went to the entrance again.

Nothing.

God! Had Sky Walker been surprised by the sheriff's

posse? Wouldn't she have heard the shots if they had found him?

If he was taken by surprise, they wouldn't have to fire a single shot, an inner voice said. He would be overwhelmed by sheer numbers.

Suddenly, she could stand it no longer. She must leave the cavern, must know what was happening. She started toward the entrance . . . then stopped, her breath caught in the back of her throat.

Yes! There it was again! There had been a movement, ever so slight, in the dense growth of cedars. She stood frozen, staring . . . waiting, until suddenly Sky Walker pushed the limbs aside and stepped into view.

"Sky Walker," she cried, throwing herself at him, wrapping her arms around his neck and flooding him with tears. "I thought they'd found you. You were so long in coming back, I thought —" She broke off, pulled back and patted his face, his shoulders, his chest, his upper arms, searching for unseen wounds. "Are you all right? Are you all right?"

"Yes," he assured her, smiling tenderly down at her. "I am well. There was no one around and we are well hidden. But we will take no chances. There are other caves leading off this one and we will go to one of them."

Gathering the reins of his mount in one hand, he led her across the cavern to a protruding rock that ran from the ceiling to the floor. When they reached it, she discovered a passageway had been hidden from view.

His horse balked at entering the narrow opening, possibly because it was barely wide enough for the animal to travel through, or perhaps because of the shadowy darkness of the tunnel. Whatever the reason, Sky Walker alternately coaxed, led, and pulled the animal through the passage until they reached a large room, perhaps fifty feet across and forty feet high.

"It's so big," Brandy said, studying her surroundings with awe. Her gaze wandered over the creamy limestone walls, stopping momentarily on the clear pool of water formed by an underground spring, before returning to Sky Walker. "Where does the light come from?"

"There are many openings into the cavern," he replied. "Although they are small, well hidden from prying eyes, they allow the sunlight to enter."

"We could live here forever and no one would ever find us." She turned to him. "I wish we could do that."

"You would get tired of living beneath the ground," he said. "We will stay here tonight and tomorrow we must return to the village."

"Will it be safe for us to leave that soon?"

"We must. When I told Hawkeye what had occurred in San Antonio, he became worried about the people in our village. Franko and his men have knowledge of its location, and we knew they could not to be trusted. Already the Texans are arming themselves and riding to stop our raids. Soon there will be reprisals. Hawkeye realized I could not stay with the other warriors and leave you in Franko's hands, so he sent me to move our tribe farther west, beyond the reach of the white-eyes who would take revenge against us."

Remembering what had occurred in the Comanche village, Brandy felt anxious for Johanna and the others. "Perhaps we shouldn't stop here overnight."

"It is necessary if we are to escape those who pursue us. They will search these hills but they will find no trace. It should be safe to leave at dawn, because the white-eyes have no patience. Perhaps it is because they are soft. Most of them have no taste for sleeping beneath the stars." His voice was scornful.

"If we don't have to worry about the soft white-eyes tonight, then let's not talk about them either," she said, arching her body against him. "Let us pretend that nothing exists outside this cave. We are the only people in this world. Just you and I."

His arms locked her to him. "I like this pretending," he whispered huskily, lowering his mouth to hers. "I like it very much."

His lips found hers in a hard, possessive kiss. It was almost violent in nature, but she made no protest, feeling the need to join with him, to feel him deep inside her body as quickly as possible.

Sky Walker, sensing her need, did not linger long on the preliminaries. He quickly divested her of her clothing, then removed his own. Their coming together was swift as he plunged deeply into her, thrusting urgently, moving against her, until she was raising herself to meet each thrust of his body. She writhed and moaned beneath him while he built a fire in her blood and continued to stoke it until the flames were almost consuming her, dancing, leaping, burning brighter and brighter, taking her higher and higher until she was poised on the brink of eternity . . . almost mindless with the pleasure he was bringing her. When they reached their peak, the sound of their voices filled the cavern, ringing out, echoing through the passages until they crested and collapsed in blissful ecstasy together.

The next morning they left the cavern and made their way to the village. Brandy felt relief when she saw the village; everything looked peaceful when they rode in.

After calling the people together, Sky Walker explained what had happened and why Hawkeye wanted the village moved. There was no word of complaint as the women began dismantling the lodges and making preparations to travel.

A week later they were safely relocated with the village hidden in the shelter of a deep canyon. While they were moving, the Comanche continued their raid through south Texas, sweeping past San Antonio, which was well defended, and wiping out Victoria. Then they attacked Linnville. The citizens of that coastal town fled in boats and watched their town burn from the ocean.

Feeling satisfied they'd taught the treacherous Texans a much-needed lesson, the Comanche headed back to the plains, driving before them over two thousand head of stolen horses.

It had been a month since the raid had occurred and during that time Brandy had never spoken of the time when Sky Walker had come to her at the hotel. But lately she had thought of the harsh words she had spoken, words that she regretted. She knew the words could never be recalled, but they could be explained, and she did want him to understand.

Brandy chose a time when they would not be disturbed, a time when the moon was a silver sickle in the star-studded sky. They were inside their lodge, nestled together on their bed of buffalo hides, when Brandy spoke softly of her reasons for doubting Sky Walker.

"I suppose I didn't really realize what the settlers had done to the Comanche until Franko and his men rode into that village." She shuddered and hid her face against his chest. Even now the memory sickened her. "They acted as though the Comanche were a subhuman species, a people who counted for nothing."

"It is the way of the white-eyes," he said. "Since they first came to this land they have tried to take it from us. Before it is finished, many of our people will be dead." He looked at her sadly. "I knew I should let you go for your own sake, little green eyes. When Franko stole you away from San Antonio, I had to follow. But I never meant to keep you . . . only to see you freed from the renegades." He cupped her chin in his hands. "When I saw you running toward me, I thought I was dreaming. When I realized I was not, my heart sang with gladness. Nothing could have kept me from you when I knew that you wanted me."

"And I always shall," she said. "Don't ever think of sending me away from you. I could never stand the pain of losing you."

"Nor could I. Even though I know I am being selfish." He looked at her longingly. "I want your children, little green eyes. I want to see them grow healthy and strong. Is it so wrong, so selfish of me to want our children to travel our land without fear as I have?"

"Our children will be able to ride this land," she said, her eyes holding a secret that he did not see.

"The Texans are fierce fighters. They will not be able to live side by side with us in peace. They will keep pushing us until we must leave the land of our fathers."

"Then we will leave," Brandy said calmly, smoothing his brow. "We will do whatever is necessary to live free. But if we must go to war to survive, then I will learn how to become a warrior and fight beside you."

"You would fight against your own people."

"Thy people shall be my people," she quoted softly. "And I will go wherever my husband takes me."

318

"If only I could promise you a lifetime of happiness." He clutched her against him, as though afraid she would be wrenched from his grasp. "If only I could guarantee you that."

"I don't expect any guarantees," she said.

"What about your father?"

"Someday, perhaps I'll contact him. But not now. The wound is too fresh." Her expression was pensive. "I believe he would like to see his grandson. He always was partial to boys." Her voice held no bitterness now.

"Your father's grandson will be my son, little green eyes. And first we must make him."

Leaning closer, she whispered against his ear. "We have already done that, my love."

She felt him stiffen, pull back slightly, and stare down at her with an expression that was both wary and hopeful. "You don't mean . . ."

"Yes," she said, grinning impishly up at him. "I can and I do. Little Brazos will have himself a friend to play with. And I anticipate the boys will be as close as their fathers are."

"You are so certain the child will be a boy?" His palm stroked the satiny flesh of her stomach. "Suppose you carry a girl in your belly?"

"Would you mind very much?" she asked quickly.

"Not at all," he said solemnly. "It would only mean that, instead of a friend, little Brazos would have a wife."

"Sky Walker"—Brandy's eyes were anxious—"I don't think our daughter would like her father choosing her husband."

"Why not?" he asked softly. "Her father chose her mother's husband."

She struck his cheek lightly with her palm, laughing up

at him. "I will have to admit you did a good job of it too."

Feeling an urgency in her loins, she snuggled closer to him. "Love me, Sky Walker. Please love me."

"Always," he whispered, moving against her. "For the rest of our lives."